LITTLE MONSTER!

'You've got amnesia,' Becky said confidently, 'That girl on 'Eastenders' had it, she didn't even recognise her baby. She got it from a bang on the head.'

'Have you had a bang on your head, Anna?' asked Laura.

'Did you get it in hockey?' asked Ava.

'I can't remember,' Anna said trying very hard to remember.

'Ah,' Becky said, as if that explained it.

'Becky,' Anna complained, 'that doesn't mean anything.' She felt her head. 'Look I haven't got a bump.'

'Someone gave you a forgetful pill,' suggested Olivia.

'A forgetful pill!' said Becky sarcastically, preferring her bang on the head theory.

LITTLE MONSTER!

Tamsin Adams

Wire
Bridge
Books

ISBN 978-0-9930326-6-0

Typeset by Wire Bridge Books
Front cover design by **Eric Celebrates Design**

Wire Bridge Books
378 Morningside Road
Edinburgh
EH10 5HX

Many thanks to my family for all their suggestions
... some of them useful

Chapter 1

'Don't Anna!' Caroline bleated. 'You're such a little monster! Dad ... DAD! Anna's eating all the peach bits from the muesli again,' she complained.

'Yeah Caro, enjoy your breakfast!' Anna said fiercely.

Elizabeth, her other stepsister, interrupted, she'd seen Anna swinging on the doorframes.

Anna punched her on the arm.

Elizabeth was four years older and far bigger, but she squealed and ran away, calling out 'Dad!'

'Anna! Don't hit your sisters,' her father said sternly, 'I've told you before about eating just the bits you like, you're twelve, you should know better. I've told you not to swing on the door frames and I expect you to do what I say.'

Anna gave Eliza a really black look; if she'd had the chance she'd have punched her again ... harder. 'Don't, don't, don't, that's all I ever hear. How am I supposed to practice?' she demanded.

'You're not!' her father replied. 'I banned all that park running stuff.'

'Parkour,' she corrected, 'and anyway I'm into free running, like the guy in the James Bond film and mum wants me to do it.'

He ignored the correction. 'When I tell you not to do something, that's it! It's for your own good, you'll end up hurting yourself. The people who do it, tattoos, lack of personal hygiene and barely literate, are not who I want you associating with. I doubt even your mother could find something nice to say about them …'

'Tattoos, what tattoo …' she started.

Dad didn't let her finish, 'Anna, you must think I'm an idiot!'

Anna opened her mouth to tell him he was, but he didn't give her the chance.

'What did I tell you?'

The last time he'd told her off he'd said something about no telly for a week, which would be a nightmare, so Anna pretended to look blank, 'god knows.'

'Language Anna Templeton! Since cutting your television privileges didn't work, perhaps taking away your allowance will have a better effect.'

'WHAT!'

'Learn to do what I tell you,' he continued, 'and maybe I'll reinstate it, but until then no more money.'

'That is so unfair,' she complained, 'you never said you'd stop my pocket money! God you're bloody mean!'

'Don't swear,' her father said angrily, 'I didn't have to warn you Anna, but I did,' her father continued. 'You've got to start listening, perhaps then you'll make the link between actions and consequences.'

Her sisters didn't say a word and kept their heads down in case Dad started on them.

'You never …' Anna insisted, she would definitely

remember if he had said he was going to take away her allowance.

Dad put his newspaper down, looked at her over his glasses, then without saying a word picked it up again and that was the conversation was closed.

Anna glared at the paper, 'I hate living here!' she said and stirred her muesli angrily.

Anna was slight, 'I'm almost the average height for my age,' she would argue. She had inherited her mother's looks, so she was even featured with big green eyes, dark hair and a warm smile. Unlike her mother, who was known for her calm and poise, Anna was a bundle of fizzing energy, always involved and always demanding to be heard. Nothing tired her out, she was constantly on the move, forever talking and she always had a better idea. She hadn't inherited her mother's elegant, understated dress sense either. Anna adored colours and the more colours she was wearing the better, nothing was too bright or too clashing. She wore green spots with orange stripes, bought different coloured tights, cut one leg off each pair so she could have different coloured legs and loved fluorescent t-shirts. Her father was always ordering her to tone it down and they constantly fought over that too. While everyone agreed she looked like her mother, no one could say what she'd got from her father. She wasn't top in anything at school, except maths, she didn't have any interest in history, politics or science. She hated the disgusting health food her dad cooked. She hated the judge who made her live here. She hating living with dad where she was always being told not to do stuff and longed to be living with her mum. Behave, her father insisted, like your sisters, do what you're told it's for your own good. She didn't think it was; she thought he just liked bossing people.

What Anna would give for a bowl of Frosties or a Poptart in the morning? Instead she chewed morosely on the nut, dried fruit and bran mush Eliza had put in front of her. She had on the boring blue skirt, checked blouse and maroon cardigan the school insisted they wear and she was soon to find out the day wasn't going to get any better.

'No, no, no Anna, you haven't been paying attention.' Mr Stanford, the form teacher, groaned.

'What!' she turned from the electronic board to point out that of course she couldn't do the translation as they'd never done most of these words.

'Sit down Anna, we don't have time for a better idea from you. Someone else,' Mr Stanford looked at the class, 'please come up and put us out of our misery!'

Susie Mitchell rushed up and took the stylus from Anna's hand.

Anna stomped back to her desk, muttering about all the awful things she would like to happen to Mr Stanford. He always picked on her and this time it wasn't fair. These French words were all new, so how could she possibly know what the sentence meant. At the front of the class Susie finished the translation, to Anna's surprise, and got a well done from Stoneface.

How did Susie do that?

In English they were told to discuss chapter twenty-three in their novel, but the plot didn't make any sense to Anna and she didn't have a clue what was going on. In history everyone had started a project on the Vikings and she didn't even know they had a project. She complained loudly and was bluntly told to stop attention seeking.

It was a pretty bad morning and it spoilt her good mood. Right up till then Anna had been feeling pretty happy about things; it felt like she'd been on a roll recently.

At lunch she complained to her friends about the French test. 'Susie must have cheated or perhaps she's been getting extra lessons!'

'What are you talking about Anna? We did those words in class last week,' said Olivia.

'You should stop daydreaming, you know,' Ava added.

'I don't daydream,' she said angrily, 'what about the Viking project, they didn't tell us about that in class.'

'Yes they did,' her friends contradicted her.

'We even started it,' Laura said. 'Don't you remember Eilidh spilling the glue and getting her sleeve stuck to her longboat?'

Anna thought they were teasing. 'Stop it,' she said, 'it's not fair!'

'Stop what?' asked Laura, 'don't you remember any of this?'

Anna had to admit she didn't.

Chapter 2

As the day went on Anna discovered everyone had jumped ahead in all her classes and she couldn't work out how. Then to round off the day as she left for home one of the dads waiting outside the school, a big fat one, said 'afternoon Miss Templeton' and she didn't even recognise him. She smiled weakly and said hi back. He looked so rueful she felt obliged to add it was a lovely day.

She was very relieved to get home.

Over the next few days, Anna discovered two weeks had passed since her last firm memory. She found all the stuff she thought she hadn't done, her preparations for the French translation, her bookmark was much further in her English book than she thought and her Viking project was on her homework pile.

'You've got amnesia,' Becky said confidently, 'That girl on 'Eastenders' had it, she didn't even recognise her baby. She got it from a bang on the head.'

'Have you had a bang on your head, Anna?' asked Laura.

'Did you get it in hockey?' asked Ava.

'I can't remember,' Anna said trying very hard to remember.

'Ah,' Becky said, as if that explained it.

'Becky,' Anna complained, 'that doesn't mean anything.' She felt her head. 'Look I haven't got a bump.'

'Someone gave you a forgetful pill,' suggested Olivia.

'A forgetful pill!' said Becky sarcastically, preferring her bang on the head theory.

'Why, why would anyone do that?' Anna asked, raising her eyebrows.

'Do you have to ask?' she replied and gave Susie, who was walking across the playground, a black look.

'Oh come on,' Becky interrupted, 'that's just so not likely, even if there was such a thing where would Susie Mitchell get it, how would she get Anna to eat it and would it really be worth it for a stupid little French test?'

'And anyway Susie is nice,' Anna pointed out.

Their discussion went on all break and the suggestions became more and more unlikely until Anna started to think some of the less bizarre ones, like poison in her father's organic potatoes, might be true; even an alien invasion was beginning to sound normal. Anyway whatever the reason, losing her memory was mega annoying because now she had double the work, her usual homework and then the stuff she'd forgotten.

Her father noticed she was spending twice as long studying. 'I'm glad you've started to knuckle down to your schoolwork,' he said and offered to help.

'Yeah, well there's no telly, is there?' she said bitterly, 'and I don't want your help!' He was always such an arse about homework, she couldn't stand the constant nagging. Mum was never like this when she stayed with her. 'I've not suddenly got interested in being a stupid scientist, dad, I'm just getting it out the way so I'll have more time to practice hockey. Anyway I won't need any of this stuff because as I've told you enough times I'm going to be a stuntwoman!'

'You're going to have to think about a proper career soon, Anna,' he said. 'It's okay to dream, but dreams don't come true.'

'Mum's did!' she contradicted him.

The expression on his face flickered.

Anna continued, 'she dreamed of being a star and she is one! She listens to what I want to do and doesn't make me do boring stuff I'm not interested in, I mean "hello", when I'm on set in Hollywood and my special suit is on fire and I'm waiting to leap out of a top floor window when the director shouts action, will I care Berlin is the capital of Austria?'

'It's the capital of Germany, actually,' her father said, 'and you're right, your mother doesn't make you do what you call the boring stuff! But it still has to be done. Your teachers complain to ME, and I'm the one who has to be the bad guy' he said coldly. 'Look Anna I don't expect you to be top of your class, but if you'd put even half the effort into your other subjects as you put into maths, I'd be happy.'

She didn't bother explaining again, he never listened. She didn't try harder in maths she just picked it up quicker than the rest of the class.

'Yeah, well I hope the Germans are proud you know their capital,' she said as sarcastically as she could. She turned her back on him and started on her homework again. He didn't leave immediately but she didn't turn back.

Catching up meant Anna was busy. Double homework on top of dance class, dad was okay about her learning to dance, he didn't like her judo class, but mum paid for it, like she paid for her private school, so there wasn't much he could do. Anna knew school was one of reasons her sisters were depressed. Caroline and Eliza's mother was dead, Anna's mum had been Dad's second wife but they'd divorced when Anna was six. Since her mum was an actress the judge had said Anna had to live with dad: even though she had told him she wanted to live with mum. Mum didn't talk to dad because of it. Anna's mum was rich and Anna knew she had offered to pay for Caroline and Eliza to go to the same school but dad said they couldn't, so they went to the local one. Anna also knew they really wanted to come when she visited mum but dad wouldn't even let them mention that.

Of top of all the official things Anna was doing, she also had to sneak off to practice free running.

At least by Friday she'd caught up with her schoolwork and cheerfully packed her bag to go to her mum's for the weekend. Before she went to wait for the driver, she popped her head into her father's office. 'See you Sunday evening.'

He gave her a look, 'I thought your mother couldn't have you this weekend. You said she had people to see.'

'Did I?'

'Yes.'

'Yes?' she said, 'oh ... yes I forgot.'

'You haven't been yourself this week,' her dad said.

'I'm fine,' she claimed. This amnesia was turning out to be

a real pain in the butt.

She went back upstairs and looked in her diary; she had crossed out "visit mum" and written 'big film discussions – fingers crossed'. She was about to put the diary away when she saw the edge of business card sticking out. Dad was just outside the door so she left it and picked up a magazine instead. He looked in, probably to check she hadn't run away, then carried on down the corridor to Eliza's room to help with her homework.

For a moment Anna mused on how opposite her father and mother were. She had a theory they had got married by mistake. They were going to marry different people but there had been a huge cock-up by the vicar and he had married them to each other, by the time they had realised what had happened it was too late. Thinking about it made her sad, because she missed her mum.

She remembered the card and pulled it out of her diary. It read 'P. Goodman, "National Solutions Department" and underneath was a barcode. She wondered where it had come from. There was nothing else in her homework diary only what she had to do each evening and a few jokey drawings. Mr Stanford must have been particularly mean in the middle of the week because she'd drawn a big hammer smashing a rock.

She searched the internet for the "**National Solutions Department**", but didn't find anything so gave up and went back to her magazine.

Mum phoned on Sunday night just before Anna went to

bed. She'd been offered the part, she was going to be starring in a huge Hollywood film, it would be her name at the top of the poster! Excited, Anna squealed so loudly dad came to see what see what the fuss was. When he realised she was on the phone to her mum he left instantly. Mum was ecstatic; she was going to come and watch Anna play hockey on Tuesday and suggested they sneak away for coffee and cakes afterwards.

They found a quiet out of the way cafe and Anna got a chocolate muffin as a special treat. Most of the film was going to be shot in the studio but there would be a big chunk when they'd go on location to shoot some of the scenes.

'Perhaps you could come for some of the time, would you like to come Anna?'

Anna couldn't think of anything she would rather do.

As soon as she got home she told dad her fantastic news, a day later mum got a letter from dad's lawyer basically saying no way, but using a lot more words. Anna would miss too much school, it wasn't a good environment for a young girl, Anna needed to be in a stable situation. Her mum got her agent and her lawyer to write letters, Anna shouted, screamed and sulked and said she would hate dad forever if she wasn't allowed to go.

She was still giving her father black looks weeks later. It wasn't missing out on a trip it was not being with mum that hurt. Eventually Caroline persuaded her to start eating down stairs again but now she was even more contrary with dad.

The only silver lining about staying in there was there was more time to practice free running at the weekend. Although Dad had starting acting like Big Brother, insisting on knowing what she was doing every moment of the day and she had to make up elaborate plans with her friends to get away. Then just as she'd got settled in a routine, he spoilt things and announced he had hired a tutor to give her extra English lessons.

'You're deliberately doing this to upset me,' she shouted and stomped off to her bedroom in another huff.

When the tutor turned up, it was a woman. Anna's father introduced her as Miss Rae. Miss Rae was wearing the most boring, colourless clothes ever, her hair was pulled back into a neat bun like she was really old ... except if you looked closely you could see she wasn't even thirty.

It was going to be a total waste of a Saturday morning and Anna was far from making the best of it. 'Dad,' she said, 'why can't you just be happy there are things I'm good at, like sport and maths and things I'm not? Why do I have to be good at everything?' He didn't answer, so she pointed out that Caroline and Eliza were rubbish at sport. 'If I have to do extra English, they should have to join the local hockey team, or be made to go swimming or do something active at least. It would do them good, they're such lazy slobs!'

She was so angry at the unfairness of it all she didn't notice her father's expression and carried on complaining until he lost his temper and she was sent to her room.

That was the first lesson gone.

As she furiously paced her room she had the feeling she'd seen Miss Rae before.

Chapter 3

The next Saturday Miss Rae turned up again, Anna got to the door first and managed to tell Miss Rae she wasn't wanted but her father arrived and apologised. She got another telling off but wasn't sent to her room.

By the middle of that lesson Anna decided Miss Rae was the worst teacher who had ever lived. It wasn't because she didn't like her, which she didn't, but because Miss Rae couldn't teach and worse, she actually seemed to know less about English than Anna. Her spelling was appalling, her grammar confused and her teaching mainly consisted of telling Anna to read thirty pages of a very dull book called Uncle Silas. She was also very edgy. Anna wondered if it was because Dad was there, but he wasn't paying any attention to the lesson, so what was her problem? At the end Anna raced off without saying goodbye. She'd wasted too much time already. She heard Miss Rae asking her to hang on a second but she didn't. When she got back in the evening she was surprised to discover Miss Rae had stayed for lunch and been there most of the afternoon too. Eliza said she was okay and dad said she was hard working and smart. 'You know Anna she's got an MA in Biological …,' he started to add

Anna interrupted to say she was useless at English and couldn't teach to save herself. 'It's a waste of money paying her,' she said, as dad hated wasting anything, 'if I have to be stuck inside on a Saturday, shouldn't I actually be learning something?'

'Yeah!' said Eliza, 'like you're the expert in English, you're like in the bottom class.'

'And it isn't a waste of money, since I don't pay her,' dad said smugly, 'she's a volunteer teacher, so just get on with it.'

Anna wasn't prepared to just get on with it. She told them in great detail what she'd do if she was dad, then she explained how she knew far more English than miserable Miss Rae and finally because it just popped into her head she told them what she thought was going to happen in 'Eastenders'. They were both so relieved when she stopped she was able to raid the fridge and head to her room before they could stop her. She vaulted onto the banister, jumped up to the next landing and had just straightened up when Caroline came out of the bathroom.

Caroline gave her a look, sure Anna had been doing something she shouldn't be doing but not sure what that something was.

Anna distracted her, 'you look really pretty, Caro.'

Caroline looked pleased and flicked her hair.

'But you've still got a big bum,' Anna said grinning.

Caroline stopped smiling, gave her a "I couldn't care what you say" look and went into her bedroom.

On the third Saturday Miss Rae turned up early and Anna got the impression she wanted to talk to her alone. She never gave her the chance and the following week Anna felt like she was being stalked; Miss Rae seemed to be everywhere and she spent the whole way to school and back dodging her.

On the fourth Saturday Miss Rae turned up looking pale and ill. Anna's father fussed over her, but Anna had no sympathy it was a good chance to show her up. 'Could you explain the apostrophe Miss Rae? "Its"? Does that have an apostrophe?'

'Not now Anna,' said her father sternly, 'Can't you see Miss Rae isn't well?'

Anna saw Eliza going into the kitchen. 'Don't touch my water,' she called out.

'I'm not going to drink your boring water,' said Eliza, 'it's boring.'

'Are you still on that fad?' asked her father. 'I told you, you don't need to drink three pints of water, the reporter who wrote that got it wrong.'

'Pints?' said Anna, ignoring her father, 'does that have an apostrophe? Apostrophes are important aren't they Miss Rae? I'll never pass my exams if I don't know when to use them.'

'Anna!' snapped her father.

'You don't know, do you Miss Rae?' Anna persisted, despite the look on her father's face, 'aren't you meant to be teaching me English?'

Miss Rae scowled at Anna angrily, her lips white and bloodless. 'I'm sorry Mr Templeton, I think I've got a headache coming on, I don't suppose you have any Paracetemol?'

'Sure … I'm sure we have.' He went to the medicine cabinet in the kitchen. Anna glared at her teacher in silence until dad came back. He was very apologetic, there weren't any left, he explained, 'one of the girls must have used the last packet.'

'Has girls got an apostrophe Miss Rae?' asked Anna.

'It's okay,' said Miss Rae ignoring her, 'I'm sure I'll survive the morning.'

'Look, I'll nip out and get some,' he said. 'It might get worse and turn into a migraine … I wouldn't want anyone to go through that,' he was very sympathetic and left to go to the corner shop.

They were on their own.

'So,' Anna said, 'teach me some English!'

Miss Rae handed her a book, 'pages 61 to 90. Read, digest and précis, please.'

'What about …' started Anna.

'Just do it!' Miss Rae snapped and went to the kitchen. After five minutes she came back with a glass of water. She seemed to have calmed down and looked better.

Anna sat and read the book as instructed. Miss Rae concentrated on her iPhone until Anna's father returned with the painkillers. They left Anna in the sitting room and went through to the study.

At eleven, the official end of the lesson, Anna shut the book with a sharp snap. No one came through. She pulled her phone out and talked loudly to her friends. Still no one, so she grabbed her rucksack, shouted she was going out and left before her father could interrogate her about where she was going.

When she got back in the evening her father was watching a documentary about some big energy project in Switzerland, she still wasn't allowed to watch television, which was a bonus on this occasion, so she collected her chilled water and said goodnight.

Chapter 4

Anna ran up the stairs as she didn't want him catching her jumping, got ready for bed, drank her water and … and …

She looked around, she was in her room, but it wasn't right. Everything seemed larger and shinier and then to her surprise her memories from the missing two weeks started to play back in her head like a film.

It was the middle of the night, she was in bed and a noise woke her up; someone had sneezed.

She opened her eyes.

There was another sneeze and a woman's voice said 'bless you!'

She turned on her torch. Two people were creeping across the room. They stopped when the light flashed over them, the man looked up. 'Is that a car's headlight?' he asked.

A familiar woman's voice replied, 'it's a torch. The girl must have heard you sneeze.'

'You'd better get the dream machine ready, Miss Rae,' the man suggested.

Miss Rae! Miss Rae had been in her room!

Anna edged to the far side of the bed as the figures moved towards her. Miss Rae, looking as fierce as ever, raised a gun-like thing, so without hesitating Anna dived over the far side.

There was a click, then silence, another click and then repeated clicks and the sound of something being shaken angrily.

Anna cautiously poked her head up to see what was happening.

'It's not as powerful as usual,' the man said sarcastically, 'she doesn't seem to be affected.'

'No,' confessed Miss Rae, weakly, 'it isn't working.'

The man spoke again 'so now we know dropping it doesn't improve its performance.'

'I didn't mean to drop it,' whined Miss Rae, 'you er, you did knock … well we did collide when we were in the drive.'

'I was about to grab the little rascal. You shouldn't have got in the way. Anyway,' the man added, 'you said you'd fixed it.'

As they argued Anna wasn't sure what to do, scream and wake up dad or find out who these people were. She was curious because they didn't seem like burglars. She turned on the bedside light. The man with Miss Rae was plump and jolly looking, with a fluffy moustache and wild looking hair.

'HEY!' she said, trying to sound as stern as possible, 'what are you doing in my room?'

'She's seen our faces,' the man said and sounded worried, 'quickly give her some dreams.'

Miss Rae just looked at him. 'It's broken, that's what we were discussing,' she said bluntly.

There was another long pause while the two figures stared at their machine. The silence was broken by a beep.

The man lifted up a small black machine and stared at the screen. 'It's under the bed.'

'What is? Anna demanded. 'Look this is my bedroom and my house. If I don't get an answer quickly I'll scream as loudly as I can and then dad will come,' she threatened and added for effect, 'and you wouldn't want to mess with him he was in the SAS! He had a gun and everything!'

'Sssh, ssh,' the man said putting his finger to his lips, 'please.'

Miss Rae snapped the machine up to her shoulder and aimed it at Anna, nothing … nothing except the clicking of the trigger.

'Stop pointing that thing at me,' Anna said firmly, put her hands to her mouth and took a deep breath.

'Okay,' said the man. He motioned to Miss Rae to lower the gun. 'Look we'd be very grateful if you'd keep quiet, we're after something important …'

There was a noise.

'What was that?' Anna asked.

A small dark shape skittered across the floor.

Miss Rae scrambled round the bed, 'where did it go?'

'Hey something went under my dresser …' Anna pointed. 'Ugh, is it a rat?'

'It's not a rat,' Miss Rae looked up to the heavens as if she was exasperated, 'just stay on your bed and leave it to us.'

'Don't worry,' said the man, as he walked cautiously to the dresser, 'we've handled hundreds of these.'

'Are you from pest control?' asked Anna.

'Sort of,' Miss Rae said, staring at the chest of drawers. She pulled a thin mesh net from her pocket, but as she bent down her sleeve got caught in the drawer handle and before she could untangle herself there was a rustling and something scurried straight between her legs and headed for the door.

The man yelped. 'Not again,' he groaned as he turned.

It was Anna's turn to be critical, 'you're so slow,' she said, grabbed her blanket, leapt lightly after the animal and scooped it up. She held the ends tight, 'are you zoo people then?'

'She'll remember everything now, even if we get the "Dream-maker" to work,' said the girl. 'We shouldn't tell her any more. Let's take it and go.'

Whatever was in the blanket was thrashing about furiously.

'I suppose I could let this thing out,' Anna suggested calmly, and pulled the wriggling bundle back.

'Please don't,' the man pleaded. 'We've been after him for six hours.'

'You can have it,' offered Anna, 'if you tell me what's going on.'

He took a moment to think then held up his hands, 'okay, it's deal.'

'No,' Miss Rae said.

'I think I make the decisions,' he said. 'First let's put it away, then we can talk.'

Looking resentful, Miss Rae slipped off her rucksack,

opened it and pulled out a plastic sheet. When she shook it it fell into the shape of a box and she slotted another plastic sheet on top as a lid. 'Pass the blanket to Mr Goodman, and we'll trap the little ... er .... feller.'

Anna handed the blanket to Mr Goodman. Miss Rae pulled on a big, heavy leather glove that went up to her elbow. She took a deep breath and carefully slipped her hand into the blanket. The thing started to thrash even more, she caught hold of what ever it was and pulled it out, but before she could get in the box it wriggled free.

Anna saw it falling, snapped out her left arm, caught the creature by the leg and swung it into the box. She was so quick Miss Rae and Mr Goodman were still groaning, thinking the thing had got away, so she slid the lid shut.

'There!' she said triumphantly.

'Oh good show,' Mr Goodman said as he realised what she'd done.

Miss Rae looked sour.

Anna bent down to see what she'd caught, then stepped back in surprise. She'd never seen anything like it in her life!

Chapter 5

It was one of the very rare occasions when Anna was shocked into the silence. The creature was about the size of a squirrel, its body was covered in soft white fur but it had a really big head. Three stalks stuck out from the head and at the end of each stalk was an eye. Anna moved closer and all three eyes turned to look at her.

'What on earth is it?' she asked, unable to stop staring.

Mr Goodman, stuttered, 'uh, uh, uh, we, uh, work for the government.'

Miss Rae stood thin-lipped, 'we've got it now,' she said coldly.

'We have a deal,' said Anna.

'A deal with a eleven year old,' Miss Rae scoffed.

'Actually, I'm twelve!' said Anna, 'but a deal's deal!'

'Yes,' agreed Mr Goodman. 'A deal is a deal, we know that don't we Miss Rae?' He turned back to Anna, 'we work for the **"National Solutions Department"**, it's part of the government, and we … er … part of our remit … er … is to hunt monsters,' he admitted.

'Monsters!' Anna exclaimed and was about to tell them there was no such thing, except the thing in the box couldn't be described in any other way, so she swallowed hard and said, 'monsters … really?'

Mr Goodman continued, 'this is top secret. If you tell

24

anyone and you'll be locked up.'

Anna was so curious she swore she'd never tell anyone.

Miss Rae didn't look happy, but Mr Goodman was in charge. He explained there had always been monsters, they lived in the wilds and used to keep themselves to themselves; the locals would stay well away from where they lived, but nowadays city folk, who don't know any better, go into the country and while they don't mean harm they nose about everywhere.

'They've been disturbing the monsters and the monsters have started to wander. They're mostly harmless but they're like jackdaws and collect things,' he said. 'Miss Rae and I are employed to catch them so they can be taken back to where they came from.'

'Mr Goodman is a world expert,' Miss Rae interrupted.

'Well I wouldn't say that,' Mr Goodman said and blushed deeply, 'just scratched the surface really.'

'Catching monsters ... wow! That's brilliant, I could help,' said Anna, 'I caught this one!'

'No, no, no, no, no, no,' Mr Goodman said, flustered.

'No,' said Miss Rae, firmly, 'of course not.'

'No,' added Mr Goodman, in case she hadn't got the message.

'But they're only little,' Anna persisted, 'and you said they're harmless. I'm just the right sort of person to help the poor little things get home.'

'No, no,' repeated Mr Goodman, but he sounded as if he was wavering. Anna changed tack. The dream machine was lying where Miss Rae had dropped it so she picked it up. 'Ah,' she said smugly, 'that's why it's not working.' She put it on her bed and changed the subject. 'I'd be really useful. I've got loads of useful skills, like judo and gymnastics.'

'The machine?' said Mr Goodman.

'I'm quicker than either of you,' Anna pointed out.

'You're just a schoolgirl,' Miss Rae said.

'That boy, the diver one, he went to Olympics when he was fourteen, Mozart went round Europe playing the piano when he was six and Henry the third was only nine years old and he was king of England. I'm twelve, I don't want to be queen of anywhere I just want to help you catch these sweet little things.'

'But …' Mr Goodman interrupted.

'I'm tough as anything, I play football in a boys team.'

'No!' said Miss Rae.

She wasn't in charge, so Anna concentrated on Mr Goodman. 'I'm going to be a stunt girl and I've already been in three films,' she boasted. That was sort of true … when she was a baby she had been used in her mum's films, but she wasn't going to tell him that. It was obvious he didn't have children, so he didn't know how to say no and mean it. 'Please,' she wheedled. She looked up at him, trying to make her eyes as big and sad as possible, which was very big and sad. Once she had used her big, sad eyes on Caroline and despite an allergy to horses, which made her wheeze and come out in a rash, Caroline had personally taken Anna for riding lessons.

Mr Goodman looked flustered and uncomfortable.

'I'd be really useful and helpful,' Anna kept looking up at him and tried to force tears out.

'It's just …' stammered Mr Goodman under the onslaught.

'I'll tell you what's wrong with your machine,' she offered, her eyes as big as saucers.

Mr Goodman was beginning to crack, 'It's against the rules … I I I … we could think about it.'

'I'd keep it a secret,' she insisted, 'I really wouldn't want anyone else to know.'

'I hope you don't think you can blackmail Mr Goodman,' said Miss Rae, coldly.

Anna ignored her.

Mr Goodman scratched his head nervously.

'This is important government business, not some silly school project,' Miss Rae insisted.

Anna continued to ignore her and concentrated on looking up soulfully at Mr Goodman, he was the boss and he was weakening.

'Your schoolwork …' he tried, 'you'll be far too busy.'

'The holidays are coming, I'll have plenty of time.' Anna managed to blink out a tear.

Mr Goodman concentrated on a spot above her head so he didn't have to look at her eyes. He coughed nervously 'er … what's wrong with the machine?'

They'd find out when they checked it, so Anna told them. 'It's switched off!'

'Switched off?' Mr Goodman turned to Miss Rae.

'It must have happened when you ... er when I ... er when it fell on the ground ...'

'See how useful I'd be,' Anna chirped, 'I'd spot things like that and I'm good at catching things, aren't I?'

'Yes ... no.' Mr Goodman replied. 'What I mean is, yes you are good at catching things, but no I really don't think you should help.'

'You said it wasn't dangerous,' Anna pointed out.

'Little girl ...' Miss Rae said patronisingly.

'I'm very public minded, people often remark on what a public minded girl I am, I'm always helping people and I'd like to help you,' Anna interrupted.

Mr Goodman tried to get the initiative back, 'three things - first, as we've already said, you're far too young, second you'd need your parent's permission, third, you haven't had any training, fourth, there are the health and safety issues, fifth, insurance is only provided for employees of the department, sixth ...'

'You said three,' Anna said in her littlest girls voice, trying to sound as upset as possible.

'Pardon,' said Mr Goodman completely losing his train of thought, worried she was about to cry.

'You said three things, but you've already listed five and you've started on a sixth and that's so not fair,' she complained. 'We could phone mum, she'll be pleased if I have something to do in the holidays, it would stop me pestering her. This would be perfect and it would help me become more mature.

I'm always being told to act more grown up and this would help wouldn't it? Perhaps we could put it down on my voluntary service sheet. I have to do fifty hours this year, I've been helping at a café for grannies …'

'I'm sure mummy wouldn't want her little girl chasing monsters.' Miss Rae argued.

Mummy! How old does she think I am, wondered Anna and gave Miss Rae her grown up look. 'Mum will think it's great,' she said 'she lets me do anything.'

'Look,' said Mr Goodman and gave a rueful smile, 'twenty years ago things were different … but now, now we're drowning in red tape and risk analysis, so however good, however enthusiastic a volunteer is,' he was wavering …

Miss Rae interrupted. 'Mr Goodman says no,' she said briskly. 'Thank you for your help tonight, we have to go.'

She wasn't going to let Mr Goodman say yes.

'Goodbye,' she said, her tone firm and emotionless, then she pulled a futuristic looking device from her pocket.

'Wow! Are you going to transport out of my bedroom?' Anna asked. 'That is so cool!'

'Er, no,' Mr Goodman replied, 'those are the keys to our van.'

A white transit van was parked outside the house.

'Goodbye,' he shook her hand, 'and thank you,' he squeezed out the window and climbed down a ladder propped there. Miss Rae didn't say anything, didn't look at Anna, just hurried after him.

At the van Mr Goodman turned and waved. Miss Rae

didn't, she got straight in, sat at the wheel and as soon as Mr Goodman had done up his seatbelt she drove off.

Anna shut the curtains and got into bed.

She lay there back disappointed, it would have been fun to go monster hunting and she was sure she would have been good at it if they'd given her the chance.

Chapter 6

A few days later Anna was practising running up walls after school and she'd vaulted onto a flat roof to think about things when she heard a familiar voice.

'Miss Templeton,' a man called.

She peered cautiously over the edge. It was that Mr Goodman. He was on his own.

'You're a long way up,' he said.

She jumped off and did a somersault before she landed to show off. 'I know you,' she said as she straightened up, 'is your little monster okay?'

'He is. Safe and secure and soon he'll be on his way home.'

She looked up at him and used her big eyes again.

Mr Goodman didn't last long. 'The other night,' he said, 'you were very good, you know, at catching the creature.'

She kept looking up soulfully.

He gave in 'I wondered if you could … perhaps give me a hand right now.'

'You said …' she began, always ready to argue and then stopped as she didn't want him to change his mind.

'Yes … well,' he admitted, 'different circumstances, different situations.'

It was what she wanted so she tried not to grin.

He held out his little machine. There was a flashing dot

on the screen. 'This tells me where it is.'

She pulled it down to have a closer look, 'it's just a dot!'

'Yes?'

'I thought it would look like a monster. That would be cool.'

'Yes,' he agreed, 'it would be, er, cool. Maybe I should ask the IT people if they can change it.'

'You should!' said Anna and as they walked she told him about lots of other things that needed changing to make them cool; starting with her school uniform and finishing with her dad's car, which was very un-cool - as in fact was he, she added. She only stopped talking when Mr Goodman came to a halt outside a large building. There was a chain threaded through the door handles and secured by a padlock. Mr Goodman took a net out of his pocket, gave it to her, and then he put another machine on top of the padlock. Within seconds there was a click and the padlock opened. He put it against the lock, another click, he pushed open the door and they slipped in.

'Wow,' enthused Anna.

'Let's see if we can find the little stray,' suggested Mr Goodman.

Mr Goodman had a big stomach, his face wobbled when he talked but he walked very softly. Anna followed as quietly as she could and they made their way through the abandoned rooms, past dusty machines and round broken glass. He stopped and tilted his head. Something was there. It could be a rat, but Anna knew it would the little monster.

She wasn't scared, she was excited and she hoped she'd catch it as quickly as the first one as that would prove she was a proper monster hunter. As they went deeper into the building the noise got louder and they eventually reached a room with a great jumble of things piled up; shoes, TV antennas, mobile phones, boxes, dolls, lampshades, clothes, newspapers, car windscreen wipers, bottles, things that could have been collected from wandering the streets late at night.

They couldn't see the monster but a bottle crate on the far side of the room rocked and then jerkily shifted a couple of feet. Anna had the net so she decided it must be her job to catch it. She hoped all three eyes would be focussed on what it was doing.

The crate shifted again, scraping and banging as it slowly moved across the room until eventually the monster could be seen behind it.

It was not what she was expecting and was utterly different from the first monster. Hairless and pale, it had one little, squashed-up eye, six legs and clammy, ugly rolls of fat, which shook as it moved; repulsive was the kindest word for it. It was pushing the crate with its head, butting it when it got caught on the rough floor.

Anna didn't like the thought of touching this one, but at least it wasn't any bigger than the first monster.

She leapt out of her hiding place. The creature gave a squeak of surprise and without taking its eye off her, retreated as fast as its stubby legs would take it. Anna chased after and thought she had it trapped, but it used the wall as a springboard, bounced forward and ran straight at her, all six legs pumping madly.

She automatically jumped out the way, thinking it was going to bite her but at the last moment it veered to the side and headed for the door, moving like an overexcited steam engine, legs thrashing and head bobbing manically. Mr Goodman reached down to grab it, but it saw him just in time, gave a startled 'eep' and switched direction. It found itself back in front of Anna and determined to prove herself, she threw herself at it. It gave another 'eep', sprang just out of reach and she landed on the floor rolling as she did.

Mr Goodman gave a concerned 'oh!'

The creature retreated with 'tsch, tsch, tsch' sound, scrabbled up the pile of jumble and this time when it reached the wall it started to run up it backwards, a smug look on its ugly face.

The self-satisfied grin disappeared and it almost lost its grip as it realised Anna was back on her feet and following it, her momentum driving her up the wall.

'Don't touch it,' shouted Mr Goodman, as she reached out to grab the creature.

Instantly she switched plans, flung the net over it and caught its legs in the mesh. She kicked hard against the wall and as she somersaulted away it lost its grip. The thing squeaked and thrashed angrily but simply got more tangled in the mesh and she landed safely on the floor with it.

'Quick,' said Mr Goodman and held out a box. She

dropped the little monster in and he slid the top on with a snap. 'Well done, Miss Templeton. Very impressive, last night wasn't luck!'

'Of course not!' she said, pretending to be offended. 'Is its skin poisonous then?

'Do you think?' Mr Goodman asked and peered curiously through the see through walls.

'I don't know, you said don't touch it!'

'I didn't want you to hurt it,' he said, 'poor little thing.'

'It's a super ugly little thing,' said Anna, peering at it too, 'but I wasn't going to hurt it. I was worried it would bite me!' she complained. 'I thought the monsters all looked the same. I got a mega shock when I saw this one. For all I knew it could have had big teeth. Has it got big teeth? Was it going to bite me? It came right at me and I thought OHMIGOD it's going to bite me! You should have said it wasn't the same. I mean I thought it was going to be a cute three-eyed monster, the same as the first. You should have told me,' she said accusingly. Then before he had a chance to answer she started again. 'This thing is not cute, no no no, and you made me think it was poisonous. I was about to grab it and then you said don't touch it. I mean why not? The only reason I could think of was it was poisonous! You should have said. That wasn't fair, was it?' She shook her head. 'Still I got it didn't I?' she added after a moments reflection. Then more excited she said, 'Did you see the surprise on its little face when I followed it up the wall? It really thought it was going to get away. But also you should have told me it could climb walls, shouldn't you?' She bent down and picked up the Perspex box to look at the creature.

She stopped speaking for a moment, so hurriedly Mr Goodman took the opportunity to reply.

'Miss Templeton I've never seen one of these before. I didn't know what it could do, I don't know if it has big teeth or not. If I did I promise you I would have told you …'

'Was this a test?' asked Anna.

Mr Goodman reddened. 'I suppose it was in a way.'

'So?'

Mr Goodman looked confused.

'Did I pass?' asked Anna fiddling with the lid. 'He is so uncute and one eye is just plain scary!'

'Be careful, we don't want to let him out,' said Mr Goodman nervously.

'No,' agreed Anna, 'we don't.'

'You've done very well,' Mr Goodman praised her. 'Perhaps, er … you'd come out again … if there was another little monster in this area.'

'I don't know,' said Anna, trying not to seem too eager.

'I'm sure we could increase the reward,' Mr Goodman said, a little too quickly. 'I've often thought £50.00 a bit paltry,'

Anna swallowed hard, fifty pounds was a fortune, 'yes I'd love to, anytime really, even if I have to skip school. Are there any more about now? We could just go and get them, couldn't we? That would be cool. Should I get some special clothes or can I wear my free running stuff? Will I have one of those machines too? If I had one and I found a monster I could give you a call and we could grab it super fast.'

Then she was back in her room. She tried to work out if she had just had an amazing dream or had it been real. She jumped to her computer and logged into her bank . She hadn't looked for ages, not since dad had stopped her allowance. There were five new payments. One from mum, every now and then she put money into her account, usually if they hadn't had a chance to spend time together but the other four had no details and each was for £75.00. She was sure they were from Mr Goodman. It couldn't have been a dream. But how? How did her memory come back and for that matter how did it disappear in the first place?

Wait a minute, Anna looked suspiciously at her water bottle. She had drunk from it just before her memory came back, perhaps there was something in it. She put it close to her nose and she wasn't sure but maybe it had a bit of a chemical smell. Hmm she thought back. In the morning Miss Rae had heard her talking about her water and then she'd gone into the kitchen on her own. Miss Rae was something to do with Mr Goodman. Mr Goodman had lots of cool gadgets, maybe Miss Rae's thing was pills, maybe she had lots of weird pills, and one of them was a pill that could bring your memory back.

Anna didn't like and didn't trust Miss Rae, but she did want to know what had happened, so if there was something in the water and she drank some more, perhaps the rest of her memories would return.

She lay back, took another swig and shut her eyes.

Chapter 7

She was outside the school gates. Mr Goodman was there, he held out his hand and Anna automatically held out hers and they shook.

'Good afternoon Miss Templeton, are you well?'

'I am, thank you. How are you Mr Goodman?'

He smiled, 'I'm well. Did the payment reach your account?'

'How did you find out my account number?' Anna asked.

'Miss Templeton, I work for the government. Now I have a new sighting, are you in?'

'Well …'

'You have a free afternoon, don't you, since hockey was cancelled? A shame, it's an excellent game. I used to play for Wales when I was younger.'

'How …' Anna began.

'A lot of training and I guess an innate skill with the hockey stick.'

'No, how did you know MY hockey was cancelled?'

'I work for the government,' he said smiling. 'So?'

'You know I'm going to say yes, don't you?'

'Know,' Mr Goodman arched his eyebrows, 'how would I know that?'

'You work for the government!' said Anna.

Sitting on the bus Anna asked why they weren't in the van and Mr Goodman waffled about how difficult it was to get parked. So she asked about Miss Rae. 'Where's she?'

'To be honest,' admitted Mr Goodman, 'which I'm not usually because I work for the government. Miss Rae has many excellent qualities, but she can be less coordinated than is necessary and her aptitude for catching anything, balls, jokes or monsters is well below average.'

'I've only met her once and I don't like her either,' said Anna.

Mr Goodman huffed, 'hang on, it's not that I don't like her, I've got to catch monsters. The poor girl has two left hands and more often than not helps them escape rather than traps them.'

'Yeah, tell me, my sisters are just as useless.'

Mr Goodman grinned, 'Miss Templeton you must be a handful for your father.'

'And he's useless too,' said Anna vehemently, 'not like mum. She can do anything, she's almost perfect!'

'Is she …' said Mr Goodman, 'look we're here now' he added as he looked down at his machine.

Anna opened her mouth.

Mr Goodman stopped her, 'no, I don't know what this monster looks like, what it is or how to deal with it.'

It was her turn to grin, 'good! This is fun isn't it? Dad would never let me do this.'

'What!' Mr Goodman looked worried, 'I thought you said your parents would be happy about you doing this!'

'I never did! I said mum would be fine. Of course Dad would hate it, he's that sort of father, he hates everything I do! I can't imagine him being happy with me doing anything that isn't related to studying or science. The trick is to make sure he never finds out, right? Or … I'll be banned from watching television for ever, I'll never get my allowance back and he'll probably get the police to tag me.'

Mr Goodman had gone white.

Anna ignored his obvious concern, 'so which way? I hope it's a tricky one. This time you should try and catch it and I should watch. That way I'll learn. How quickly do you think you could catch it? We could have a bet and the loser has to do a forfeit. We did that at school, Olivia lost and we said she had to wear her underwear on top of her clothes. Actually she didn't get out of the changing room because a teacher came along and stopped her. We could do that, whoever loses has to wear their underwear over everything else!'

'You think I can't catch it,' complained Mr Goodman. 'You think because I'm fat I'm past it.'

'Yes,' agreed Anna, 'You'll look funny with your pants on top of your trousers.'

'No, we're not going to do forfeits! With an attitude like that I'm surprised you've made it to your twelfth birthday!'

'My step sisters keep saying I won't make it to the next one, they're ugly by the way … and cruel … and their feet are much bigger than mine with huge warts, horrible nails and they're really hairy!'

'What ...' asked Mr Goodman.

'Stepsisters – Cinderella, doh! Surely you know Cinderella?'

'Stop calling me Shir ...'

'OLD JOKE!' interrupted Anna.

'I'm going to have to be quicker aren't I?' he suggested.

'Yes you are,' Anna agreed, 'so losing a few pounds would be a good idea ...'

'Miss Templeton, you are so rude,' he laughed. 'I've been catching monsters for the last fifteen years.'

'But just the slow ones! That's why you need me. I'm fit and because I'm fit I'm fast.' She started to explain what her diet should be and how important it was to have the right balance of carbs, sugars and proteins. 'My mum's dietician designed my diet, would you like me to ask him to do one for you? That's another reason why I hate dad, he ignores my special diet and gives me his organic muck. I have to try to get back on track at school. For a scientist you'd think he'd be a bit more sensible wouldn't you?'

Mr Goodman smiled and said that he thought organic food would be good for her too.

'But it tastes like cra ...'

The machine beeped and it was time to concentrate. The green dot was in an area of scrubby wasteland near a dual carriageway. There was a path, but it didn't look as if it had been used recently; brambles, thorny trees and bushes had gone wild and straggled over it.

'In there,' whispered Mr Goodman pointing to a

particularly dense looking area of undergrowth. There didn't seem an obvious way in so they walked round as quietly as they could. On the far side was a well-worn path with enough headroom for a small creature to make its way into the centre. Mr Goodman set up a net over the entrance, he whispered to Anna to go to the other side of the undergrowth and make lots of noise. He said he would trap it this time as an example. She went round until she thought she was opposite, then yelled and shook the bushes as hard as she could. A minute later Mr Goodman shouted excitedly, almost immediately he swore loudly, then he shouted 'sorry' very loudly, before swearing again.

'Has it got away?' Anna called anxiously and started to run back as fast as she could, worried Mr Goodman was in big trouble and needed help.

She rounded the corner and stopped on the spot.

Chapter 8

Mr Goodman was holding the net, which was good, the creature was in the net, also good. It had big brown, friendly eyes, six or seven of them at least and a cheerful expression, which made it look quite endearing. However what was not so good were the feeler things that spouted from its body. They bulged slightly every couple of seconds and then sprayed sticky gunge over poor Mr Goodman.

He was covered in the stuff.

When the creature heard Anna it sprayed goo in her direction. Fortunately she was too far away but poor Mr Goodman was soaked again. He didn't swear this time; he just looked resigned.

'Well done,' said Anna cheerfully, 'I wish I'd seen you catch it, I'm sure I'd have learnt a lot.'

'Feel free to pursue your studies up close,' Mr Goodman replied sarcastically.

Anna didn't move.

'I think,' decided Mr Goodman, 'it's time to contact the office. Could you phone for me, we don't want to discover if this stuff affects phones.' he nodded to his bag. 'There's a business card in there. Use the camera on your phone to scan the barcode and automatically your phone will dial. Ask reception to send some one, and please, ask them for a towel and a change of clothes.

Anna did as he asked and when he wasn't looking she carefully pocketed the card.

Mr Goodman was still periodically getting gunged so he suggested Anna head home, 'I'll see you the next time I need help and I hope it will be a drier experience; at least for me.'

Anna said goodbye and headed home. She was buzzing and full of energy so on her way back she leapt over the street furniture, vaulted the bins and did cartwheels down steps. At the shops closest to her house she saw a familiar face, she couldn't think who it was, then later on she realised it was that friend of Mr Goodman, that Miss Rae. Anna was glad she hadn't stopped as Miss Rae was not nice.

Some of the guys who taught her free running were practicing so she stopped to say hi. Roy, a big tattooed French man, came over and just as he did a car stopped.

'Anna!' It was her dad. 'Get in the car.'

'Hi Dad, just a mo ...'

'Anna I can't stop here, so just get in.'

She said bye to Roy, said she would see him later and got in the passenger seat.

'Who was that?' asked her father.

'Just one of the guys who teaches free-running.'

'What a yob,' Dad said. 'All those tattoos, I wonder if he ever washes his hair.'

'So,' said Anna. 'He's just about the best free-runner in London at the moment, some of the jumps he can do are 'mazing.'

'I don't want you associating with him,' her father

informed her. 'If I see or hear you've been talking to him or even doing any more of this stupid running stuff, I shall stop your allowance.'

'What's wrong with you dad? What …' started Anna before she was cut off.

'Don't talk back young lady, you'll do as you're told. I only want to hear about school and homework from now on. I told you last time if I caught you at it again there would no television for a week, so that's it no television!'

'WHAT!' she exploded. 'God you're so bloody mean!'

'Don't you swear Anna Templeton,' her father said in a warning tone of voice, 'it's rude, it shows a lack of imagination and an inability to form a coherent argument. I don't want any daughter of mine swearing.'

'Fine, but if I can't watch television I won't know what's going on, my friends won't talk to me, I'll lose the support of my peer group and that could harm my development and my ability for social interaction.' She had lifted the phrase from what one of the social workers had said in the teen soap opera she was watching, 'and my ability to concentrate on work.' She added to try to persuade him.

'You need better friends. If they're so fickle they won't talk to you over a television programme then you're better off without …' They were home and as soon as the car stopped Anna leapt out before the rest of the stupid lecture. She stormed up to her room and immediately phoned her mum to complain. She was desperate to get away from living with dad. He always put down her friends, he kept lecturing her telling her what to do all the time and he had a total lack of interest in any of the things she liked doing. 'Thank god I'm coming over next weekend,' she said.

'Oh Anna,' said her mother, 'you can't. I've got to meet the director and producers. This is it, the biggest film I could ever be in and they've green-lighted the sequel already.'

'Oh ...'

'There's tons to talk about ... and they want to choose two small indie films to give me credibility. They'll put them out just before the blockbuster, they say it'll help with the award.'

'Award mum?'

'Oscars, Anna. But I've got to spend the weekend with them, just so they can be sure I'm committed to doing the press and all that stuff.'

'Yeah ... of course, no probs,' said Anna.

'I miss you,' her mum said. There was a long pause. 'I'll call them and say I can't make it.'

Anna knew how hard it had been for mum to get to this point and she couldn't spoil it just so she could have a weekend away. 'No, don't mum, it's okay, I'd have to come back to play hockey and the choir is singing on Sunday morning so I'll have to come back for that too so we'd spend most of the time travelling.'

'I'll have my fingers crossed for the game and I'll look past school on my way to the offices. I've got lawyer Ken to put together another appeal. I still can't believe your father got full custody or he was even going to demand it. I shouldn't talk about conspiracy theories but it feels like that. It never felt like the judge was looking at the facts, I mean I can't believe all actresses fail to get custody.'

'Dad just wants some dumb, little robot who does everything he says and eats the crappy organic stuff he makes,' complained Anna. Then she added, 'I feel sorry for Caro and Eliza, they're not allowed to do anything they want, they have to do whatever he says and it's just not fair!'

Mum calmed her down and then insisted she would sort it out. She said if Caroline and Eliza wanted they could come stay with her whenever and for as long as they needed. That cheered Anna up and she was a bit less angry by the time Caro banged on the door and said dinner was ready and she should get her butt downstairs.

Chapter 9

Of course Anna ignored her father and everything he told her to do from then on. Mr Goodman met her at the school gates twice more the next week and she went both times, they caught two more monsters, each quite different from the previous ones. The last one was tricksy, but in the end both little monsters were carefully put in perspex boxes ready to be taken back home.

Anna was having a great time and the only cloud was the occasional appearance of Miss Rae. She was obviously trying to follow her, but was making a terrible job of it and Anna spotted her every time; in fact on one occasion Miss Rae walked into a dustbin and knocked it over with a tremendous clatter so everyone looked. Miss Rae was so clumsy she'd make a useless spy, Anna on the other hand knew she'd make a great spy, she pretended she'd just stolen a memory stick with a secret code on it, she jumped over a garden wall and raced off.

On Friday Anna eagerly looked for Mr Goodman outside school in case another monster had turned up but annoyingly Miss Rae was standing where he usually stood. Anna went up to challenge her but before she could speak Miss Rae held out a small package. 'Mr Goodman asked me to deliver this,' she said, her tone of voice implying that delivering things was far beneath her and delivering to Anna was even lower, as she plainly did not like Anna. 'I would do what he asked,' she continued, 'for your own good.'

'What?' said Anna, but Miss Rae was already stalking away.

Anna waited until she was away from her friends before opening the parcel. 'Dear Anna,' the printed note read. 'I've enclosed some tablets. They will protect you from any scratches or cuts you get from the monsters. Cheers P.G'.

She swallowed them right there and that was the last of her memories; she was back in her room.

So Mr Goodman's pills had given her amnesia. Now she realised what she was missing she felt sad. She'd enjoyed their adventures and had liked Mr Goodman. Her uncles and aunts were all from dad's family, they were all as dull as him, but Mr Goodman was very much the sort of person she'd have liked as an uncle. She wondered why he had given her the pills, had she done something wrong or said something to someone? She looked for his note, it would be nice to have something to remember him by. She rifled through the papers on her desk, had a rummage in her school bag, checked the waste paper bin, the pockets of her school jacket and finally found it scrunched up in her trackie trousers pocket. She read it, her bottom lip quivering; it was a horrid way to end her adventures. She turned on her computer to play a game and then read the note again. Why had Mr Goodman written "Anna", he had never called her anything but Miss Templeton? She put it down and went back to the computer. She looked at it again and it also bothered her he had signed it PG; she had only known him as Mr Goodman. The more she thought about it the more she became convinced it wasn't from him, it was from horrible Miss Rae. Of course it would be just like Miss Rae to ruin everything that's exactly the sort of thing she would do.

As she lay on her bed trying to fall asleep, the question rattled round her head; why would Miss Rae want her to lose her memory and then eight weeks later why would she make it come back? Anna decided she would find Miss Rae in the morning and ask her nicely to explain what that was all about.

Chapter 10

The next morning, fired by righteous indignation Anna gave everyone the benefit of her opinion at breakfast and her opinion of breakfast. Her opinion of breakfast was, as usual, very low.

Eliza repeated what dad said but without much enthusiasm, organic food was good for her, good for concentration, good for energy and good for growth.

'Which I think we all agree you could do with, shorty,' said Caroline.

'It hasn't done much for the growth of your bosom,' retorted Anna.

Caroline squeaked outrage to Dad, but Anna was already listing what her friends ate for breakfast and how much tastier their meals were. 'They're also perfectly nutritious,' she claimed. 'Dad, we should do an experiment!' she said trying to get him on her side by playing the science card. 'I'll go on a diet of modern convenience foods. In five years time we'll compare my school reports with Caro's and Eliza's. If mine are better you buy me a Mini Cooper, if they're worse I'll gracefully accept defeat and if they're the same we all shake hands and go to MacDonalds. You could turn it into an interesting scientific study. Perhaps you'll win the No Bell prize!'

'Anna,' said her dad irritably, 'just eat your muesli, it's too early for one of your schemes to get out of doing something that's good for you.'

'Why don't we get Caro to eat Poptarts for a month and see if they have any effect on her.'

'They'd give her spots,' suggested Eliza.

'Then she'd have a nick name,' Anna pointed out.

'No Poptarts,' said dad, 'and no rubbish convenience foods. I've expressively forbidden you to eat that junk stuff.'

'For scientists none of you are very curious,' complained Anna. 'I keep coming up with great ideas and you just sit on your lumpy organic bottoms turning them down out of hand. Right I've finished this muck. See you later.'

She was gone and without her fizzing energy, it was like the colour had drained out of the room. After a brief period of silence her father asked the older two girls how they were getting on with preparing for exams. Deprived of the bubbling vitality of their younger sister they both felt quite dull and answered in monotones and told him what he wanted to hear.

Meanwhile Anna was out the front door and running. She liked to run, but today she was going to check all the places she'd seen Miss Rae. If she couldn't find her she was planning to use Mr Goodman's barcode business card and trick Miss Rae so she could ambush and interrogate her.

She was almost on the next street when someone called her name. She stopped dead. It was Miss Rae, she was standing just behind dad's car. Right thought Anna, let her do the talking, leave lots of gaps so she gets embarrassed, make her do all the work, never show any emotion. Together they walked round the corner in silence.

'Hello Miss Rae,' she said.

Miss Rae opened her mouth …

'What the hell are you playing at!' said Anna. 'I can't believe it, omigod! You gave me pills that made me lose my memory didn't you! Do you know how awful it was at school? Everyone thought I was a moron. Everyone thought I hadn't been paying attention and couldn't hold a thought in my head for more than five minutes! I worked so hard on that French translation and then I couldn't remember anything and Susie Mitchell got a "well done" from Mr Stoneface. That should have been my "well done". He hates me and already thinks I don't pay any attention and that was my chance to show I do. Dad was angry too and I got a telling off from him and then Eliza recited a poem in French to show off and Dad made me listen to the whole damn thing. I had to pretend I needed the loo because Caro started on a German poem. It was all your fault, wasn't it? I've had my television privileges revoked AND my allowance stopped. Caro and Eliza have been getting MY money for the last eight weeks! Worst of all I've just found out I was having a great time and doing something I was really good at. You stopped that. What are you like, spoiling everything, are you some sort of Grinch?'

She remembered she was going to make Miss Rae do all the talking so she stopped abruptly. Then she remembered the wasted time doing the supposed English lessons and began a new rant that lasted even longer. When she was finished she started to walk away in a huff, which she did when she didn't want to hear dad telling her off. She was already round the corner before realised she still didn't know what was going on and she was going to have to find out what Miss Rae had to say so she went straight back. Miss Rae was standing where Anna had left her, looking shell-shocked.

'So where's Mr Goodman?' Anna asked.

Miss Rae opened her mouth.

'Is he dead?' said Anna, 'did one of the monsters kill him?'

Miss Rae said 'N ...'

'You put something in my water, didn't you?' said Anna.

'Anna,' said Miss Rae, 'give me a chance to ...'

'I saw you trying to follow me! You'd make an awful spy. I'd make a great spy, I wouldn't knock over a bin like you did ...' As she was speaking Anna knew she would have to listen at some point and she decided that point was now so she stopped. The sudden silence un-nerved Miss Rae who couldn't speak for a full minute.

Chapter 11

'Er ... Mr Goodman is well, very well,' said Miss Rae. 'He's in Germany ...'

'What's he doing there?' Anna interrupted, 'why is he in Germany, he should be here doing his job! Is he in Berlin? That's the capital of Germany!'

'He's working with our counterparts in the German department; sharing information. We're not the only country who have monsters you know.'

'But what about OUR monsters, who's catching them?' Anna demanded.

'I am, of course,' said Miss Rae.

Anna blinked in amazement, 'I find that hard to believe.'

'Your father remarked on your general lack of comprehension' replied Miss Rae.

'He did not!' said Anna, hotly.

Miss Rae breathed in deeply and closed her eyes. When she opened them she said, 'we got off on the wrong foot, Anna.'

'We didn't, you did!'

'I'll make a deal,' offered Miss Rae.

'With a twelve year old?' Anna said sarcastically.

'A deal,' repeated Miss Rae, gritting her teeth. 'Help me capture the monsters and we'll forget the Saturday English lessons.'

Miss Rae needed her and Anna was torn between turning her down to teach her a lesson and wanting to be back in the exciting world of monster catching.

'Mr Goodman gave me a reward for every monster we caught,' Anna pointed out.

Miss Rae needed her so Anna started to imagine how much she might persuade her to increase it to; a hundred pounds, maybe two hundred pounds!

'The rate is £75.00 per monster,' said Miss Rae and Anna realised Miss Rae wasn't important enough and couldn't change it even if she wanted to.

Decision time! Anna wanted to get her own back because Miss Rae had been horrid, but it was that or catching monsters. Catching monsters won. 'Okay,' she said, and held out her hand, 'it's a deal'.

Miss Rae looked relieved and held out her hand too.

'I want one of those machines too,' Anna added.

Miss Rae hesitated, but only for a moment and they shook hands.

'Right let's go,' said Miss Rae.

'WHAT!'

'We've got to start catching them, duh!'

'Duh! No one said right away. I had some awful mush for breakfast I need something decent before I faint from lack of proper food.'

'But your father cooks only organic food, it really is very good for you!'

'Miss Rae, it's mush and it could only be improved if it

was tasteless, because at the moment it tastes of cardboard, I should be allowed to choose what I have for breakfast and the first thing ...'

'Okay, Anna, for god's sake stop,' Miss Rae gave in, 'I'll buy you something if we can just get on!'

Anna nodded.

They stopped at the first corner shop, where Anna made her buy a bag of crisps, a Mars Bar and a can of Coke. She secretly clenched her fist since dad never let her ever have junk food.

'Okay,' she said, through a mouth full of crisps, 'where is it?'

'Well,' said Miss Rae carefully, 'the, er, first one isn't too far away.'

'First one?' asked Anna and pulled the machine down to have a look. There were six or seven green dots in the immediate area. 'Wow, a bunch all turned up together!'

'Well not exactly,' mumbled Miss Rae, 'they've been turning up as usual, it's ... they've ... the problem is with just one person the first creature managed to avoid being captured and then the next one turned up.'

'Ah,' said Anna, 'so you haven't actually captured any since Mr Goodman went, have you?' She rubbed it in, 'and that's why you need me, perhaps we should ...'

'We have a deal,' said Miss Rae quickly, 'and you're the one keen to stick to deals.'

'Okay,' agreed Anna, 'we have a deal. Let's go. He's over that way.' She started to jog. She looked behind just to make sure Miss Rae was keeping up.

Miss Rae was following but instead of looking where she was going she was staring at her machine.

'Woah,' Anna shouted, instinctively leapt back, grabbed Miss Rae's arm and pulled her sharply to the side just before she ran, SMACK, into a streetlight.

'Let go,' said Miss Rae sharply, 'get off.'

'Hey I just stopped you from a clattering, what about a thank you?' Anna demanded.

Miss Rae gave her a black look until she realised she'd almost run into a lamppost and then just turned away. If that was her way of saying thank you Anna decided she'd let her get a nose full of concrete the next time. They set off again in annoyed silence, but Anna only lasted a couple of seconds before she started thinking aloud about what sort of monster the next one would be, she liked the one with three eyes, she said, it was her favourite, the sluggy, one eyed one was yucky and the one that sprayed gunge was just plain disgusting and she hoped it wasn't one of them. She asked Miss Rae how many different varieties she thought there were and then answered her own question, suggesting they might all be different. 'What about that?' she asked. 'Everyone different from each other, that would be cool.'

'Very unlikely,' Miss Rae said dryly, 'Genetically unlikely. They would inherit the characteristics of their parents, who in turn would have a morphological structure based on their own parents. Given that they would have developed from a base form one has to have the expectation that there would be similarities, they would share the same features, facial characteristics and body structures. Each one reflecting the base model they had come from, albeit less and less with each generation.'

'Have you forgotten how to speak English?' asked Anna, sarcastically.

Miss Rae spoke very slowly, as if to a baby, 'you have only seen a very few monsters, there is no reason why those should have all looked the same. If you visited a farm and the first creatures you saw were a cow, a pig, a chicken, a cat and a bee, it would be unscientific to assume every other animal on the farm was also completely different. The theory you presented is based on too small a sample to be of any use. In fact it's ludicrous and only an idiot wouldn't think otherwise.'

Anna instantly replied, 'only an idiot would think I meant that. I know about statistics and stuff. I said it would be cool!'

'Well it wouldn't,' replied Miss Rae.

'And you're a world expert!' countered Anna.

'However little I know, it's still more than you!'

'You haven't proved that yet,' said Anna.

Miss Rae was about to reply, but instead breathed in deeply. 'What an interesting person you are Anna, shall we agree to differ on this and concentrate on catching the next monster?'

Anna liked arguing but she didn't want to push things too far and not be allowed to hunt monsters, so she bit her tongue and agreed. Instead she asked how far away it was.

'It's somewhere in that multi-story car park,' Miss Rae said, without looking at her machine.

'Right,' said Anna, 'I'll take the net ... wait a mo, what's this one like?'

'What?' asked Miss Rae.

'You've seen it haven't you? You knew it was there without looking the tracker. What's it like then? Hey, have you got body armour on?'

Miss Rae looked embarrassed to be caught out. 'It ... it tries to bounce its way out of reach and if you get in the way, well it bounces into you.'

'Bounces into you! I don't have body armour,' pointed out Anna. 'You could have said!'

Miss Rae put her hands on her hips, 'you gave me the impression you can deal with anything. I didn't think a little bouncy monster would bother you.'

'Well it doesn't! I'm well used to getting bashed when I'm playing games. Dad of course might be bothered if I go back covered in bruises!'

A look of alarm passed over Miss Rae's face. 'Your father?'

'Hates me doing anything dangerous, in fact he's tried to ban me from football,' said Anna cheerfully, adding 'and free running.'

Miss Rae stopped. 'Perhaps this is a bad idea.'

'Come on ... you want these monsters caught, don't you?' Anna said. 'Or doesn't it matter?'

'Of course it matters,' Miss Rae replied angrily, turned

her back on Anna and stomped into the car park. Anna followed, it was time to switch on. During the two weeks with Mr Goodman he had insisted she tried to focus, he said she had to be ready to deal with whatever was out there 'and who knows,' he said 'what we may come across.'

He had been a lot more serious for a moment and Anna realised he meant it. It was like when Roy rolled his shoulders before teaching her a new free running move, it meant she had to really concentrate or she could get properly hurt.

Miss Rae headed straight for the stairs, stopped halfway down and pulled a cycling helmet from her bag.

She held it out to Anna. 'Put this on!'

Anna shook her head. 'No, I'm not used to wearing one. It would distract me. You keep it.'

Miss Rae gave her a look that said - I've given you a chance so don't blame me. She put it on herself and continued down.

Anna's senses were heightened now and while Miss Rae barrelled along eager to get the monster caught and boxed up, Anna was more cagey.

At the next level Miss Rae called out for her to be ready, 'I've got the boxes, you'd better have your net handy!'

Anna scanned the area.

Miss Rae was already marching down the aisle. 'Keep up,' she barked.

Anna didn't, she'd heard something, so she stayed where she was and watched from the doorway.

There was scuffling sound, an intake of breath and a

thump. Miss Rae only had time for a surprised shriek before a hairy football bounced from the side, caught her a glancing blow on her shoulder pad and knocked her over. The little monster, growling happily, bounced across the floor towards one of the pillars. Anna was about to give chase when she heard a sound to the left of Miss Rae.

It was a second monster. There were TWO!

The new one was bigger, it had a bald patch on the top of its head and looked older and tougher. Miss Rae hadn't seen it, she was back on her feet again and trying to spot where the first one had gone.

This second monster looked far more dangerous than any of the others and it was lining itself up, targeting Miss Rae's head. Anna moved in to action. She sprinted as fast as she could, swung the net just as it bounced and it landed right in the middle with an 'urk' sort of sound. Its sharp, little eyes widened in surprise and it looked unsure of what had just happened. Anna had been off balance when she cast the net and the monster's momentum pulled her forward. She didn't want to let go, so as she fell she spun onto her back so as not to bang her elbows.

'What are you doing! Can't you let me concentrate?' Miss Rae turned to glare. It took her a moment to take in the scene. Anna flat on the floor her arm stretched out and tightly gripping the ends of the net and in it the monster twisting and squirming frantically.

'Oh ...' said Miss Rae, 'oh gosh.'

'A box,' demanded Anna.

The first monster had ricoched off the wall and was heading back.

'Duck you idiot, DUCK!' Anna yelled.

Miss Rae wasn't listening but luckily just as the monster bounced she bent over to sort the box and it flew over her head. Anna sprang to her feet, swung the monster she'd caught off the ground before it could jump again.

The first monster hissed angrily, reached the wall rebounded and targeted her instead. Anna waited as long as she could before swaying out of the way and it landed right beside Miss Rae who dropped the perspex box in surprise. Anna instantly leapt on top of the little creature before it could roll away.

'Quick,' she shouted as both monsters wriggled furiously, trying to free themselves.

It took Miss Rae a maddingly long time to get the box ready; she was so flustered she kept getting it wrong. Eventually just when Anna was sure one or both monsters were going to get away it was complete and she shoved the big one, still in its net, into the perspex box. The second one wasn't as frantic and she was able to hold it upside down by a leg until its box was ready and then she dropped it in.

They stared down.

'Why didn't you come when I told you to?' asked Miss Rae.

'Because I don't just charge in without checking if it's safe,' replied Anna

'But I told you to and I'm giving the orders.'

'It was a stupid order,' said Anna. 'When you say something sensible I might listen to you. Anyway we've caught two monsters so you should be pleased, I am, I've got a hundred and fifty quid.'

Miss Rae was still angry, 'but …'

'If I hadn't stopped the big one, it would have knocked your block off!'

'What do you mean?' asked Miss Rae.

'Hadn't you better get someone to pick these up,' said Anna without answering the question. 'The big one looks like he really wants out of there.'

It was battering at the sides of the box with its powerful legs.

Miss Rae muttered to herself and pulled her phone out.

'Are we going to get another one, today?' asked Anna. 'I'll probably need some lunch if we are.' She was determined to get as much out of Miss Rae as possible.

'Yes,' said Miss Rae. The phone answered and she told the person on the end to come and collect the boxes. 'Yes two,' she repeated, 'I've got two to be picked up.' She listened for a moment. 'No it's not a joke!' She turned off the phone. 'Okay, let's go. If you behave yourself I'll get you lunch, what do you want?'

'MacDonalds' Quarter Pounder with cheese, fries and a coke.'

'Is that your favourite …' Miss Rae asked.

'I don't know, it's the only one I've tried,' admitted Anna. 'As if you hadn't noticed Dad is a health fanatic.'

'Doesn't your mother take you?'

'She's a mega movie star! ... like we can just pop into Burger King or McDonalds! So, they were surprised you caught two monsters ...'

'No.'

'I think they were. I think that since you haven't caught any in six weeks, they might be a little taken aback.'

'Look!' snarled Miss Rae and then changed her mind '... look I'm not arguing with a kid. Do your job, take your seventy-five pounds, the monsters will get taken back to where they came from and if you keep your mouth shut maybe I'll enjoy myself too.'

'What made you so sour?' asked Anna.

'I've just discussed a modus operandi that would work,' replied Miss Rae, 'let's stick to it and maybe we'll get through this without saying anything we'll regret later.'

'You mean, you'll regret later!' said Anna. 'I don't regret anything I say.'

'You think you're precocious, but you're just rude.'

'Am not!'

'Are!' Miss Rae clutched her forehead, 'you're making me do it again, you're so bloody annoying! Just shut up. SHUT UP!'

'For a grown up you're not very grown up,' pointed out Anna. 'Let's go, my tummy needs lunch and then we can chase down another monster.' She led them onto the street. 'Actually none of them are actually monsters are they? They're more like bunnies.'

'Bunnies!' Miss Rae replied in surprise.

'Yeah, I mean I know monsters. Monsters are huge and scary, lots of big teeth, horrible slimy drool, red eyes and plenty of roaring.' She roared loudly, giving Miss Rae a start. 'I've read loads of books and seen tons of telly about monsters.'

'They're not like bunnies.'

'Are!'

'Look they're plainly … Mr Goodman says we have to round them up so they don't get harmed.'

'That big one definitely wanted to do you harm. An' he definitely would have done you big harm even with your bike helmet on.'

Miss Rae didn't contradict her this time, but stared dead ahead.

'Lunch then,' said Anna.

As they set off a big black van turned the corner.

Miss Rae pushed her into a doorway, hissed to stay there and keep quiet and then walked forward as quickly as she could and signalled to the driver.

The van stopped beside her, she had a whispered conversation and then the guy drove on to the warehouse.

Anna waited until it was well away before she stepped out and caught up Miss Rae. 'They were from your office?'

Miss Rae started to walk on.

'They've come to collect them two we just caught,' Anna continued, 'but you don't want them to know I had anything to do with it, because that would be against the rules. Actually can I have a milkshake instead of a coke?'

Miss Rae stopped walking for a moment.

'No you can't blackmail me. We agreed a coke. Now zip it.'

They walked on in silence. Anna wasn't bothered about the milkshake she just wondered how far she could push things. She liked walking on edges.

At MacDonalds they went to the counter together and Miss Rae did order her a milk shake instead of Coke and Anna said thank you as nicely as she could manage, which sounded relatively sincere for her.

'You did catch two monsters,' Miss Rae said as an explanation.

Miss Rae bought herself a Big Mac too, although she had bottled water rather than a fizzy drink. They went upstairs because Miss Rae said there would be more seats but Anna decided it was because no one could see them from the street.

'Isn't this great? Macdonalds are so good.' Anna evangelised, taking a big bite out of her burger. 'They're nice and clean, the places dad takes us too look like they been breeding chickens on the floor. I hate touching anything, it always looks scummy and the food tastes like they made it the day before. That girl is doing a great job cleaning. I bet they keep their toilets clean. If I was prime minister I'd make it a rule all toilets had to be kept clean so they don't smell like toilets. You can get horrible diseases from toilets can't you? And I'd make another law that everyone has to wash their hands after goin'. I hate the idea of someone shaking your hand and they haven't washed and they've just been to the loo.'

Miss Rae shivered and for once agreed with her. 'That would be a good law. It's a horrible thought.'

Anna then went on to tell her some of the other great laws she would make to stop every thing being so filthy and she had a very pleasant lunch.

Before they left they had a secret check of their machine.

'That's the closest one,' Miss Rae pointed to a flashing green dot.

'Have you seen it, what's it like; I hope it's not one of the squirty ones? If there are only a few different types we're going to keep coming across the yucky ones so we're going to need waterproofs' said Anna. 'Mr Goodman was covered in slime, at least it didn't smell I hope there isn't a squirty one that has a smelly slime. Think on that! Grim!'

There was a small window when Anna wasn't talking and Miss Rae managed to say the next one had no fur and one eye.

'That's okay, we caught one like that, it was tricksy but it didn't bite. Look I have an idea. You should make up the box when we get there but before we see the monster. That way we'll be ready. That's a good idea isn't it?'

Miss Rae agreed to try it and they set off.

'It's in an old supermarket,' Miss Rae explained, 'we can get in the back door.'

'You have lots of cool equipment,' Anna tried to concentrate on things that wouldn't cause an argument, since they seemed to be getting on okay at the moment.

'There's a special laboratory and they make these things for us,' Miss Rae explained.

'The lock thing is really clever. Have you got one of those?'

'Yes …'

'Does it open every lock?'

'I …'

'Imagine if it did?' Anna thought of all the places she could get into, that really would be cool.

'It's not a toy!' Miss Rae was back to being her normal self.

Hmmm, Anna speculated, the Big Mac must of affected Miss Rae's brain and made her a bit nicer. Perhaps she should make Miss Rae have a Big Mac whenever they went monster hunting and eventually she'd become a normal person.

She glanced over at the machine to see how close to the next monster they were.

Miss Rae let them in the back door and Anna carefully shut it.

'I bet the monster has it's own special ways of getting out but we don't to make it too easy,' she said and suggested that if it looked as if was trying to run away Miss Rae should try and try to herd it back. 'I'll have more chance to catch it then.'

They were actually very lucky, the little one-eyed monster

didn't realise they were there and Anna caught it completely by surprise.

'Hey we boxed that one up super-quick!' She jumped on to a counter and did a victory dance.

Miss Rae phoned her back-up people, told them there was another one ready to be collected. From what Anna could hear they were super-surprised but she didn't say anything and they left as quickly as possible.

Anna asked how the back-up people knew where to go and Miss Rae said each box had a chip. Anna made a joke and asked if they were guided by the smell of salt and vinegar and Miss Rae almost smiled.

'I'd better get off now,' decided Anna, 'dad thinks he's running Ford open prison so I have to be back to check in.

'He's worried about you …'

'No he's not, he's worried I'm having fun,' Anna said. 'Anyhows do you want to give it another go tomorrow? There're four still out there.'

Miss Rae said yes and then mumbled thank you as they parted company.

Chapter 12

Of course Anna wasn't actually going home. She knew if she said she'd been with Miss Rae, Dad wouldn't be too nosy. She'd tell him Miss Rae had met her in the street and insisted on making up some of the lesson time they'd missed. She'd go on a tirade about how useless Miss Rae was and what a complete and utter waste of time it had been and she was sure if she went on for long enough he'd be convinced.

Right now she was going to find Roy.

She sprinted down an alley ran up the wall and then made her way full speed over the rooftops, leaping the gaps, hurdling chimney pots and practising tumbles just for the hell of it.

At the hall the free runners used, a few of the regulars were there and Roy was putting them through some training routines. She dropped down from the open window above him without making a sound.

'Do you think I should get a tattoo?' she asked.

He looked round in surprise.

'Where did you spring from petite caracal?'

'I'm magic! I magicked myself here with a clever spell,' said Anna. She was about to start on a long description of all her magic powers and what she intended to do with them but Roy told her to shut up and get to work.

'I can work and talk,' she said.

He sighed and said he knew she could but everyone else needed quiet so they could hear his instructions. He gave his shoulder a roll. 'I have something new for you to learn.'

That shut her up.

It took a good hour of practice before Roy said she just might have an vague idea of what she was meant to be doing.

Since that was his way of saying she'd got it – she shouted 'YEAH!' then she was up the wall and out the window; it really was time to head home.

She whirled into the house and both Caroline and Eliza felt a buzz course through the building. Even though she was a complete nightmare and there was no filter and no off button Anna had energy to spare.

'Where have you been?' her father demanded.

'Chasing bulls in Pample Homer!' she announced. 'I caught the biggest one and won a cow, we can keep it in the garden and Caro can get us fresh milk everyday for our morning mush.'

'Pamploma,' her father corrected, completely distracted by the ridiculous answer.

'It's fields ahead of the herd, the cleverest cow I've ever seen,' continued Anna, 'I'm going to call it Friesian Crane after that brainbox on the telly! So what's happening here? Doing an exciting jigsaw puzzle, sorting out the laundry, the fun never stops does it?'

Then before she could be quizzed properly she was off, hammering up the stairs so Dad knew she wasn't doing any free running. The radio flicked on and they could hear her singing along joyfully to the music.

Eliza looked over at her sister and gave a little grin. The house was better when Anna was there, even if they couldn't join in the fun and had to sit while dad muttered po-faced to himself.

At dinner dad asked her again where she'd been during the day and she started describing the thrill of chasing bulls and then switched and said she'd had the most boring day in the world because she'd got stuck with stupid Miss Rae. 'She really hasn't a clue about grammar you know, she insisted we do some more of that awful book. It's exactly like her, dismal!'

'Miss Rae is not dismal,' her father replied.

'Got a pash for her?' asked Anna.

'ANNA!'

'Her lips are so thin you could open letter with them so I suppose she'd come in handy when the mail is delivered!'

'She has two degrees ...'

'If she got a third one she could form a singing group. When I have a singing group I'll call it "Annachy in the UK" and I'll have so many chart hits I'll make Beyonce seem like a beginner ...'

'You will not,' interrupted Eliza.

'I WILL! I'll be rich and famous, but I won't forget you lot. When I travel the world Caro can look after my private jet, plan my schedule and arrange my taxis and Eliza, you can sort my laundry and sneaker collection, I'll visit everywhere and people will adore me even more.'

'Even more? No one adores you at the moment Anna,' said Caroline.

'They do! Even gloomy Miss Rae is under my spell and gives me extra tuition!'

Her father took the opportunity to point out Miss Rae had a degree in biochemistry, a second one in pharmacology and she'd got a PhD.

'What's that "a pink hair do"? She must have washed it out then. If I was going to change my hair colour I'd get it bright orange …'

'No hair dye!' ordered her father.

Caroline looked glum.

'Miss Rae is a clever, sensible and hard-working young lady and you would do well to take her as a role model Anna Templeton.'

'The only roll I want is a fresh, white roll with bacon and ketchup.' She spooned out some of her dinner and stared at it. 'Speaking of food what's this muck doing on the dinner table? Let's get Miss Rae to analyse it and see if she can identify anything nutritious in it.'

'It's all organic, all fresh and all good for you!' her father replied.

'It might be good for a sheep, but it's no good for me … or Eliza and Caro, look at them, they're fading away day by day, soon they'll just be ghosties wandering the house gnashing their teeth and wailing "pizzas … piiizzaaaaas".'

To her satisfaction she noted her sisters agreed with her,

even if they weren't going to say anything in front of dad.

Anna toyed with the stuff on her plate, gave her opinion on the Prime Minister's new dress and then she was gone.

'Anna! ANNA! I didn't give you permission to leave the table!'

It was too late. The telly was on and she was dancing in front of it copying the moves the performers were making.

He went through and turned it off.

'Anna. You didn't have permission to leave the table and you don't have permission to watch TV, remember your TV privileges have been revoked and even if they weren't I don't want you watching this rubbish!'

'Don't, don't, don't! Actually what is wrong with you dad? Still disappointed you never got a job as a prison warden?'

'Go to your room Anna!'

She was off in an instant and her bedroom door could be heard slamming shut.

It was exactly what she wanted, she would have at least three-quarters of an hour before he came up to lecture her. and that was plenty of time. She had a full bank account, no one knew about the extra money she'd got from monster hunting, so she was going to skip off down to Fernando's for a bag of chips and a sausage.

A second floor window was no problem for her and the moment she hit the ground she was at full speed, leapfrogging bollards, pillarboxes and wheelie bins, bounding up and over the phone boxes and was there in no time.

She scoffed her meal in the shop, telling them that chips

were great for a growing girl and they made the bestest. Twenty minutes after she'd slammed her bedroom door she was safely back on her bed, her favourite book in front of her and trying to look as innocent as she could. They were mighty fine chips she gloated.

Dad knocked on the door an hour later and came in.

She stared at him, he must have been giving her a talking to because he was opening his mouth a lot but she wasn't listening. She was imagining him being chased by lots of hairy, bouncing monsters, squealing like a baby and running like Miss Rae. The monsters chased him so far away he never found his way back and mum came to collect her in a helicopter. As they were leaving Anna felt sorry for Caro and Eliza, who'd been forced to eat lentils, beans and cabbage all their lives and she asked mum if they could come and live with them; mum said yes but only if they didn't recite any poems in French. They said wouldn't and they all went to live in America where mum won an Oscar and Anna became the best stuntwoman in the world!

It looked like dad was winding up so she nodded and hoped she wasn't agreeing to anything stupid.

'So that's no television for the next month and I hope you learn a lesson from this, don't be so disobedient in future.' He left closing the door behind him.

She stared at his back. He really didn't like her and she wondered why he wouldn't just let her go and live with mum and then he wouldn't have all this hassle. Being difficult was part of her plan. Anna lay back, she wished Mr Goodman was still there. He was clever, he knew stuff and he worked for the government … maybe, just maybe he'd be able to help sort it out for her. Funny how Miss Rae scoffed the Big Mac after she'd said nice things about organic food and how the lunch dad had cooked for her had been tasty. Bloody grown-ups they don't know their own minds. Unlike her, she knew her own mind!

She got ready for bed. Turned out the light and then slipped the iPhone mum had given her from its secret place. She plugged in the headphones, logged into catch-up TV and caught up with her favourite shows. When she was done she carefully hid it away again and was about to turn the radio on because she liked music playing as she went to sleep when she noticed how quiet the house was. Usually there was the drone of some dull documentary. It was about the only thing dad watched. Maybe they'd run out of the dull ones and he didn't want to risk seeing anything too exciting just before bed.

Chapter 13

The next morning Anna bounced through the kitchen, and straight out to the front door. She wasn't even going to pretend to eat the muesli and she wasn't allowed coffee.

'Breakfast young lady,' dad ordered.

'We all know it'd be tastier eating the packet it comes in,' she retorted.

'Toast then.'

That was an improvement so she turned and went back in.

She opened the kitchen cupboard. 'Jam, jam, jammy jam jam,' she sang, 'strawberry jam or raspberry jam or apricot jam or blackcurrant jam …' She stared into the cupboards. 'NO JAM! I think it's well time I was allowed to do the shopping.'

'You don't need jam Anna …'

'You don't need a tie, but you wear one. I need jam because soya spread is boggin' and I need something to take the taste away. Am I right Eliza?' She didn't give her sister time to reply, 'I am! There are minimum standards for bringing up children and giving them jam on their toast is one of the most important ones …' She saw Miss Rae walk past. 'Oh God, there's that bloody woman again, packing extra lessons in her manky handbag …'

'Anna, I've told you about swearing …'

The doorbell rang interrupting him. He went to answer it.

'Oh hi Miss Rae,' he smoothed down his hair. 'Come in, we're just having breakfast.'

'Without JAM!' yelled Anna. 'You'd like jam wouldn't you Eliza?' she asked and when she actually left a gap Eliza said yes … very quietly.

Anna was so surprised her sister was agreeing with her she was momentarily speechless. She recovered quickly enough. 'Dad, Eliza would like jam too. We're quorate so that's two votes to one in favour of jam. Democracy in action, right in your kitchen; you must be very proud. Now pop to the shops any flavour as far as I'm concerned … except onion!'

'Jam, Elizabeth?' Dad said sternly.

Eliza quailed under his gaze, 'it … it was a joke …' her voice tailed off and she took a big spoonful of the muesli.

'ELIZA!' Anna reproached her.

Dad offered Miss Rae something to eat.

She surveyed the table. 'Er, I've … er … had my breakfast, a cup of tea would be nice though.'

'Ginger, camomile or I've just sourced some Milk Thistle and Dandelion.'

'Just "builders" for me, Mr Templeton,' she replied, her thin lips closing tight.

Dad looked appalled and fetched the box of Typhoo he'd bought when they'd had the plumbers in.

'How nice to see you.' He turned on the kettle.

'Er … Anna and I were making some progress yesterday

so we … er … we thought we'd try and build on that.'

'Adverbs? Should that have an apostrophe?' asked Anna. 'I've always wondered about pronouns are there amateur nouns too? If you're writing a letter to your mates you can use the amateur nouns, but if someone's paying you, you gotta use them professional ones.'

'It's Latin,' Caroline showed off, 'pro means "for" you use a pronoun "for" the noun, "she" instead of Anna, for example.'

'You're a bundle of laughs Caro. Do you want jam?'

'It rots your teeth,' she replied.

'You don't cover your teeth with jam and then leave them, of course it'd rot your teeth if you did that. No what you do is …'

'Anna we've had enough of your views about jam. Remember we have guests,' dad interrupted

'Does guests have an apostrophe?' she asked.

'Look Anna …' her father started.

'Perhaps I'll skip tea, we should get on Anna,' Miss Rae interrupted before Anna was sent to her room and spoiling her plans for the day. She stood up and Anna torn between pursuing the jam issue and catching monsters decided the monsters would be more fun and stood up too.

'I've just got hold of a new recipe for fennel, Miss Rae,' said dad, 'if you're not busy this evening …'

'That would be a treat … except I can't, I've something on. Another time perhaps.'

'Don't cook any for me,' Anna called as she hurried out, 'I'll just chew on my bedroom carpet!'

The door slammed behind them.

'Fennel!' said Anna, 'urgh, you're lucky you've got an excuse.'

'I'm not keen on fennel I must admit,' Miss Rae said.

'It's bloody disgusting,' Anna ranted. 'And so is beetroot, kale, cabbage, pumpkin, broccoli, chicory, broad beans, green beans, butter beans …'

She stopped to take breath.

'You don't need to list every vegetable you hate right now Anna.'

'Course not, have you got an email address?'

'Email?'

'Yes, I'll send you the full list this evening.'

Miss Rae pulled out her monster-tracking machine. 'If you promise to shut up about vegetables or jam I have something for you.'

'I can let you off the vegetable list,' offered Anna, 'but I'm still not done with jam. I mean you have jam on your toast don't you?'

'That's neither here nor …'

'You do though?'

Miss Rae clenched her lips tightly and massaged her forehead. 'Okay, I have strawberry jam on Mondays, Wednesdays and Fridays and raspberry on the other days. Now can we get on?'

'Do you? Cool. Don't you get bored on Sundays?'

'On Sundays?' asked Miss Rae.

'Saturday and Sunday, you have raspberry jam two days

in a row!'

'Anna I was just trying to shut you up …'

'You didn't do a very good …'

'Anna please, please, I'll give you one of these trackers if you shut up?'

Anna's mouth snapped shut and she pretended to pull a zip across it.

'Good,' said Miss Rae. She handed over a machine and Anna held it reverently.

Miss Rae turned her own machine on and started to check the screen. 'Did Mr Goodman show you how to work it?'

Anna looked up.

'DID MR GOODMAN …' Miss Rae said more loudly, annoyed at the lack of response.

Anna nodded vigorously.

'What is it now,' asked Miss Rae.

Anna unzipped her mouth. 'I thought you wanted me to shut up.'

'I wanted you to concentrate on the matter in hand, obviously I still wanted you to be able to communicate.'

'We make a great team, don't we?' suggested Anna.

Miss Rae searched in her bag, found a box of Neurofen and took two.

'The closest monster is the same type as the one we caught in your bedroom.'

'I caught,' corrected Anna.

Miss Rae ignored her. 'The others are not ones we've seen

before ... so let's see if we can pick this one up and then go after one of the others.'

'Okey dokey super smokey.'

They set off.

'These machines are so cool,' said Anna. 'It's so clever you can see where the monster has been in the last half hour. This one, he's been a wandering ...'

'What are you talking about?'

Anna held the machine up to let her see.

'I didn't know they did that, why didn't Mr Goodman tell me?' Miss Rae complained.

'Perhaps he didn't know, I just found it now. This monster looks like something gave him the heebies, he was all over the shop.'

The green dot was skittering all over the screen. Anna pressed one of the buttons and the green dot was stationary.

'Did you pause it,' asked Miss Rae.

'No that's now. I think he must be hiding. I wonder what he's hiding from. It's not another monster because that would show up on the screen. Perhaps someone is in there, perhaps they looking for it.' Anna had a sudden thought. 'You know lots of people must have seen them, they can't be completely secret can they?'

'Obviously,' Miss Rae became very superior again. 'That's why we have the dream machine.'

'Yeah yeah, but you're not there all the time zapping people, you're only there when you're trying to catch one. What about all the times the bunnies are out there but you haven't tracked them yet?'

Miss Rae stopped dead in her tracks. 'Oh … right … I see what you mean.'

'They're going to start talking aren't they, Miss Rae? A lot of times they aren't going to be believed, people'll just say they're talking rubbish, but if enough people see the bunnies well … you know if you keep saying stuff eventually people hear it.'

'Like you and jam!'

'Exactly, jam jam, jam I have to make a hell of an effort to be heard by dad - but if I keep at it maybe jam will get on the shopping list.'

'We won't worry about it now Anna, I'll say to Mr Goodman in my next report.'

'Are you going to tell him I'm helping?'

'I've … I've not decided yet.'

'He's moving again,' Anna nodded to the screen.

They were soon outside the building, an old workshop, and they stopped at the door.

'Miss Rae?'

'What Anna.'

'Mr Goodman taught me a clever trick. He does know his stuff even if I gave him a hard time for being fat. I wonder why he's fat I never saw him eat anything, do you think he just has a very big breakfast, probably with jam, he'll be a apricot jam man I bet …'

'Anna, tactics?' Miss Rae interrupted.

'Oh yeah! If I go round the other side and you go in this

way, you could make lots of noise and the little bunny will run away and maybe run right into my net and we won't have to chase him. That's another good plan isn't it?'

'Mr Goodman is a clever man.'

Anna turned.

'Wait Anna, how will you get in?'

'The local neds have smashed windows on the second floor I'll get in that way.'

'But we don't have a ladder.'

'Pssht, I don't need a ladder, Miss Rae. See you in there.'
She was round the corner before Miss Rae could say anything else.

Miss Rae put her lock tool against the door. Nothing happened.

She checked it.

It was definitely on because the little light was flashing.

She had carefully charged it over night; she didn't want Anna discovering she'd let the battery run down.

She tried again.

Nothing. No metallic click, the cylinder didn't turn; there wasn't even a creak.

'Grrrr!' she said to herself, why did things work for that bratty, little kid but not for her?

She grabbed the handle, rattled it fiercely and the door swung open.

'Oh ...'

It hadn't been locked after all.

She went in, walked down the small corridor and according

to the machine the creature was in the next room just beside the door. She got quite excited, it was so close there was no way it could get away before she caught it.

'HA! to you Anna Templeton,' she said to herself.

She pulled the net out of her pocket, crept up and peered round.

There it was, sitting in the hallway; all three eyes focussed on a rusty spanner.

YES! This was going to be easy, she gloated.

She spread the net out, focussed on the little monster and edged forward carefully.

Then everything went wrong!

She hadn't noticed a sticky up bit of floorboard, caught her foot on it, tripped and arms flailing wildly she fell forward and crashed into the half open door with a big bang.

The monster didn't even look to see what made the noise but instantly raced away in the opposite direction.

'Damn!'

She rubbed her knee, cursed the floor and pushed herself to her feet disappointed and frustrated; that would have been her first catch!

Thirty seconds later Anna appeared, singing to her self about jam and swinging the little monster in a net.

'Well done Miss Rae. That was massively perfect, it ran straight into our trap. I think the big bang you made, gave it such a fright it just wanted to get away, it practically jumped into the net.' She held it up to look at it. 'You are so the cutest of all the monsters aren't you,' she cooed, 'with such fluffy fur. Have you got a box then?'

Miss Rae still peeved pulled a folded pack from her rucksack, pulled the edges so it made a box and put it on the floor. Anna carefully put the little monster in it and slipped on the lid.

'This stuff must be strong then?' Anna suggested, tapping the perspex.

'Yes it is, I developed it specially because it needs to be light, but really strong.'

'You didn't buy it?'

'No,' she replied, irked at the suggestion.

Anna nodded. 'That is mega cool. I tell dad all the time, girls can do anything and be anything they want, you know be stuntwomen, footballers, be good at maths or be brilliant inventors. He thinks girls should do what they're told and he thinks he's the one who should do most of the telling. I'm going to be what I want to be and it's cool you're a scientist because you can't write English so you'd find it tricky to get work where you have to write in English.'

'Anna!'

'What?'

'It doesn't matter,' said Miss Rae, she could only take Neurofen 4 times a day so she have to save them until she really needed another dose.

'So?'

'So what Anna?'

'So are you going to phone your pick-up people? I'm glad you made these boxes strong, those hairy, bouncy ones were tough. Can anyone open it?'

'They shouldn't be able to, not without the zapper.'

'Good, because if someone came in and found it, they could just open the box and take the little pirate away.'

'Pirate?' Miss Rae asked bemused.

'Eye Eye Eye Captain,' Anna replied and laughed. 'If anyone comes and nicks the box your pick-up people can follow it can't they?'

'Why would they take it?'

'I don't know, people take anything that's not nailed down. Someone nicked my gloves. I had a blue one and an orange one so they didn't match but they still took them. I didn't care I still had an orange one and a blue one, but it's the principle. I made dad report it to the police. He didn't want to but I guess reporting it was easier than listening to me complain about it.'

'I can imagine.' Miss Rae's mind was on the Neurofen. Could she have another two now?

'Well? Are you going to phone them?'

'Yes, yes of course.' She took out her phone. 'That's the one in QS 23 boxed.' She listened for a moment. 'No I'm not having you on, look just come and collect the bloody thing …' She turned off her phone.

'You shouldn't fucking swear in front of a minor,' said Anna gleefully.

Miss Rae pulled out the packet of Neurofen and quickly swallowed two more.

'Anna if I take you to Kentucky Fried Chicken could I

have twenty minutes of quiet?'

'Do they do milkshakes?'

'Yes.'

'You're getting good at deal making.' Anna held out her hand.

The twenty minutes silence obviously didn't include the walk to Kentucky Fried Chicken because on the way there Anna gave her opinion of people who stole gloves and a detailed description of what their punishment should be. However when she got there she stuck to the deal and clammed up.

After five minutes Miss Rae got so unsettled by Anna sitting opposite, staring at her in silence she went back on the deal and asked her what she thought of her chicken meal.

Anna got out a piece of paper and started to write.

'No, no you can speak,' she said.

It was curiously comforting to hear Anna's stream of consciousness. She alternately raved about how immense her chicken dippers were and derogatory about the meals her father cooked. She talked non-stop for ten minutes before she remembered she had fried chicken to eat and stopped briefly to take a bite and eat some chips.

'Do you like this?' Anna asked.

Miss Rae hadn't expected a question, then she realised it was her chance to talk.

She was too slow.

Anna, energy pulsing through her, was off again and this time she explained why fried chicken should be part of her diet and how it wouldn't just feed her muscles but provide nourishment for her brain too.

Miss Rae tried to keep a straight face, it really was very annoying how Anna's enthusiasm was catching.

She had assumed Anna's grasp of science would be sketchy at best but she seemed to know her stuff about nutrition and made a number of salient points about what she should be eating in relation to her energy outputs.

'Dad's a scientist but he doesn't have a clue about food.' she said, 'look at poor Caro and Eliza and tell me if they look healthy?'

Miss Rae opened her mouth.

'They don't do they? They look ill and underfed. They're not getting the stuff they need …'

'No they're not …' Miss Rae managed to interject.

'You're agreeing with me?'

'Like you said, Anna, if you say something sensible …'

'Huff, huff,' Anna pretended to be hyper-ventilating, 'I am always sensible!'

However it was time to move so they finished quickly and headed for the old greyhound stadium.

'Do you know what this one looks like?' Anna asked, 'have we caught one before?'

'No … I came down when it appeared and tried to catch it, it isn't specially quick, but it managed to squirm away through a tiny gap and I couldn't follow.'

'Like a snake?'

'Not really, more like an otter …'

'What's an otter?'

'They look a bit like a cross between a seal and a dachsund ... a sausage dog,' she clarified

'Ooooh, with big sweet eyes?'

'Sort of ... it looked pretty slimy.'

'SLIMY! Ugh. I'm not going to touch anything slimy!'

'Use the net!'

'But what if it slimes me? Dad was out one night and I persuaded Caro to let me watch Ghostbusters, it was brilliant by the way, but one of the ghosts slimed Peter Venkman, the ghost was called Slimer, not very imaginative if you ask me, he got covered in green goo, that's Peter Venkman, although I suppose the ghost was too, and I do – not – want – that!'

'It was very small ...'

'I need protective equipment,' Anna informed her, 'and a towel ... and plenty of wet wipes. Could you invent a special anti slime ...'

'Anna let's just try and catch it, we have to work with what we have.'

'If we had a hairdryer we could dry it off before we try to catch ...'

'Anna ...'

'Okay, okay.'

Miss Rae unlocked the gate with her machine and they carefully stepped through.

Anna held up her detector. They could see the little green dot pulsing; the monster was at the far end of the stand. She zoomed in. 'Look it's underneath where the seats are. You got your net ready.'

Miss Rae nodded.

'I'll go round the far side you go this way.'

They split up and Anna raced along the track before disappearing round the end.

Miss Rae cautiously headed under the banked seats.

The little creature was crouching in the middle. It had short legs, a thin but strangely long body, stubby little arms and its fur was slicked down with slime, or goo or something. Despite the slime it looked strangely endearing, with a curious look on its face and the right number of eyes.

It was holding an old bottle, it placed it on the ground, spun it round and watched as if hypnotised as the bottle slowly came to a stop, then it spun it again.

Anna appeared at the far end. She had seen the monster too, she stopped, nodded to Miss Rae and took a step forward.

Miss Rae took a step closer to the creature too.

It was concentrating so hard on its bottle it hadn't realised they were there.

It was closer to Miss Rae and when she was almost on top of it she raised the net above her shoulders, the little thing didn't have a chance.

She got ready to throw the net over the monster but couldn't move, her right arm was stuck. Grrrr … her jacket was snarled on a bit of the stand above her. She wrenched it hard and there was a loud tearing sound.

Startled by the noise the monster turned, saw her, sank

back on its haunches and sprang forward. With her arm caught she was a sitting duck, it landed on her shoulder, slid round her neck, slithered down her back and was away.

'Yeurgh,' she whimpered. She felt the slime ooozing down inside her jacket; cold, glutinous and disgusting!

Anna raced forward but it was too late and the little thing slipped noiselessly through a tiny hole in the wall. She stopped and stared at her screen.

'It's gone for now.' She turned to Miss Rae and saluted.

'What are you doing Anna.'

'I thought you were saluting so I'm saluting back.'

'I'm stuck!' She gave her arm a sharp jerk her arm but that didn't help, she was indeed, absolutely stuck.

'People always say I'm short,' said Anna, 'I'm not, but even if I was it would be better than being too tall. You're quite tall and that's why you got snaggled, another bad thing about you being tall would be if we wanted our photo taken together you'd have to bend down or the top of your head wouldn't be in the photo.'

'Yes, yes can you just help me get free?'

Anna stretched up but couldn't reach. 'That's one of the downsides of me being average height.'

Miss Rae sighed.

'But don't panic, I have a plan.' Anna took one of the perspex boxes out of Miss Rae's rucksack and shook it into shape. She put the lid on and used it as a step.

She pulled the material back.

'It's caught on a screw, Miss Rae. I'm going to have to

cut it off. Is that okay? It's a nice jacket this, even if it is boring colour.' She noticed the gunge. 'Yuck it slimed you,' she added.

'Just get me free.'

Anna had a pair of nailscissors in her hand and she chopped the material away until Miss Rae could move her arm.

Anna was staring at the back of her neck, 'it's dripping down inside your jacket, I have tissues would you like some?'

The cold slime oozed down and made Miss Rae shiver.

'Yes ... yes please.'

Anna helped her off with her jacket and fleece.

'Here bend down,' said Anna, 'I'll give it a wipe.'

She started to clean the slime away. 'School organised a first aid day and I went on it. I passed first time, I'd make such a good doctor ... except I'd have to cut people open and that would be disgusting. Ugh, imagine fiddling about with someone's insides,' She scrunched up the first tissue and pulled another out of the packet. 'You'd open them up and all their bits would be on show throbbing away and there'd be blood slopping everywhere. I've seen a film of a heart pumping it was gross. If I was a doctor I'd have to do all that stuff you know cutting bits out of people. Afterwards I might meet the patient in a coffee shop and I'd have to say hello, but it'd weird because I'd know what they looked like ... not just all naked like, but what they looked like under their skin too. Awkward! What if I'd operated on a policeman and he came and told me off, like Dr Anna you're not allowed to park your car here and I'd be all wait a sec, you came to me because your kidney was on the blink, it was a really difficult operation and if I hadn't been the top kidney doctor in the world you'd have needed a robot kidney …' She dried Miss Rae's neck and wiped the collar of her blouse. 'I'd say I saved your life Inspector Noparkingere, you should let me park because I've got to go and save someone who's been eating too much fennel and that's made their kidneys proper poorly. There you go.' She stepped back to admire her handiwork. 'Do you think you can get fennel poisoning?'

Miss Rae was trying to keep a straight face. 'I don't know Anna. I do know if you eat too much of just one thing that is bad for you because you won't get the right balance of amino acids and proteins.'

'Caro and Eliza don't get enough amino acids and proteins. Do you want a tissue to clean your jacket?'

'Thank you.' She took the tissue and wiped the gunge off. 'It was my fault it got away.'

'It ain't gone far,' Anna showed her the machine. The green dot was flashing on the next street. 'You know Miss Rae I don't think the net would have caught it anyway. It was real slippery wasn't it? The other monsters got caught up in the net, I think this one would have got away. I think we need a different plan. The next monster is over that way. Let's see if we can catch that one first and decide how we're going to catch Donald Yuck?'

'Maybe you're right,' Miss Rae agreed.

They walked to where the next one had holed up. It was a new one too. It was a little like a turtle except it had legs all the way round its shell and its eyes were on stalks sticking out of the top. It was walking across a black and white tiled floor, it wasn't quick but its colour changed so it looked almost exactly like whatever it was standing on. If they hadn't had the machines they wouldn't have spotted it.

Anna immediately moved to pick it up, but Miss Rae caught her arm. 'Umm … do you think I could try and catch this one?'

'But I … oh … yes, yes sure.'

The little monster heard them, stopped shuffling, pulled its eyes back so they were almost flat and adjusted its colour so much it was indiscernible from the floor.

Miss Rae crept up, anxiously dropped her net over the thing and scooped it up. Anna held out a box. She carefully dropped it in and Anna slid the lid into place.

'He's a friendly looking one, isn't he,' Anna said. 'Oh … my bad it might not be a he. Of course all the monsters we've seen could be girls, perhaps she's fuming and if she could talk she'd be going – how dare you call me a boy I'm the most beautiful of all the tortoisey monsters.'

Miss Rae let Anna gabble on, she was too pleased to have caught her first monster to care.

'I'd better get them to pick it up,' she finally said when there was a gap in the Anna's stream of consciousness.

As she tried to get it sorted, the office staff were all arsey and asked her if she really had caught another one. She put her most affronted voice and said "yes". She overheard Adam, the very cool computer boy, saying she'd probably found a funny shaped stone and that brought her mood right down; they did finally stop making jokes and agreed a pick-up in the next twenty minutes.

They left the building and Anna was already thinking about how to catch the slimy creature. 'We need something that stops it slipping away don't we, not a towel exactly but like a towel, something that sucked up the gunginess and then we could get it in the box and it couldn't slip away.'

She was right and Miss Rae said so.

Anna looked pleased.

Miss Rae continued. 'There is something and maybe if the nets were coated with it they would work better.'

'Coat the nets?' Anna asked.

'Yeah, there's a polymer, it absorbs a lot of liquid, if that was on the nets it'd be more difficult for the little things to slip out.'

'That would be mega,' agreed Anna excitedly.

'But for now I think we should call it a day. We've caught two and I've got time to go back to the lab and see what I can come up with.'

'Sure,' agreed Anna.

They parted reasonably amicably and Anna cartwheeled down the road to celebrate another successful day of monster hunting.

Chapter 14

Anna stopped on her way home, bought some normal food and climbed onto a flat roof well out of sight and savoured it. She knew she wasn't going to enjoy dinner.

The smell of fennel baking wafted from the kitchen so she went in holding her noise.

'Dad, dad, there's a terrible smell in the house I think it must be the drains.'

'Don't be snide Anna, it isn't becoming,' her father replied.

'You know what, jam might make it palatable … it couldn't make it any worse!'

'It's fresh, it's organic and it's healthy,' he replied.

He'd have asked her to lay the table but she always made a point of putting everything the wrong way round and it annoyed him so much he'd stopped making her do it.

'How was your English lesson?'

'Awful. She's getting stupider by the day,' Anna asserted.

'I shall be asking Miss Rae about your behaviour, Anna, so you'd better have been polite.'

'I'm surprised you don't have MI5 following me so you know exactly what I'm doing and what I say to Miss Drea-ray.'

'I shouldn't have to, you should just tell me the truth …'

Anna was already on her way out.

On her way up to her room she popped her head round Eliza's door.

'Hi Anna, do you want something?' Eliza asked.

'Just checking you've tidied your room. It's always such a mess!'

Eliza kept her bedroom immaculately clean; so she just smiled and turned back to her computer.

Anna slipped a packet of chocolate Hobnobs onto the chest of drawers and left.

'Hi Caro,' she yelled as she burst into her other sister's room. 'What-cha doing?'

She was on her computer too.

'Making notes for the debate tomorrow, if you have to know.'

'Schoolwork, in the holidays, you need a psychiatrist!'

'It's interesting!'

'It ain't!' Anna said, 'but if you're dumb enough to be doing schoolwork then your brain needs to be properly nourished or it won't function. My brain functions perfectly and that's because every now and then I have a biscuit. Here you go …' she handed her the second packet of Hobnobs, 'perhaps this will help.'

She danced out of the room before her sister could say thank you and within seconds she had the radio on in her own room and was singing along.

If Anna hadn't been singing and dancing she'd have heard Caroline go in to Eliza's room. She wouldn't have heard the whispered conversation but she'd have known they were having one. It didn't matter to her, the gifts had been given without any desire for thanks; none of them deserved the awful food their dad fed them so she would do her bit to make sure they all had something better. When school was on, at least Eliza and Caro had a decent lunch, but during the holidays dad's muck was all they had to eat. Anna could sneak out to the shops and of course this week she'd been at two, TWO fast food places and while she wouldn't want to eat that stuff all the time she did want it every now and then.

Dad shouted dinner was ready.

'Anna did you hear?'

'Hear what?' she turned to see who was at her door.

'Dad said dinner is ready,' said Caroline.

'Joy!' she replied and followed the two older girls down.

'Ugh, it's still fennel,' she said as she sat down. 'Before we attempt to force this muck down could we know how many amino acids are in it?'

'It's one of the healthiest foods you can eat,' dad replied, 'full of vitamin C, Potassium, folate and fibre.'

'Can't we get that stuff from something that tastes nice,' she replied.

'You haven't tried it yet Anna!'

'It smells of aniseed and that is not a good smell. Okay let's do a deal, I'll try it but if it's horrid we order pizza.'

'No,' dad replied.

Anna stood up.

'Where do you think you're going?'

'I'm going to need something to wash it down.' Anna opened the fridge. 'Oh great no fruit juice.'

'There's plenty of water in the tap.'

She sighed deeply and sat back down with a glass of water.

She took a forkful of the braised fennel, studied it and reluctantly put it in her mouth. She chewed once and instantly spat it out and took a long drink of water. 'God that's disgusting!'

'ANNA!'

'Eliza, Caro what do you think?' she asked defiantly.

'It's ... er ... er,' started Eliza.

'I'm afraid it really isn't nice Dad,' stuttered Caroline.

'Rubbish,' he tried it for himself, took a second forkful but chewed reluctantly and put his fork down. 'Been busy today Caro?'

'Dad if even you can't eat it then it must be truly awful,' interrupted Anna. 'I'd prefer a delicious chicken pizza but as ANYTHING would be better than this I'm prepared to put up with a vegetarian one!'

Dad speared another piece of the fennel.

Anna shifted her chair closer and stared at him. 'Yum yum,' she said sarcastically.

He couldn't bring himself to put it in his mouth and put his fork back down on his plate. 'Perhaps we could have cheese on toast tonight ...'

It wasn't pizza but at least it wasn't fennel and as that felt like victory to Anna she offered to help Caroline make it.

She made sure there was plenty of cheese on each slice and didn't care it was on brown bread or that Caroline added sliced tomato too.

'We should put Lee and Perrins on it, that's what my friends do,' Anna said.

To avoid being subjected to ten minutes of Anna extolling the benefits of Lee and Perrins, Caroline agreed. They found some Soy sauce and as it was the same colour they used that instead.

'Best dinner ever,' Anna said at the end, 'I can already feel the nutritional benefits of cheese expanding my brain; she chanted a complicated equation that she'd just made up, but since the others didn't know they couldn't challenge her.

Chapter 15

The next morning there was a text from Miss Rae.

<Working on net's. 10.00am Tomorow.>

'Miss Rae, social skills zero out of a hundred,' Anna said to herself. She stared in the mirror and held her hairbrush up like a microphone. 'Anna "Superstar" Templeton social skills one hundred out of one hundred!'

That meant today was a free day and even better Dad was taking Caroline to her stupid debate so no hassle from the man! She heard the front door shut, grabbed the jam she'd bought the day before and jumped down the stairs.

Eliza was sitting morosely in front of her muesli.

'Look at yourself Eliza, compared to you "Moaning Myrtle" was the life of the party. Now don't get up, dad has gone hasn't he? It's okay he has, I watched the car drive off. I'm going to make you toast.'

Eliza gave a weak smile.

'Toast and da-da de-DAAA! JAM! I like all jams but I know you like strawberry best of all, so I bought raspberry … of course I didn't Eliza, I got strawberry, the king of fruits, the president of potted preserves, the …'

'Jam?'

'The heavenly spread!'

Eliza's face lit up, 'jam and toast for breakfast!'

'YAAY!' agreed Anna, 'and that's not the end of the treats

for today. You and me, we're going out on the town.'

'What do you mean?'

'I don't know,' admitted Anna, 'I presume it means going to have fun, but if it doesn't then we'll have to pretend it does, because we're going to have fun.'

'What sort of fun?' Eliza asked, suspicious now.

Anna dropped her voice to a whisper. 'I went to Kentucky Fried Chicken the other day and it was awesome; we're going for lunch there.'

'I can't afford …'

'Pah to your paltry allowance! Mum gave me money, she's off to 'ollywood to talk about a film and wanted to cheer me up. I'm going to take you for lunch, "sisters are doing it!"'

'Anna …'

'Yes Eliza …'

'I …'

'No quib-i-ling my sib-i-ling, we're going to be princesses for a day.'

Eliza stood up, 'if you're sure, thank you and the biscuits thanks for them too. Dinner yesterday looked like it was going to be the worst ever and knowing I had biscuits in my room was a godsend.'

They ladled on extra jam, ate their toast, washed up extra carefully, cleaned the kitchen just in case and then went upstairs with the jam.

Anna handed her the jar. 'You take it Eliza, I can always get more and if there's going to be a finger tip search of anyone's room it's going to be mine and that would stop any supplies in the future.'

Eliza agreed.

'You love art, let's go to the art gallery first,' decided Anna.

'You hate art galleries!'

'I don't, I hate dad taking me because he won't let me just like a painting and move on, you have learn about it and discuss it and put it in context. It's a picture of someone delivering hay, nice house, nice sky and nice river, it's lovely let's look at the next one … but dad has to talk about the history and everything … YAWN! You're not going to do that are you Eliza?'

'Course not.'

'Good,' she linked her arm with her sister's and they headed to the National Gallery. On the way Anna described her favourite paintings and what else the artists should have painted, which mainly turned out to be portraits of her.

Eliza never minded she hardly got a word in edgeways, it was fun listening to Anna joyfully rabbit on.

After the gallery it was time for lunch and Anna's excitement reached fever pitch. Eliza had never been allowed fast food so she was fascinated to find out what it was like. Anna bought some of everything and got a milkshake, a Coke, coffee and a Sprite.

'It's an experiment so we have to sample the lot,' she explained, when Eliza asked why she'd got so much.

Laden with chicken, chips, burgers, a sort of chicken popcorn, chicken salad and the drinks, they staggered to their table.

Anna opened every last box and spread out their feast in front of them.

They tried a little from each packet, shared the drinks and Anna shared her views on everything from the uniforms of the staff to what a bloody pain dad was.

Eliza had to go to the library after lunch and Anna told her she was on her own there.

Later when Eliza was sitting in the reading room with her textbooks she thought about lunch. Anna was right about the food, it was fun to try it and it was tasty; she didn't want it everyday, but she did want it every now and then. She was also right about dad, he was just too much, too controlling, she wanted to do her own things but he never let her and unlike Anna she was too scared to disobey him when he told her no.

Anna had moved on. She lived in the moment and while she'd had a great time with Eliza she was already onto the next thing. The next thing was the little monsters. She pulled out the machine Miss Rae had given her. She kept it hidden in one of Caroline's old tampon boxes. She was sure Dad would never look inside it.

She turned it on. She wasn't going to hunt the monsters on her own, that would be stupid, but the machine was very clever and maybe it could give them more information if she investigated a bit more.

The map of London came up and she pressed the button to show where she was. There were no little monsters near so she zoomed out to check a wider area, as she did she saw some older boys coming her way. She didn't like the look of them and shoved the machine safely in an inside pocket and zipped it up. As they came closer she tightened the straps on her rucksack.

'On your own?' one of them said. It wasn't a question.

'Got a phone?' another asked.

'Yes I do, of course I have a phone! Do you think I've just dropped in from the twentieth century?' ranted Anna. 'Everyone has a phone. My father is a moron and he's mean too, so my phone is the cheapest bit of crap ever but of course I have one. You have phones too but like my dad you're morons so you probably don't know how to use most of the functions. I could show you because I'm a genius but ain't got time I gotta go.'

It wasn't the reaction they'd expected, but before they could respond, Anna turned and sprinted towards a row of shops. She was up the side of the first one and on its roof in a flash.

The boys chased after, but stopped when they reached the wall.

'How the hell did she get up there?'

'Dunno.'

'Where'd she go?'

'Forget her, I'm not chasing some little kid who can do that, waste of fucking time.'

'The bitch got some attitude! She should respect us – shouldn't call us morons.'

'She was right about you, you are a moron. I 'ad to show you how to turn on your phone.'

'The crap you did, you still can't work out how to text …'

They wandered off, barging each other and swearing a lot.

Anna hadn't waited to watch them go, she was already well away. She found a spot that wasn't over-looked and pulled the machine out. Something had caught her eye as she'd shoved it away.

There was a new green dot. They hadn't caught all the ones that had arrived since Mr Goodman had gone away, but this signal was stronger than any of those.

She couldn't decide if that meant this monster was bigger or it just had more of what ever allowed the machine to see them in the first place. She wished Mr Goodman was about because she was sure he'd know.

She had to say to someone so she texted Miss Rae.

She didn't expect an instant reply so she decided it would do no harm to have a look and then she would know what they were up against.

She raced through the streets and was soon standing outside an old market building.

She sneaked in a window and found herself in a vast cavernous room with big iron pillars holding up a glass roof and round the edge a balcony. The market stalls were still in the middle but no one had used the place for a while so everything looked saggy and falling apart.

She shimmed up one of the pillars to the network of

crisscrossing metal struts holding up the roof. According to the machine the monster was on the left near the wall; it wasn't moving.

She sat and waited.

A snuffle broke the silence and the monster's nose appeared.

Before she could get closer for a proper look there was a clang and a rattle of chains. Someone barged the door and there was a grinding sound as it was shoved open.

Anna hurried along the strut to the next pillar, pressed up against it and made herself as thin as possible.

Three men came in. They were all in suits. One had a clipboard and the other two were carrying briefcases.

The one with the clipboard started explaining about the building, telling them how old it was, how big it was and how much space was available. The other two were interested in it all. The younger one then set off to look round on his own and the other one stayed asking questions and occasionally saying things like it would need a lot of work. The salesman replied that the structure was sound, that it wasn't going to fall down.

The younger man poked about everywhere and when he reached the place where the snuffle came from he shouted back to the others.

'You're going to have to check the doors, mate, looks like someone's been sneaking in and kipping here ...'

He banged one of the abandoned stalls and to his surprise a dark shape launched itself from underneath the counter, bowled him over and before he could get a proper look it scuttled away through the maze of kiosks.

'Bloody hell,' he shouted, 'I've just been knocked over by a bloody badger!'

Anna however got a proper look as it made its escape and she didn't like what she saw.

Chapter 16

'What the hell! Let me go. LET GO ANNA!' demanded Miss Rae.

Anna had a hold of her arm and was dragging her out of her local Waitrose.

'I was just about to pay for my Honey Nut Clusters!' she complained angrily.

'You must have had a brainstorm then, you should have muesli in the morning! We have muesli, it tastes bogging, but according to dad it's the breakfast of the gods so why would you want Honey Nut Clusters? You should thank me for saving you from an unhealthy breakfast.'

Miss Rae glowered fiercely, 'What do you want!' Then before Anna could reply, 'how did you know I was here?'.

'It doesn't matter how,' Anna said excitedly. 'Well if you really want to know, these machines are actually totally awesome. I discovered if we're within a few miles of each other I can tap into your machine. So this is what I did … look it's not important how I found you … actually it was pretty simple you go into the main menu …' She stopped again. 'It was huge.'

'What was huge?' Miss Rae asked.

'I went to have a look. I wanted to scout it … you know the machines must all be linked to each other, we could use that in future … hey do you know what happened to me today, these stupid boys tried to mug me and take my phone, they should be arrested, can you get them arrested Miss Rae, you being part of the government and all?'

She was so excited she couldn't finish a sentence with out thinking of something equally important she wanted to tell Miss Rae.

'Anna, ANNA' Miss Rae interrupted. 'Forget about the machines, forget about being mugged. You saw something?'

'Forget about being mugged!' Anna was outraged, 'what if I tried to take YOUR bag,' she grabbed it, pulled it sharply to demonstrate and caught Miss Rae completely by surprise.

'WAAHhh!' screamed Miss Rae.

'See!'

'They shouldn't,' Miss Rae agreed as sympathetically as she could. 'But that's not why you dragged me out of the queue! Was it a little monster?'

'It was a monster all right but …'

'But it was huge,' said Miss Rae.

'We're gonna need a bigger box!'

'How big?'

Anna stretched her arms out as she tried to judge the monster's size. 'It wasn't a bunny.' She said emphatically. 'It was about as big as a poodle or a spaniel.'

'A spaniel?' Miss Rae caught sight of something out of the corner of her eye. 'There's a dog over there,' she pointed. 'About that big Anna?'

'It was real ugly,' she said as she gave the dog the once over. 'Like all its bits, its arms, its legs, its head, its body and even its eyes, nose and ears were from different places. Its fur was long, straggly and greasy ...'

'Was it smaller than that dog?'

'Yes about half the size. It had teeth, sharp teeth and a real raggedy nose ...'

Miss Rae went and sat on a bench, beckoned to Anna and patted the seat.

Anna stood opposite. 'Miss Rae you're being a moron like all the other stupid adults, you want to slap me down just because it isn't the size of a cow or something. It's HUGE "compared" to the others we've seen, twice a big as the biggest one so far. Not just a little bit bigger, TWICE AS BIG. Imagine if I was twice as big as I am now.' She jumped on the bench and held her hand above her in the air. 'Or the bench was twice as high. You wouldn't be able to climb on it let alone sit on it. When I was with Mr Goodman we caught four and you and me we've caught another five. None of them was bigger than a baby bunny so this thing is humongous compared to them.'

'But ...' started Miss Rae.

'No buts,' Anna was fired up and started pacing up and down. 'Don't you see? Mr Goodman has been doing this for years and in all that time he said the one I caught in my bedroom was the biggest one he'd seen. I don't know how many he's caught but it must be hundreds. Suddenly one turns up and it's twice the size. I don't know about you but that's scary!'

'It ...'

'It wouldn't fit in our boxes for starters … so that's gonna be a problem and for seconds …'

'Calm down Anna, calm down' Miss Rae said. 'I am listening to you, I understand what you're saying.'

Anna stopped pacing.

'I wasn't going to slap you down,' said Miss Rae. 'Yeah I'm a bit pissed you dragged me out of the shop and yeah we're not exactly peas in a pod, but doesn't mean I wasn't going to listen to you.'

'Oh … oh okay.'

'I'm the sort of person who needs information and facts … I'm really not great at being spontaneous I need time to think.'

Anna sat beside her. 'Sure.'

Miss Rae closed her eyes.

'How long do you need,' asked Anna after a moment of silence.

'A bit longer than three seconds.'

'Longer?'

'Yes Anna.'

'Okay, I'll get some practice in, call me when you're done thinking.'

There was a high wall across the road, Anna jumped onto the top and ran along it.

Miss Rae glanced up.

Every now and then Anna would cartwheel or somersault and land back on the wall without a wobble.

Miss Rae forgot she was meant to be thinking and found

herself watching the girl instead, the skill was incredible and so balletic. Anna's control and finesse was captivating. She seemed to know exactly where she was even when she was twisted upside down.

Eventually Anna came over and sat back down. 'You done thinking Miss Rae?' she asked.

'What?'

'You know about this new monster, what should we do?'

'I'm sorry I got distracted watching you. How do you do it?'

'Practice, lots of practice … and my coach Roy, he's one of the best free-runners in the world. He was in a film, they didn't use a stunt man, he was really doing the jumps and tumbles, he did this move where he …' she caught herself. 'And I really wanted to do it, you've probably spotted I'm a bit hyper, it helps me burn off energy.'

'A film? Seeing you up there, that was just like watching a film,' Miss Rae said and then admitted she didn't know what to do if the monsters were getting bigger. 'I mean obviously we'll have to get a larger box and I guess this one you can catch but what if the next one is even bigger and then they get bigger and bigger until … well until we do come across one that IS as big as a cow.'

Anna stood up in front of her and looked her in the eyes. 'You're super clever and I'm the number one monster hunter, we'll deal with it! How did you get on with the nets?'

'The polymer I used seems to work and the nets are tough. Tough enough to trap even big animals like lions and tigers.'

'Good,' said Anna. 'Shall we try and catch the other three tomorrow. You ask for some bigger boxes or at least one bigger box and then we could try and catch Mr Ugly. By the way I had another KFC today. I took Eliza and she loved it. I've had a great day.'

Miss Rae remembered the muggers. 'Some boys tried to take your phone, you're alright?'

'Yeah.'

'What happened?'

'I gave them some lip, which confused them, then I ran away and they couldn't catch me ...'

'They were too slow,' Miss Rae suggested.

'I gotta go so I'll show you. "Ain't no wall can trap PRISON BREAK ANNA!"'

Anna turned, sprinted towards the side of the nearest building and seemed to run up the side. She caught hold of the edge of the roof, pulled herself up, stopped for a moment to wave and then it was like she disappeared, 'to the secret Annaboratory!' she could be heard calling.

Miss Rae stood open-mouthed for a moment, what Anna had done didn't look possible, but she pulled herself together and phoned the workshop to see if they could make up some larger boxes.

Chapter 17

Anna's evening passed uneventfully, which always disappointed her. Dad hardly reacted to any of her provocations as he was pleased Caroline's team had done well in the debate and got through into the next round. To celebrate he'd made a salad; it didn't have anything odd in it so she was able to eat it. Eliza kept quiet and never said anything about catching her sneaking a look at the TV before Dad turned up. For them it was a quiet evening.

She went to bed early, spent half an hour browsing the internet for how to trap animals without hurting them and at the end erased her browser history; she was sure dad checked what she was doing. She threw herself onto her bed pretty happy with life. The monster hunting was immense, she loved the thrills and taking risks was something she did.

Before she fell asleep she thought briefly about Miss Rae. She hadn't been quite so po-faced in the last couple of days, which was probably a good thing because being sour and angry all the time made her look like an old lady.

Chapter 18

"Ain't no stopping us now, we've got the groove."

Anna could be heard singing as she leapt down the stairs.

'Don't do that,' ordered dad.

'Sing?'

'Jump down the stairs, you might hurt yourself.'

'Don't feed us so much vegetarian muck, you might not provide us with enough nutrition.'

'Don't talk back!'

'If they took the word "don't" out of the dictionary, you'd never have anything to say,' she retorted.

Dad had a fierce look on his face, 'are you looking for trouble Anna Templeton?'

'It be much easier if you just let me go and live with mum, then you could eat your rabbit food and contemplate paint drying in silence.'

'That's not going to happen,' he replied and turned to his scientific journal.

'Why not?' Anna demanded.

'The conversation is closed.'

'The conversation is closed, it's always closed and I don't see why. I want to live with mum, mum wants me to live with her and it's obvious you're fed up with me. When I'm sixteen, "ZIP" I'm outta' here!'

'You won't be leaving home until eighteen at least. That's what the law says and I'll get the appropriate warrant to make sure.'

Anna was about to contradict him when it struck her how certain he was about a warrant. She'd been on the internet and found a page called "*the Care of Children Act*". It said a child can legally leave home at sixteen and the parent can only get a warrant if the child was at risk. She wasn't at risk and she wouldn't be at risk with mum. What was that about? There was something fishy going on. She would say to mum what he'd just said.

Caroline and Eliza looked miserable. What was the deal with them, were they stuck, but forever Anna wondered? Oh well she didn't have time for this now, she was off.

Before Dad could react she was out the front door, it slammed behind her and she sprinted down the street before he could call her back. She had a route along the alleys behind the houses and there was no way he could follow her; she was just too fast.

They had agreed to go after the slimy monster first. Anna arrived early so she found a handy roof where she could see people coming and going but no one could see her. She checked the machine. The creature was still there and she opened another screen so she could see when someone with a machine was getting close.

She didn't have to wait long and a little red dot soon appeared. She watched until Miss Rae came into sight. She was going to leap down with a yell and give her a surprise but stopped because Miss Rae looked sad. She called out "hi" instead, waved and somersaulted down.

'You're sad! Why are you sad? Is your dad making you eat boring muesli instead of letting you have the Honey Nut Clusters you bought special for breakfast?'

'I'm not sad Anna, just a bit worried.'

'Worried? Why are you worried? You've got me helping.'

'Yes and I'm very grateful …'

'When I'm not being the best stuntwomen in the world I'm going to be a singer. I could sing to you, that's guaranteed to cheer you up!'

Miss Rae gave a weak smile.

'Okay, okay … what are you worried about? Should I be worried too?'

'You shouldn't be worried about anything Anna, you're twelve that's not an age when you should have worries.'

'I have my own special worries,' replied Anna. 'Mainly about Dad. He doesn't like me, he gets fed up with my nonsense, he's always telling me not to do things but he won't let me go and live with Mum. I don't know why. I'm worried about Caro and Eliza too. They were really down this morning. More down when dad said he was going to keep me with him until I was at least eighteen and I think they were down because that meant they were stuck too … but for ever. He doesn't let them do anything. He's always on their case. You know what would be best? It would be best if Dad had to go away but we couldn't go with him so we had to go and live with mum. But you've got worries. I've told you my worries so now you have to tell me your worries.'

'Okay Anna ...'Miss Rae pursed her thin lips. 'I'm worried because I'm not a real monster hunter. I'm just a trainee. I was only out with Mr Goodman because I can drive and he can't. I was driving the van and carrying the equipment. I mean eventually I'd have done some actually hunting but when I met you that was just my fifth trip and only the second time he'd let me come after a little monster. He got sent to Germany and because I was the only one who'd even been out they told me I had to go and collect them. I didn't catch a single one. I knew you could catch them so that's why I gave you the memory water. Now they think I've got the hang of it and when I told them the monsters were getting bigger they just said they were sure I'd soon work out how to deal with them.'

'Oh.'

'Yes,' agreed Miss Rae.

'But you are a real monster hunter. You caught that one the other day.'

'I didn't really, it was just sitting there pretending to be a bit of the floor.'

'But you still caught it! You know I was thinking about stuff too,' said Anna. 'It's all well and fine and dandy us catching them but where are they coming from? What the government has got to do is stop them coming, not waiting until they get here and then hoping we can catch them!'

'That's true.'

'Okay,' decided Anna. 'There's four left so let's get them

boxed up today and then you can go back and say "hey government, you listening to me, you've got to stop them coming".' She pulled out her machine. '… and …'

'What?'

'That's funny one of them is missing.'

'Missing?'

'Yeah,' said Anna. 'Look.' She held up the machine. Three dots were visible on the screen; the slimy one, the big strong dot and a few blocks away another dot. 'Where's the other one gone. I hope the poor little bunny hasn't been run over or something. I wonder if that happens a lot, that they get run over? They don't like being seen but a car might squinch them without them knowing anything about it?'

'People would see the bodies … and … well people like odd things don't they?' suggested Miss Rae. 'So they'd tell the newspapers and there'd be photos on the internet as well. Wouldn't we have seen all that?'

'But we haven't been looking! They might be all over the place just not in the papers we read. To be honest I don't read any papers.'

'I'm sure the government would have noticed,' Miss Rae decided, 'but you're right, none of that explains where this one has gone.'

'He might have gone home, you know got bored, or he was scared, or he didn't like the smell of the buses, maybe he found what he was looking for or he had to go back and do his homework,' suggested Anna. 'I hope he wasn't run over though.'

They thought about that for a moment and decided they'd better catch the others sharpish.

'I've brought you an upgraded net,' Miss Rae handed it over. 'I came in the van and I've got towels and stuff in it. I've got a couple of bigger boxes too.'

'Have you got more nets?'

Miss Rae looked up curiously.

'I've a plan,' Anna said.

They sneaked through a door well away from the monster, set up nets in the corridors and then went out. Anna led them round the building and back in through the other door. They had a net each just in case, but Anna said if they were noisy it would run away and hopefully get caught in one of the nets.

'I really don't want to get slimed!' she said.

They started rattling things, banging on walls and stamping their feet and soon heard the sound of something scurrying away.

They followed its progress on their machines and it looked like it was going the way they wanted. After five minutes it stopped moving and when they caught up, they found it wriggling glumly in one of the nets. It really was very slimy, Miss Rae slipped on her gloves and gently put it in the box.

When she phoned to organise a pick-up, the people on the other end didn't seem as surprised as they were before.

'Sweet,' said Anna, 'that didn't take long.'

'That was a good plan,' said Miss Rae.

'It wasn't really my plan, I found it on the internet. I'm

glad it worked.' Anna crouched to look more closely at the monster in the box. It was tentatively touching the sides as if couldn't work out what was stopping it from moving about freely. 'You'll be better off back home,' Anna told it. 'This isn't a good place for you.' She stood up. 'Where do you think it lives?'

'I haven't a clue, Wales, Cornwall somewhere remote ...'

'I meant what sort of place, a pond or a marsh or something? It's slimy so does that mean it likes wet places or is it slimy because it lives in a dry place so the slime protects it?'

'Oh ... I see,' said Miss Rae, 'well snakes often live in very dry places and their skin is dry.'

'I held a snake once. It was like holding an old bit of rope that shiggled about in your hand. It was okay. I wouldn't want to have to hold them all day, like as my job or something.'

'Newts live in wet places and they're slimy, so perhaps this one comes from a wet place.'

'What's a newt? Dad talks about drunk people being pissed as them. Not in front of me, but when he thinks I can't hear. I think kids must have supersensitive hearing when it comes to adults swearing because we can always tell exactly what they're saying, while the rest of the time we just hear random mumbling.'

'Newts are small reptiles, from the salamander ...'

'What, what, speak up you're mumbling ...'

'Small reptiles from ...' started Miss Rae, she stopped.

'You almost smiled Miss Rae!'

'You set me up ...'

'"You gotta be bad, you gotta be bold, you gotta be wiser,"' Anna sang joyfully. 'I'm a lean mean foolin' machine and I got you good!'

'You got me Anna. Come on let's get the next two.'

Anna took one side of the box and together they carried it to the van, slipped it in and shut the door.

Anna got the machine out to check. 'Hey! It's gone.'

'What?'

'The one we've just caught.'

Miss Rae looked at her machine. 'The metal of the van must stop the signal getting through. The one that disappeared, it could be in a car.'

'Perhaps it's caught the bus, maybe it's off to the shops for some Honey Nut Clusters, what if ...'

'You suggested we can't be the only ones who have seen them Anna, I wonder if someone else found it and took it away.'

'It'll reappear if they let it out won't it?' Anna suggested. 'We can go and get it back when they do. Do you have a search warrant? That would be mega. We could go to their house and be all arsey and demand they let us in and they'll say "can I see your search warrant" and we can flick it in their face, "here's your search warrant you rotten thief, you're going down!" And I could say "book him, Sergeant Rae," and you could say "you've been a naughty boy, you're going to do time ..."'

'I don't have a search warrant ...'

Anna switched to an American accent, 'we'll gonna hafta sneak in and pick up the liddle critter, because we've gotta job to do, y'all!' she said.

'Do you watch a lot of television, Anna?'

'As much as I can.'

They got in the van and in between giving directions to where the next monster was, Anna explained the plot of the latest show she was watching, she sang the theme tune and acted out the more thrilling parts.

Miss Rae listened to her excited monologue and was actually disappointed when they got to their destination.

'What's this one like?' Anna asked.

'It's one of the three eyed ones …'

'Good, they're sweet, they're my favourites.' She used the zoom on her machine. 'I'd say it's collecting stuff. Look here's where it's been in the last half hour.' There was a pattern of pathways radiating from a central point. 'We should wait until it goes off to pick up something and then sneak in and and wait for it to come back,' she suggested. 'If we're real quiet we might be able to catch it with out any hassle.'

'Anna I think you should go on your own, I'll wait here, I … I don't want to knock into something and give the game away.'

'But …'

'I'm quite clumsy …'

'Well okay, but just this time. Look I'll set up your machine so you can see where I am. I've got my crappy dad phone and you've got your amazing iPhone so we can keep in touch; if it gets away no probs we'll try again.'

They waited until the little green dot left the centre point and Anna disappeared, as silent as a ghost.

Miss Rae followed Anna's progress on the machine and she reached the monster's nest long before it started heading back. The little green dot returned, reached the red dot and stayed there. Moments later her phone rang.

'Got it,' Anna said happily. 'It's been collecting old cans, there are thirty or forty here. It's smaller than the first one, but it's got lovely fur. I'll bring it out ...'

There was a noise behind Miss Rae. A door opened and a security guard appeared.

'OI! What are you doing here?' he asked in a gruff voice.

She kept the phone on so Anna would know not to come.

'I work for the government,' she said and pulled out her ID card. 'I'm checking the buildings in this area for subsidence.'

'Subsidence?' the man asked.

She stamped on the floor. 'There's so much underground nowadays, water pipes, electric wires, tube trains, internet cables and of course the sewage system so we have to do regular surveys – we don't want anything collapsing. Imagine if you were in here checking the building ...' she realised she was sounding just like Anna, '... and the floor collapsed ... well you might just end up in the drains.'

'Yeah I wouldn't want to be up to my arse in sewage,' the man agreed. 'I didn't know you wuz doing this, it should be on my schedule …'

She claimed her department sent out notifications but admitted that doesn't mean they get passed on.

'Too much bloody information, that's the problem. Even if I 'ad it, it'd probably be buried in the middle of the file.' He complained and held out a big wad of paper. 'I 'ave to fill in forms every day but I reckon they just get stuffed in a filing cabinet and no one ever sees 'em. You going to be much longer?'

'Just a few more checks.' She moved her machine about as if it was a subsidence-checking machine.

'Well I've got do a circuit of the outside so once you're finished wait by the door and I'll know you're not in 'ere any more.'

'Will do.'

He went off.

A minute later Anna appeared. 'Very cool, that was a nice lie.'

'Well I do work for the government …'

Anna just grinned. 'Tell you what, I'll meet you in the van, we don't want him seeing the latest bunny.'

When Miss Rae got back to the van, Anna was in the front seat singing.

'"Because I'm happy, clap along if you feel like a room without a roof, because I'm happy" … Do you want a looksee?'

They went round the back and checked the monsters. The three-eyed one was brushing its fur; it had one eye on the slimy monster, one on what it was doing and one turned to look at them when the door opened.

'Isn't he lovely?' said Anna admiringly before turning to the other one. 'Do you think the rest of the slimy monsters think Donald Yuck here is lovely? He might be the super star of the monster world and they might all want to look like him. Perhaps he's on their tellies, "I use Slimealot it keeps my fur wet all day long". Perhaps all the other monsters are desperate to be just like him and rush out to buy it. Some of the girls at school do that. A popstar will wear something, or put on special make-up and the next day, they're in that dress and all made up the same.'

'But not you Anna?'

'Not me because I love my bright clothes and I really can't be bugged doing make-up; it's a waste of time. You don't wear make-up!'

'No ... I ... I never learnt, always had my nose in book.'

'I s'ppose it gives us more time in the morning for breakfast; you for your delicious Honey Nut Clusters, me for my repellent home-made muesli; I'd prefer to eat make-up than that. One more monster to go then we can "parteee!"'

They got in the van.

'We should get a dog shouldn't we, a big humungous one that talks? I'll paint your van so it's like the Mystery Machine – the monsters will all be like, we'd have got away if it wasn't for Miss Rae and that meddlin' kid!'

Miss Rae couldn't help herself and joined in when Anna sang, "Scooby Doo where are you", out aloud. They sang the whole song and before they knew it they were at the old market, where Anna had seen the big monster.

'This one really is super ugly,' Anna said. 'It knocked a man over so it must be strong too. This time you're going to have to help.'

'I ...'

'You have to Miss Rae, I am quite little you know ...' Anna looked up soulfully.'

'You didn't give me a chance to reply so you can stop doing that big, sad eye thing of yours, of course I'll come. I'll just ... I'll be careful.'

'We're a team,' Anna decided, 'Team Anna Savannah, we're the best, the Manchester United of monster hunters!'

They checked their machines. The monster was moving slowly along the back wall.

'Let's check round the outside first,' Miss Rae suggested. 'we don't want any interruptions.'

'Jinkies ... that's a good idea!' agreed Anna.

They walked all the way round. The building was next to a main road but the area was run down and they passed no one.

'How did you get in the first time, this door is double locked?'

Anna looked up.

'Oh of course ...' said Miss Rae, 'I forgot you can fly.'

'Took me an age to learn,' grinned Anna.

Miss Rae unlocked the padlock and the main lock with her machine and then carefully closed the door behind them with a snap.

'These machines are so cool, we can see where the little bunnies are and we can see each other.'

Miss Rae agreed.

Anna tapped Miss Rae's chest, 'I'm glad you've got your armour on, it's tough little critter.'

'What about you?'

'I'm a tough little critter too. I did wonder if I should wear some but I thought it might slow me down and maybe that's not right for me.'

'What are we going to do then?' Miss Rae asked.

'I think the same plan as we did for Mr One-Eye. You go on one side and sort of chase it towards me and I'll try and catch it. We don't want to get too far apart because I might need a help to keep a hold of it.'

'I'm really not very strong …' admitted Miss Rae, 'and I'm not exactly fit.'

'Sure you are, Girl Power!'

Miss Rae managed a weak smile and set off round the building, staying as far from the monster as she could. She checked the machine, it hadn't moved and neither had Anna. When she was opposite she walked up as quietly as she could until she was no more than ten metres away. She stopped for a moment, breathed deeply and then stepped forward and banged one of the abandoned stalls. She took another step and shouted.

There was frantic scurrying and a dark shape scuttled from under a table and headed in the opposite direction. Anna stood up, she looked focused and there was a determined expression on her face.

The dark shape stopped dead when it saw her, changed direction and headed off at a right angle.

Anna bellowed not let it get away and followed.

Miss Rae started yelling and banging the stalls to try and keep it from getting away on her side of the building.

'Yee-ha!' Anna called with glee and Miss Rae caught glimpses of her as she raced through the building, sometimes running, sometimes cartwheeling but always with a smile on her face.

Anna got ahead of the monster, stopped and screamed. The dark shape backpedalled rapidly and headed to where Miss Rae was standing. There wasn't time to panic, so she spread the net out and braced herself.

The monster saw her at the last moment and swerved, she turned to follow, tripped and fell in front of it. The net was in the thing's way and it ran straight into it at full pelt. Caught in the folds, it struggled frantically but quickly became so entangled it couldn't move.

She lay on the ground, grimly holding the net as tight as she could and breathing heavily. She heard Anna singing above her and looked up.

'Is he okay? You almost squashed the poor thing when you fell over.' Anna shook a box into shape, scooped up the monster and slid the top shut.

'I did not …' Miss Rae started, before realising she was being teased.

Anna helped her up.

'Now you've caught two monsters, Miss Rae - queen of the world!'

'You planned that! You chased him straight towards me.'

'And you caught him!'

'But I might not have and then he'd have got away.'

'Naw, I'd have 'ad him! When I saw him the first time I saw how he dodged about and anyway I'm plenty faster than he is. But I didn't need to did I? Actually that was a pretty neat catch.'

'Was it?'

'Yeah. You swooped down on him like an eagle ...'

Miss Rae laughed. 'No I didn't, I did actually trip and was lucky to fall in front of him.'

'We've all got to start somewhere, maybe you were a bit lucky, sometimes I'm a bit lucky in class and get the right answer but I'm not for telling anyone. What's important is we got him and we got 'im together didn't we? Starsky and Hutch, Shirley Holmes and Dr Watson, Batwoman and Robin, Pinky and the Brain!'

'Anna you are incorrigible.'

'Am I? Cool. What does incorridable mean?'

Miss Rae repeated it correctly. 'It means you don't change, you're always yourself.'

'Yeah I am.'

They carried the box together and put it in the van. Anna was right, the monster was very ugly.

The two other monsters looked at it when they put it

down. They didn't seem bothered but neither did they seem curious either.

'What are you thinking Anna?'

'When I see dogs in the park they rush up to say hello and sniff each other. I can't think all those dogs are mates but they're sorta pleased to meet. Do this lot care there's another monster nearbye?'

Miss Rae looked closely at each one in turn. The ones they caught earlier had settled down as if they were making the best of things. The most recent one was moving about, checking the size of its box and occasionally tapping the sides.

'Hey, maybe we could go eat, you know to celebrate you catching a monster?' suggested Anna. 'Not a burger, not fast food, maybe noodles, yes noodles are cool and a juice … or a smoothie. I can pay.'

'You don't need to pay; I have an allowance for lunch. The government gives me an allowance.'

'A good thing too, it would be real bad if you starved, to death especially for the bosses, they'd have to gather everyone together … "we've got some bad news, Miss Rae died of hunger this year because we didn't pay for her lunch, but we've got some really good news too, Superstar Monster Hunter, Anna Templeton has kindly agreed to help us when she's not topping the singles charts all over the world and making supercool blockbuster movies in Hollywood."

'I don't think I'd starve to death.'

'I hope not. If you were starving you could come for your

tea, god knows what revolting vegetable dad would boil up for you, but if it was that or an empty stomach ... Do you like dad?'

'I don't know how to answer that.'

'Up to you. I hate him, but that doesn't mean you have to. Some one must love him, it might be you.'

'It's not me Anna.'

'Why not?'

'Anna, that might be personal!'

'Well is it?'

'What?'

'You said "might be", is it personal? I think there's something wrong with him.'

'I've looked at his records. He's well respected in his job and is doing some good work at his company.'

'So why is he such an arse at home?'

'All I've seen is a file with some facts, I don't know what he's like outside of that. He's not someone I'd go out with, I mean he's handsome enough, I can see people would be attracted to him.'

'Can you? Oh. I suppose that's not something I'd see is it?' decided Anna. 'He doesn't treat me well and he's proper bad to Caro and Eliza. They're trapped in the house and can't do anything on their own without him.'

'He's looking out for them,' Miss Rae suggested.

'But that's no good, they've got to get out there and make their own mistakes.'

'What if they get hurt or people take advantage of

them.'

'They've still got to go,' Anna said firmly. 'It's not really life if you're not allowed to get into trouble, or you never bang your elbow or scrape your knees, or people never say horrid things to you. I know it's not nice but you've got learn to deal with stuff,' Anna opined. 'Just think if Dad suddenly disappeared and we were left to look after ourselves. I'd be okay because I'm a bloody pain in the neck, I know what it's like when things go wrong and I can pick myself up and try again. You should see the bruises I've got when I've been trying to learn a new free running move, or when I've been playing football and the boys have barged me over. Caro and Eliza don't know any of that; he won't let them play games, he's always there telling them what to do, I mean he even helps them with their homework so they get that perfect mark.'

'I suppose you could be right.'

'I'm always right,' said Anna, 'and when I'm not I pretend I am anyway, then I stick it away in my head and the next time I am right. So you don't have your eye on the prize?'

'What?' asked Miss Rae.

'Being the new Mrs Templeton, if you were my step mum we could fight all the time and not just in the mornings. You could poison me with an apple and I'd have to hope there was a handy prince passing to give me a snog.'

'No … no definitely not.'

'Have you got a boyfriend or a girlfriend then?'

'I'm not going out with anyone.'

'Which would you have?'

'ANNA!'

'I've got a best friend at school who when she was born she was a boy. I go to an all girls' school so she's a girl now. It doesn't matter stuff like that, what matters is inside you. I don't mind if you like girls or boys,' she shrugged. 'I think I like boys. I had a crush on Lou's brother. Although when I finally talked to him he'd turned out to be a smelly prat and that stopped my crush. Lou thought it was funny because that's what she'd told me. It was a real pain because he followed me about for days until Minnie told him she liked him and then he forgot about me. So what do you think, boys or girls? Of course you might not like either, our teacher said some people aren't bothered at all.'

'You have very wide ranging lessons!'

'We do, that was our geography teacher. I asked him if he had a girl and he said he didn't but he wasn't interested in boys either. So is that you?'

Miss Rae reddened but Anna plainly wasn't going to let it go so she decided to answer truthfully.

'I like boys, Anna.'

'There you go. I bet you didn't want to tell me because there's a special boy you like. It's not Mr Goodman is it? Were you jealous when we went monster hunting together?'

'No Anna, it's not Mr Goodman.'

'Who is it then?'

'If I tell you can we move on to something else?'

Anna looked up expectantly.

'He's one of the IT boys.'

'But he doesn't even know you exist and you're pining for him …'

'He does know I exist, he … er … keeps making fun of me,' corrected Miss Rae.

'He's the one who said you'd caught a rock?'

'Yes.'

'Maybe he likes you but he's too shy to say. Perhaps I could carry notes between you. There was a film on the telly and a boy had to do that for an older girl who had a secret crush, I never saw the ending because dad came in and turned the TV over to a documentary about the history of the printing press, that was well interesting … NOT! You could write notes and I could take them, I could read them to him and see how he reacts. Perhaps he'll swoon at their loveliness, then again your English is so bad he probably wouldn't understand what you're trying to say.'

'No I don't think we'll be doing that …'

'Hey, hey, think about it, Miss Rae, it might be the nudge he needs.'

'You're good at catching monsters, perhaps you could concentrate on that and leave the match-making until you're a little older.'

'If you had liked girls that would have been all right you know. At school they say you should respect everybody, it doesn't matter if they're different from you. I mean if you don't like someone because they're a different colour, or they fancy girls then what's to stop them not liking you because you have green eyes or your favourite animals are cats or something?'

'Your teachers are right. I wish it had been like that at my school.'

'Why?' demanded Anna.

'Enough revelations for now.'

'Fair enough,' Anna accepted, 'I bet you've told me a lot more than you planned to. Jam, jam, jam!'

'Yeah, you're a persistent girl.'

'So Dad's going to have to look else where for a new Mrs T. Do you think if he found one he'd let me go? I wonder how many of my friends' mums are single. Do you think if I could get him hitched up he'd let me go?'

'It's not that bad is it, being told what to do?'

'Do you think if I didn't have him laying down the law I'd be off taking drugs , joining a gang and nicking stuff. Mum has rules too, lots of them actually, but they're more about respecting other people.'

'I think I'm going to tell the office you've been helping,' Miss Rae changed the subject.

'They might stop me …' Anna pointed out.

'But if I don't, when they do find out it'd be worse. I can't catch any on my own so if I come clean now they might let you keep helping.'

Anna thought for a moment and then agreed it was probably a good plan. 'There's only one out there at the moment. If they say no to me helping, you could ask your boy to give you a hand, that'd give you a chance to talk. You and me we've had a chance to talk and we've found out loads about each other, maybe if you had him trapped in the Mystery Machine you'd find out loads about him and then you'd be able to force him like you.'

'I don't want to force him ...'

'No?'

'No Anna, if he likes me, that'd be good. If he doesn't well ... well he's a smelly prat and I'll have to move on.'

'That's very grown-up.'

'Yes,' Miss Rae agreed, 'I'm quite grown up really.'

Chapter 19

Because she was sure dad would be watching, Anna stomped down the drive, a grim look on her face, and slammed the front door shut.

'Bloody woman, another morning wasted. That Uncle Silas book is the worst book in the world. I've read screeds and screeds and still nothing has happened. Who on earth would write a book like that? Perhaps Senor Fanny was paid by the word so he stretched it out as long as he could.'

Dad was waiting in the doorway of the kitchen.

'Anna ... what is this doing in your room?'

He held up the iPhone mum had given her.

'Damn,' she said to herself, but before she could make up a convincing lie, Eliza came forward. 'I was wondering where I'd left it ...'

'Eliza?' stuttered Dad.

'A ... a friend lent it to me, it's ... part of the holiday club homework, we're looking at modern design and these are meant to be iconic so we have to report back on what we think makes them ... iconic.'

'Why was it in Anna's room?'

'I was showing her ... er ... a grammar App and then it was dinner time.

'I didn't want to leave it lying, it's exactly the sort of thing burglars would take, if I was a burglar I would so look out for iPhones, so I hid it …' Anna added.

'Oh,' said dad.

'Thanks Anna,' said Eliza. 'It would have been a nightmare if it had been stolen, Rosie would have had conniptions.' She took it from dad. 'I'll put away out of sight just in case.' She disappeared up the stairs.

'I want an iPhone,' demanded Anna. 'They are so cool. My phone is basically a tin can with a bit of string attached compared to it.'

'Well you're not getting one …'

'Don't even think about it …' Anna said mimicking his voice and pulling a face.

'Don't try and wind me up,' demanded dad. 'You'll thank me when you're grown up.'

'I doubt that very much,' Anna replied coldly and went up to her bedroom.

Later on in the evening she slipped into Eliza's room.

'Thanks,' she said.

'Do you want it back?' Eliza asked.

'Can you look after it for now?' Anna asked. 'It'll be safer in your room. Mum gave it to me so I can use Skype to talk when I'm missing her.' She sat opposite Eliza on the bed. 'Do you miss your mum?'

'Yes, I miss her a lot.'

'At least I get to see mine. I wish dad would let you come when I visit. Mum loves you and Caro.'

'Yeah I wish he would.'

'Things might change,' Anna offered. 'In fact I'm going to

make sure they do.'

'What can you do Anna?'

'If I can change dinner from revolting fennel to delicious cheese on toast I can do anything,' she said with a grin, 'and I will. Dad's really odd, I wonder why, he's not like any of the other dads at school.'

Eliza agreed, but couldn't suggest any reason.

'I want it to be the other way round. I want us, you, me and Caro to live with mum and visit dad if we want; I probably wouldn't you know.'

'That would be brilliant,' said Eliza, 'but it'll never happen.'

'It will,' Anna asserted, 'it will.'

She went back to her own room even more determined. She wasn't going to dream about it, she was going to make it come true. She didn't know how, but she felt Miss Rae was on her side now, so maybe she would have a good idea.

"I'm burning through the sky Yeah! Two hundred degrees - That's why they call me Miss Fahrenheit,"

'Stop singing and go to sleep,' dad bellowed.

"I'm trav'ling at the speed of light - I wanna make a supersonic woman of me," she sang back even louder before heading to bed.

Chapter 20

Miss Rae was going to speak to the people in the office in the morning and suggested they'd meet for lunch so she could let Anna know how it had gone.

'What are you doing today?' dad demanded.

'There's a careers thing at school,' she lied, 'Careers with Maths. I'm going to that, I want to be able to do my own accounts when I'm the world's best stuntwoman.'

'Just give up this stuntwoman nonsense, Anna, I'm sick of you going on about something that's not going to happen.'

'Did you want to be something when you were growing up, Dad?'

'Yes. I wanted to be a engineer and by hard work and application I achieved my goal.'

'And what's so different? I have a goal, I'm prepared to work hard towards it, you know put in the effort.'

'Because I don't want you to go into something so superfluous.'

'Can't you see it's not about you,' Anna replied. 'Anyway it's going to be amazing. I'm going to work my way up until I get a job in a blockbuster movie, then I'll tell you and you can get a big group of your engineer mates together to see it, and you'll be sitting there with your party box of pickled gherkins and you'll be able to turn to them and proudly say, "see that actress crashing through the plate glass, that's not really Miss Holly Wood, that's my actual daughter Anna." And they'd all go "Wow!" and "Cor!" and "can she tell us the calculations for how much force times speed was needed to break the glass". And you'd feel great pride because they'd be mega impressed and then you'd email me and I'd send you all the equations and they'd be real complicated and your mates would be all, "she knows her calculations, doesn't she?" Life will be rosy then. You'll be proud of your daughter, I'll be rich, there'll be jam on my breakfast toast EVERY day, but people will think it's famous actresses jumping off roofs and killing vampires and they won't know it's me, so I'll still be able walk down the street without being hassled. That'll be sweet. I'd better scoot and get that information about being an accountant and then no one will rip me off and steal my dosh. Cheery bye.'

She'd have liked to go out the back door and jump over the fence, but decided he'd probably make her come back and give her another lecture so she went out the front way. Caroline was just coming down the stairs and she grabbed her and gave her a hug.

'Love you Caro! I have two favourite sisters and you're one of them.'

Caro held her tighter than normal, but didn't say anything. When she let go Anna was out the front door and down the street singing loudly and skipping happily.

She headed first to check if Roy was about, she wanted to see if he'd got any new moves for her to learn. When she arrived she discovered one of his friends was with him. She was French too, she had cropped blond hair, lots of tattoos and was dressed in black.

Anna instantly recognised her and for the briefest moment was stunned into silence.

The silence did not last long.

'Meraud Barbier! MERAUD BARBIER!' she squealed.

The girl turned round.

'OhmigodIcan'tbelieveitsyouyou'rejustincredibleyoudid thatjump,youknowthejump, THEJUMPitwasthebestthing Ihaveeverseen!'

'This is the little caracal I was telling you about,' Roy said, 'Anna Templeton.'

'Ah yes,' said Meraud, 'you are Miss Anna.'

'Now Anna you must slow down,' said Roy, 'English is not our first language.'

'Slow, slow, slow,' Anna told herself and breathed in deeply. 'MERAUD BARBIER! I watch you all the time you are just the coolest person in the world when you crossed Paris in that video it was so amazing you were so fast and the moves were unbelievable I – DID – NOT - BELIEVE - some of the moves.' She grabbed Meraud's arm. 'Your tattoos are amazing, your moves are amazing, you're amazing, has anyone told you, you are amazing?'

'Sometimes,' Roy said to his friend, 'Anna will talk for a whole morning and no one else gets a chance to speak.'

'You are excited?' Meraud asked.

Anna was staring at her open-eyed, 'so-so,' she said and then launched into a description of one of the videos she'd seen starring Meraud and began to demonstrate her favourite jumps from it. 'You jumped like this and then the bad guy, the one with the scar he ...'

'Anna,' interrupted Roy, 'would you like Meraud to teach you some moves?'

'Would I?' she nodded vigorously, 'I would like that more than anything in this world!'

'If you promise to keep the talking to the minimum, Meraud will spend the next hour with you. You have one hour because other people would like to learn from her too.'

Anna nodded again.

It was the quietest hour they had ever experienced when Anna was training. She listened to Meraud without interrupting. She watched in awe when any of the moves were demonstrated and concentrated so hard when it was her turn she forgot to speak.

At the end they made Anna do one of the moves she had just learnt and when she managed it there was spontaneous applause.

'She has almost got it,' Roy said loudly to Meraud.

'Oh ...' Anna said plaintively, 'and I worked so hard.'

'It was excellent ...' Meraud started.

'Cha! She fish for compliment, you should see her use the big eyes,' said Roy. 'We have to be careful what we say to Anna or her head will grow too big to lift.'

'Meraud, what do you really think?' asked Anna directly.

'Five minutes, Roy. Come with me Anna.' She led her out

of the hall. 'You follow.'

She set off across the road into the park, hurdling the obstacles, flipping over pathways, leaping from one balustrade to another. Anna followed, copying what she was doing and laughing as she tried to keep up. After a couple of minutes Meraud led her onto a monument and stopped.

She let Anna get her breath back.

'Anna, the most important thing to learn is you should never stop learning. Every move is step towards next move. So you work hard and you learn show-off trick, that is not end that is beginning. You understand?'

'Yes, yes I think.'

'Good. Now you ask what I think. You have skill, you work hard and you learn quickly. You can get better but you remember always to enjoy. Just now we run though park I see you smiling. That is good, free-running you speak with your body. I see you, I see joy, the rest the most difficult tricks they are nothing if there is no joy. The next time I visit, no teaching, no lessons, we run through city you and me, we celebrate life, okay?'

'Yes, yes, yes!' Anna's eyes were gleaming. 'We could go now.'

'I promised to help the others too.'

'Yeah you did,' Anna agreed. 'Meraud?'

'Yes.'

'Thank you.'

'Mon plasier.'

They went back to the makeshift gym and Anna watched

the next training session. She didn't take her eyes of Meraud, although she did manage to give Roy a comprehensive and very personal review of the latest download chart and didn't hold back when she didn't like something.

Eventually she had to go to meet Miss Rae. She thanked Meraud again, high-fived Roy and then made her way out of the high window as usual. 'I love you Meraud,' she yelled as she disappeared.

'I wonder if she enjoyed herself,' Ray commented as the multi-coloured figure disappeared with loud whoop.

Chapter 21

Anna arrived at the café still bubbling with excitement, saw Miss Rae and plonked herself down beside her.

'I've had the most AMAZING morning ...' she stopped. There was another person at the table, a lady she'd never seen before. 'Who are you? Are you with us? Are you Miss Rae's mother, are you Mrs Rae?' she asked. 'No you're not her mother you don't look anything like her, who are you?'

'Anna, please calm down. This is my ... um ... head of department. Mrs Gra ...'

'Mrs Gray, is that planned, Mrs Gray and Miss Rae. Is that how you're picked to work in your office if a Mr Hay, or Miss May or Mrs Day turned up looking for a job would you give them one right automagically?'

'Mrs Graham,' Miss Rae finished.

'Or Kay, Faye, Jay ...'

'Anna, serious head on,' Miss Rae said severely. 'This is important for you too.'

'Oh ... right.' She zipped her lips.

'Anna is very enthusiastic,' Miss Rae conceded.

Mrs. Graham held out her hand. 'How do you do Anna?' Anna shook it.

'Mrs. Graham wanted to meet you Anna. I've told her how you've been hunting the little monsters with me.'

'I've come to understand we put Miss Rae in an invidious

situation, with little preparation and elevated standards to live up to,' said Mrs Graham. 'It was an unreasonable responsibility to put on her which she achieved by circumventing our habitual procedures.'

Anna unzipped her lips, 'are you speaking in Latin,' she asked. 'I'm only understanding half the words.'

'Anna is twelve,' said Miss Rae.

'My apologies,' said Mrs. Graham. 'When Mr Goodman was asked to help out in Germany poor Miss Rae was left holding the baby, so to speak. It was an unfair situation, which we should have thought about. Luckily you were able help her and from what I understand you're a natural at hunting monsters.'

Anna understood that. 'Yeah, I'm an ace monster hunter.'

Miss Rae nodded in agreement.

Anna wasn't quite sure what all this meant. Mrs Graham didn't appear angry so she didn't think she or Miss Rae were going to get a row.

'As a government organisation we're meant to do everything by the book,' Mrs Graham continued.

'Book, "the book"?' asked Anna, worried she was going to have to start reading Uncle Silas again.

'But,' said Mrs Graham, 'on this occasion I'm going to pretend the book doesn't exist.'

'Good, because it's well boring ...'

'What?' asked Mrs Graham.

'Uncle Silas!' said Anna.

Before she could tell them both about its short-comings,

Miss Rae said she would explain about Uncle Silas to Mrs Graham later.

'We can't employ you as such,' continued Mrs Graham, 'but you can volunteer and we're happy to give you something to say you've been doing community service. In addition there is the reward system and I think, given your skills it could be £90.00 per … er …pick-up. What do you think?'

'There's no point in me pretending to think about it because I love monster-hunting. Miss Rae and I have stopped fighting and I get a chance to practice my free-running so yes … yes, yes, yes.'

'Excellent. Since that is settled I think we should eat,' said Mrs Graham and picked up the menu. 'Oh good they do sausages and mashed potatoes.'

'Yeah Soss and Mash for me too,' said Anna.

'Why not?' agreed Miss Rae.

When the waiter came they ordered three plates of sausages and mash, Miss Rae and Mrs. Graham had tea and Anna had a lemonade ice-cream float.

After Mrs Graham left, Anna confided she thought they might have been in big trouble so she was relieved it was okay. Miss Rae admitted it hadn't gone well at first. She had asked to speak to Mrs Graham and when she admitted Anna had been helping Mrs Graham went off the deep end and she got a huge telling off.

'For a while it was touch and go, I thought she was going to sack me, but eventually she gave me a chance to explain and I was able to tell her how unfair it was that I'd been told to go hunt monsters on my own and how useless I was at it. I was able to tell her that you were a natural and how you'd even worked out how to use more programs on the machines and that had made things easier. I was in her office all morning and eventually she agreed with me.'

'Good for you Miss Rae, did you use the jam technique?'

'A bit – and I think she was worried about people finding she'd replaced an expert monster hunter with some kid just out of university who hadn't got a clue and two left hands as well.'

'I wonder if the monsters are getting to be more of a problem?' Anna asked. 'I guess they're trying to keep it under wraps aren't they. It's probably better keeping me happy than letting me go blabbing about it to everyone. What did she say about the one that's been monster-knapped? Is she going to sign a warrant?'

'I never asked. I should speak to her about it.'

'Yeah you should. Do you always wear the same trousers and jacket?'

'What?'

'You always look the same, have you just got one suit?'

'NO I don't!' said Miss Rae, outraged at the suggestion.

'Well you're not going to reel in your IT boy if you always look the same. You need to wear something more lovey dovey, I don't mean like a popstar girl but you can't always look like Men in Black. I can't help you, but Caro could. She likes fashion and when dad's not about, she practices doing make-up, she could help you.'

'Help?' Miss Rae squeaked nervously

'Yeah, she could do a makeover on you and all the boys in the yard would swoon!'

'Anna, life is not like the television.'

Anna stood up and spun around "'who run the world? Girls! Who run the world? Girls!'" she sang. 'But it doesn't matter if it's not exactly like the telly, we can give it a try! We can't do it do today, I'd have to ask her and I'll have to get the big eyes as big as possible if she's going to say yes. So we've got a free afternoon and we're going to play catch.'

Miss Rae stared at her, 'we're going to do what!'

'Play catch, I want to play catch. I've brought a ball, won't you play catch with me …' Anna looked up, her big green eyes wide open and the saddest look ever on her face.

Miss Rae decided she'd been spending far too long with Anna Templeton, the look hadn't worked when they first met but now the girl only had to stare for a few seconds and she was giving in.

They crossed the road.

'Okay we'll play catch, but I'm really not very good at catching.'

'I know,' said Anna, 'that's why you need to practice.'

They spent an hour in the park, but even Anna had to accept Miss Rae wasn't getting any better. 'Oh well,' she conceded. 'You'll just have to concentrate on being the brains of the team.'

Chapter 22

When she got home Caroline and Eliza were in the sitting room watching telly. She stood at the door and announced she'd had a brilliant day and she hoped one of dad's disgusting vegetarian specials wasn't going to spoil it.

'You can come in,' said Eliza, 'he's not here.'

'Had to go to some event, won't be back until after ten!' explained Caroline.

Anna cartwheeled in, jumped over the sofa and plonked herself down between them.

'No way!'

Her sisters grinned.

'He's left a salad in the fridge,' Caroline added.

'Salad! Ptoo!' replied Anna, 'we're going out. We could go for a pizza, or fish and chips or for an Italian, what else is close by? There's an Indian isn't there, but I don't know, I've never had a curry so maybe not tonight.'

'Go to a restaurant?' asked Caroline nervously.

'What if he finds out?' said Eliza.

'We'd be grounded for weeks,' added Caroline.

'He won't find out,' said Anna confidently. 'I want to eat out!'

'But …'

'No buts, I'm going so you've got to come to look after me. Where do you want to go?'

'You don't need looking after,' said Eliza.

'Do!' Anna claimed.

'We can't afford it,' Caroline tried.

'I've plenty of dosh from mum,' promised Anna. 'So no worries there ... what's it going to be?'

'We have to come?'

'Yes,' said Anna and her sisters recognised the look.

'Then pizza!' Caroline sighed, there was no point fighting a losing battle. 'We have pizza at school and I'd like to try it from a restaurant.'

'You've made the right decision, I'll get everything sorted.'

Anna washed three plates, three knives, three forks, three spoons and three glasses and put them on the drainer then she put the salad in a rubbish bag and washed the bowl.

'In case he checks the garbage I'll take it with us and put it in one of the wheelie bins down the road. Do you want to change?'

Caroline thought it would be best if they looked like they did when he left.

'I look fabulous anyway,' said Anna. 'I always do,' she boasted as Caroline locked the front door. 'I think it must be something to with my eye for colour and a natural gift for putting looks together. You two of course look like telegraph poles, with your excessive height, it's like I'm walking in a ditch when I'm beside you.'

'Anna, we're completely normal, height wise, you're simply shorter than average.'

'You're more of a muppet than a sister,' decided Eliza.

'Would you like a footstool for your birthday?' asked Caroline. 'You could carry it with you and when you want to join a conversation, simply stand on it and voila you're on the same level as the rest of us.'

Anna responded with a long rant about being normal in a house full of giants and in that vein they soon found themselves at the Pizza restaurant.

'You really have enough money,' asked Caroline.

Anna opened her purse and showed her.

'And you don't mind spending it on dinner?'

'Course not.'

They had a great evening. They laughed and talked and joked and giggled but they avoided talking about dad because that would have brought the mood down. When the pizzas arrived Anna waited until her sisters were munching away before asking if they would help Miss Rae.

'You want us to help her Anna, but you're always saying how awful and stupid she is,' pointed out Eliza.

'Yeah, subtle aren't I, secret things, plans and stuff so I have to pretend.'

'You have a very complicated double life Anna,' said Caroline.

'I'd make a great spy,' she suggested. 'Is there anyone you'd like spied on?'

Caroline ignored the offer and asked how she wanted them to help Miss Rae. Anna said how Miss Rae liked a boy in her work but he didn't pay her any attention. 'I thought if she looked a little less like a teacher and a little more like a girl maybe he would be nice to her. I know I look great … but I admit it's not a look everyone goes for …'

'Simon Robinson did, he followed you about for weeks,' Eliza remembered, 'what happened to him?'

'He wasn't quite the boy I thought he was.'

'He had a very powerful odour,' said Eliza. 'He definitely needed super-strength Right Guard.'

'He was the lamebrain, wasn't he?' asked Caroline, 'you mooned about him for ages I'm sure his sister tried to put you off …'

'Can we get back on topic, please.'

'You want US to help Miss Rae, because you're worried if YOU do, she'll only meet smelly lamebrains.'

'I want YOU to help because I'M a busy person, with MANY irons in the fire and I don't need any more.'

'I s'ppose we could give her some tips for you, so long as we can get out of the house.'

It was a deal. The rest of the meal passed in no time and reluctantly they made their way home. They brushed their teeth, washed their hands and faces and checked the house in case they'd left anything that might give the game away.

Anna went to her room, she didn't want to be caught watching telly and she'd just sat at her desk when her phone rang. It was her mum, everything was signed and sealed. Anna screamed so loudly her sisters rushed it to see if she was okay.

'Everything's sorted for Mum's film!'

They grabbed her and the three of them jumped up and down in excitement.

'Caro and Eliza, are pleased too,' she managed to gasp down the phone when mum asked what was going on. Eventually the thought of dad coming back calmed things down and she told mum she loved her and she was looking forward to seeing her and turned the phone off.

The three of them sat on her bed chatting until they heard the front door then Caroline and Eliza went back to their rooms and Anna slipped into bed.

'That must be the best day in the history of the world,' Anna said to herself as she settled down. 'Meraud Barbier gave me a personal lesson, I became an official monster hunter, dinner was amazing and to top it all, mum is officially in a blockbuster. Wow!'

Chapter 23

Anna was awake really early as it was her first full day as an "official" monster hunter. She put on her most multi-coloured outfit because she felt so cheerful. She hoped she'd get a badge or an identity card. 'I don't want a uniform,' she said to herself. 'That would be a bummer.'

Dad had laid the kitchen table and there was a choice of homemade muesli or branflakes. She didn't care because she was going to grab something when she went out and poured herself a glass of milk.

She was drinking it when dad came through.

'Right Anna you're coming to work with me today.'

'WHAT!'

'Yes. I want you to see what life is like in the real world and not in the world of your imagination.'

'NO!'

'Don't you contradict me!'

She could tell by the look on his face she wasn't going to get out of this. She screamed inside.

'Go and change into something smarter.'

'I am smart. You wear what you like why shouldn't I?'

'You've got to learn to dress for different occasions. We're going to a place of work so you have to dress appropriately.'

'I don't have a suit.'

'Just something smarter and avoid the usual mishmash of

clashing colours. And do it now!'

'Grrrrr!' she growled.

'Just go!'

She headed back up stairs and it was all she could do to stop herself going ballistic. As she was stomping on each step a brilliant plan popped into her head.

She came back down in the dull skirt he'd bought her and the tweed jacket he'd got Grandma to give her one Christmas. Possibly they fitted two years ago but she had grown since then so the skirt was very short and the jacket actually looked fashionable now it was too small.

'I'd forgotten about this lovely jacket from Grandma,' she said. 'Doesn't it go well with the skirt you bought me?'

He looked her up and down.

The skirt was really short, but he had bought it and if he told her to change again it would mean admitting he was wrong. 'That's smarter,' he said finally. 'Now eat some breakfast.'

'Can I have toast?'

'Yes okay …'

She stuck some of the wholemeal bread in the toaster. 'Still no jam. They make organic jam, you know. We could have that or honey, that's organic too and if we bought lots of honey that would help the bees meet their sales targets wouldn't it?'

He ignored her.

'We've got a really interesting project on at the moment,' he said instead, 'designing a new production line for a company producing screens for smart phones.'

'Can I have a proper smartphone? Do they make the screens for iPhones? Can I have an iPhone?'

'No.'

'If you bought me a new smart phone that would mean they'd need to make more screens so your production line would be even more important. That would be a good thing. Then you'd become indi-pencil-able.'

He corrected her pronunciation, 'indispensible!'

She continued to come up with more reasons why she should have a smartphone until he went to get the car out.

The moment he was left the room she texted a long rant to Miss Rae, she complained about breakfast, she complained about the man on the radio, she complained she couldn't get out in the morning and for good measure complained about dad's car and then she said she would text her later if things changed.

It was probably the longest text Miss Rae had ever received and it took her some time to work out what Anna was trying to tell her, there were so many other things she wanted to get off her chest.

Anna waited at the kitchen table until dad came back.

'I said I was getting the car out.'

'I'm not deaf, I was trying to digest the toast; without jam it's quite indigestible.

She always made a fuss about sitting in the front and sat down quickly to bag it, in case Caroline or Eliza were coming as well.

She turned the radio on and immediately put it onto a pop music station.

He put it back to Radio 2.

'HEY!'

'My car, my music,' he said.

'But your music is rubbish!'

'At least my music has meaning and melody.'

'So does mine and what's more it's relevant to the modern world – I mean …' she pointed at the radio 'Ra Ra Rasputin … what's that all about?' She pointed out the short-comings of the music he liked all the way to his office.

She had been to his work before, but usually had to wait in the car. She had never been the least interested in seeing what was inside and she still wasn't, but it was time to put her plan into action and that plan was not to speak or at least speak as little as possible. It was probably the most difficult thing she had ever tried in her life but it was worth giving it a go because he wouldn't expect that.

They took the lift to the sixth floor where his office was. She recognised some of the people but just said "hello", he introduced her to the others and then brought her a chair to his desk. Once his computer was open he started to explain what he was working on. She stared at the screen but kept her lips tightly sealed and as he wasn't getting any response he quickly ran out of things to say and stopped.

She sat there furious, the sun was shining and there were so many things she could be doing and she wanted to shout at him but she stuck to her plan. He managed to endure her silent staring for fifteen minutes but eventually cracked.

'Why don't you have a wander round the office,' he suggested. 'Have a look at what everyone is doing.'

'A look? Okay.' She wheeled her chair to the man at the next-door desk, sat directly behind him and stared at the back of his neck.

'Hi Anna.'

'Hi.'

'I'll explain what I'm working on.'

'Please don't!'

'Oh.'

She stayed there, silently staring until completely freaked he called to one of his friends. 'Tania, could you show Anna the CAD of the new production line layout.'

She moved to the next person, did the same to her and was satisfied to see it had the same effect. In fact the whole office was starting to be affected.

A man in a suit came through and said a cheery hello. The muted response surprised him.

'And you must Iain's daughter,' he held out his hand.

Anna gave his hand a very limp shake and nodded.

'Planning a career in engineering then,' he said as heartily as could.

'No.'

'It's an exciting time to be an engineer.'

'Is it?' she replied, in a dull monotone raising her eyebrows in mock surprise and then stared at him.

Dad came up. 'Lots of opportunities,' he said trying to be

as enthusiastic as possible.

'Lots eh?' she replied and continued to stare at the boss man.

There was a long silence until the man in suit said, 'yes … exciting,' and shuffled his feet edgily.

'I'm going to get a coffee,' said Tania.

Most of the other people said they were too and disappeared.

The man in the suit said he had to make some phone calls and went back to his office so she and dad were left standing in an almost empty room.

'Better get on,' dad said.

She followed him to his desk and sat so she was just behind him. He could tell she was there but couldn't see her face with out turning.

When the people making coffee came back, one of them called to dad.

'Iain can I just get your input on this … er …transfer point.'

Dad stood up and they went into one of the empty offices and shut the door.

Anna watched through the window and it was obvious dad was trying to explain himself. He must have told them how loud and opinionated she was, so her silence had caught them on the hop.

The other man starting speaking, waved his hands about a lot and dad's shoulders slumped.

When he came back he stuttered a bit and said

unexpectedly they needed to have a big meeting to discuss the project. 'It isn't really appropriate for you, so you'd better head home. I'll ... er ... give you some money for a taxi.'

She was torn between demanding to know why she couldn't go to the meeting and cheering because her plan had worked. She mumbled 'okay,' then she couldn't help herself and asked 'are you going to swear and that's why I have to go?'

He said of course not and she managed to stay shut up after that.

It had worked! Her plan had worked and much sooner than she'd expected; she was ecstatic and as a bonus she had an extra tenner and she sure wasn't going to waste it on a taxi.

'Now go straight home Anna,' he ordered.

She shut the office door but stayed just outside and listened.

'I thought you said you couldn't shut her up, it was like having Banquo's ghost looming over my shoulder,' one of them said.

'She's normally a nightmare and challenges everything I say, even obvious things like if I give a mug of tea she'll say she asked for a cup, or I'll say something is red and she'll instantly argue it's more of a scarlet or something. I don't know what's come over her.'

The boss man joined in, 'just don't bring her again, brought down the whole atmosphere, god it was like a morgue, I half expected to find someone laid out on a slab of marble.'

She left them to it. She had a free morning and it was time for a decent breakfast. She found a café near the office, bought a coffee and a pastry and chatted to the people eating their breakfast and told them how cool all the cakes were and how a curranty pastry was the perfect start to her day.

She phoned friends and they went to Convent Garden to look in the shops, grabbed lunch and watched the buskers. In the afternoon she phoned Miss Rae, who actually sounded pleased to hear from her.

'I could buy you a coffee,' Miss Rae suggested.

Anna immediately agreed.

Miss Rae was waiting when she arrived.

'Have you got lipstick on?' Anna asked. 'Is that because you like to look smart when you buy me coffee.'

Miss Rae reddened. 'I ... er ... thought maybe you were right and I could look just a little bit more like a girl ...'

'Rather than a policeman,' suggested Anna. 'The good news is Caro and Eliza would LOVE to give you a makeover. I could phone them now.'

'I said I'd only be out for a quick break.'

'Tomorrow morning?'

Miss Rae looked like a deer in the headlights.

'Great,' said Anna without giving her a chance to say no. 'They're not going to make you look spangly and half dressed like, just look cool so your boy will see you and say to himself, I'd never noticed how cool Miss Rae is. She's the sort of cool girl I'd like to talk to. I mean that's what it's about isn't it, talking. I talked to my boy and discovered he was a yoyo and you've got to talk to yours and find out what he's like. He might be a yoyo too but then you'll know. But he might be that boy from Star Wars!'

'Who on earth is he?'

'You don't know the boy from Star Wars, haven't you seen Star Wars? It doesn't really matter if you haven't, he was cool and sensitive and he made the right decision in the end. Your boy might be like him but you've got to find out. So tomorrow morning I'll bring the beautiful sisters along. You know when we talked to Mrs Graham and she said about voluntary work, I need something that says I'm doing it. I don't know what, a bit of paper, a letter? You know what, you should meet my mum, the way she dresses is really cool, that might help you, she can wear practically anything and look amazing! Yeah, something about helping with animal welfare, you're clever you can decide what. Then when dad says I've got to go with him or he tells me I've got to have elocution lessons, or that he's putting me on an anti-swearing program I can say "can't today I'm building up my community service hours," and show him the paper and he'll think, "at least she's not practising her bloody Parkour," that's what he calls it, "maybe she's got a conscience after all," and I can laugh all the way to the bank, hahaha!'

Miss Rae managed to untangle in her mind what Anna wanted and said okay, but for now she'd better go.

As she was leaving Miss Rae said Mrs Graham couldn't get a warrant. If someone has kidnapped …

'Monster-knapped,' corrected Anna.

Miss Rae smiled '... has monster-knapped the little guy, we'll have to go and assess the situation and decide on the best way to fetch it back.'

They said goodbye and Anna headed off. She was home first and when dad came back he started to give her a row for her conduct in the office.

She looked up with her best innocent face. 'What do you mean, Dad? I thought you wanted me to behave.'

He looked flustered. 'Yes I did ...'

'I didn't think they'd want me chattering away like I do and disturbing them.'

'No of course not ...'

'It's a proper place of work.' she pointed out, 'isn't it? Not a place for chatter. A place where people need quiet so they can concentrate on transfer points; they sound real tricky transfer points ... I thought that's what you'd want.'

He growled to himself, looked frustrated and eventually changed the subject and instead told her off for not eating all her dinner.

Chapter 24

'I want you to be nice to her,' Anna said to her sisters as they set off to meet Miss Rae.

'We've got to be nice? But you hate her and you're really nasty to her,' Eliza pointed out.

'No I'm not!' Anna shrugged, 'that was weeks ago! Now you have to promise to properly help her. You can't just slap the make-up on and stick her in a push-up bra because if you do, her boy is going to say to himself, "what's going on 'ere?" It's got to be subtle, just make her a look a little less like a prison guard and a bit more like someone who would be fun to spend an evening with. I think she's shy with boys so you've got to make her think, well actually I am quite pretty and I do look nice and when my boy sees me he'll think that too.'

'He's not her boy yet!'

'I know and he might be a terrible person anyway, but she's got to find out, because if it's not him she can cross him off the list and maybe the next one will be the one who makes her laugh and smile. Have you got a boy Caro?'

'What with dad stalking me all the time? What you don't need is dads hiding behind bushes with binoculars …'

'So you can snog?'

'That too, but mainly like you say, so you can get to know the other person.'

170

'What about you Eliza? You got a boy in your sights?' Anna demanded.

'I like Robbie Nash and I think he likes me, but it's as Caro says, dad's always there and that frightens him away.'

'God what is he like, is dad some sort of Harry Potter "Dementor", sucking the happiness out of everything?' ranted Anna.

'Miss Rae was pretty stand offish when she stayed for lunch,' said Caroline as they hung about the front door of the department store waiting for her.

'She's proper clever,' said Anna, 'but all her cleverness has gone into schoolwork so she's never had time for being mates with people and I don't think she knows how. She'll have to work that out for herself, your job is to … is to … well make her as nice on the outside as she is on the inside.'

'You think she's nice?'

'Yeah,' agreed Anna. 'She's like an Easter Egg, we've just got to get the hard plastic wrapping off to get to the tasty chocolate inside.'

'Do all your metaphors revolve around food,' asked Eliza.

'Perhaps you're a cookie monster,' offered Caroline.

Anna ignored the insults and dug in her purse. 'I don't think Miss Rae has a lot of money, so you could use this.' She handed over a bundle of notes.

'Where did this come from, Anna?' asked Caroline. 'You haven't been taking it from Dad's wallet have you?'

'I've got a special, secret, hush-hush job.'

'There's a hundred pounds here!'

'I thought what you could do is choose the clothes and then tell her the price after you've taken this money off. So if she can only afford fifty quid you could get her a hundred and fifty quids worth of stuff. Tell her there's special discount or you've got a store card or something. I don't think she shops much so she's not going to know.'

Before Caroline could reply they saw Miss Rae in the distance.

'Hey Miss Rae, I've assembled my crack team,' said Anna, 'we're like the New Avengers of makeovers.'

'I'm not really sure I need a ... a makeover,' she said nervously.

'No you don't, you just need a fresh eye and Caro and Eliza are great at this sort of stuff. I'm useless at fashion and make-up so I'm going to do my own thing for a couple of hours, I'll meet you back here and we can go for cake.'

Before anyone could argue she was gone.

Chapter 25

Three hours later Miss Rae, Caroline and Eliza were back at the main door. They had a bundle of carrier bags and were smiling and chatting.

Anna reappeared, eyes sparkling and breathing heavily.

'Hey team,' she shouted, 'time for cake. I've found a great place, the cakes are huge - huge, creamy, jammy and chocolaty. How did it go? You've got loads of bags, let's have a look.'

Caroline slapped her hands away. 'Patience Anna, we'll show you when we're sitting down. '

Anna stared up at Miss Rae. 'You look great, I told you Caro was amazing at make-up. Your boy is going to be intrigued.'

Miss Rae smiled.

'We thought maybe it was time for a hair cut too,' said Eliza. 'Miss Rae says she always wears it tied back so perhaps it's time for something new.'

'Cool,' agreed Anna.

She took them to the café and "oohed" and "aahed" at the clothes they'd bought.

'Caroline and Eliza are incredible at finding bargains,' said Miss Rae. 'I got all this lot and paid less than a hundred and forty pounds.'

Anna winked at her sisters.

'So I think I can just about afford a haircut …' she continued, 'so long as it's not one of these West End salons.'

'You'll be able to do the make-up again?' asked Caroline.

'I think so, it was simpler than I expected.'

'Good,' said Anna. 'We should have our own telly show, "The Anna-lysers", do you get it? We'll analyse how to bring the best out of people!'

'Why would it be called after you, you haven't done anything,' Eliza complained.

'I pulled it together,' said Anna, 'I'll be the host, you'll be the assistants, scurrying about helping people and bringing me jam pieces! I'll start on this and then they'll ask me to do everything, Strictly Come Dancing, Britain's Got Talent, reading the News, in fact when mum wins an Oscar they'll ask me to present it to her.' She sighed at the glory of it all.

'ANNA!' said her sisters together.

'What?'

'You're impossible,' Caroline told her.

'Impossibly talented,' she retorted and stole a piece of Eliza's cake.

Even though it was the holidays Caroline and Eliza had classes to go to so they headed off when they were finished.

'Well?' asked Anna, when she and Miss Rae were on their own.

'They were very good and I hardly knew I was being bullied into buying clothes.'

'You've got some great boy-catching kit now,' decided Anna, having another peek in the bags. 'She's done your make-up real nicely. How old are you?'

'Er ...'

'Tell me!'

'Twenty-five.'

'WHAT! I thought by the way you dressed you were, ancient, forty-two ...'

'I do not look forty-two.'

'Or older.'

'Anna!'

'But you don't now. You're going to get a haircut. What are you going to ask for?'

'Caroline gave me this.' Miss Rae held out a magazine. One of the hairstyles was circled. 'She said she thought it would suit.'

Anna studied it and then stared at Miss Rae. 'I think she's right. She's pretty smart at this sort of thing isn't she? I think she'd like to do fashion or beauty as a job. Dad wants her to go into engineering or building things. Do you like my sisters?'

'Yes,' admitted Miss Rae. 'They're lovely.'

'Are they more lovely than me?'

'Anna you can't ask people questions like that.'

'Why not? If you don't ask this sort of stuff then you'll never know. You can say "yes Anna they are far more lovely than you, you are a rude, nosy, annoying little kid." If I don't like the answer, well tough because I asked the question. I can go away and work on being less rude, nosy and annoying, or I can say well that's me take it or leave it. So?'

'Anna I'm not going to compare you to your sisters. They're different so I'll have a different relationship with them than I will with you. If I think they're lovely that doesn't mean they are any more or less lovely than you.'

'Okay,' Anna agreed, 'not a bad answer. So we go get your haircut and then we've got work.' She showed Miss Rae the machine. 'Another bunny has appeared. That's where I was this morning. It's the same size as the first ones, but mega different.'

'How do you mean?'

'It has silky hair all over its body and it's a bit like a hairy bat, you know its skin is stretched between its arms and legs, so I think it can glide. It's the first one that looks proper fierce.'

'Fierce?'

'Yeah, got all these teeth and they look a bit like the sort of teeth sharks have.'

'Oh …'

'Miss Rae, we've got to see how we can work as a team. You're really no good at catching them and if we spend time trying to let you catch them they're more likely to get away and then we'll have to try again.'

'You have a plan. Anna?'

'It's more sticking to what worked. If you concentrate on making a noise so they run towards me then I can concentrate on catching them. We've got to make sure we don't get in each other's way. You do that and make sure the box is ready and maybe that would work.'

Miss Rae agreed and admitted she had wanted to catch them because as she was in charge; she thought that's what she should be doing. 'But you're right we have to play to our strengths.'

'Good,' said Anna. 'I was worried you were going to be an arse about it.'

'Does your father mind you swearing?'

'He hates it, that's why I swear whenever I'm with him. I've never sworn in front of mum because I love her so much. Okay team Anna-chester United, let's go'

Chapter 26

Firstly they stopped at the hairdressers and when Miss Rae was taken off Anna talked to a lady waiting her turn and informed her that the hairdressers had the best magazines ever. She'd gone to the dentist and all they had were car magazines and they were dull as hell. 'Why do they have so many magazines about cars? It's not like they come up with new cool colours or shapes, they're just bigger or faster or ... or they've got more leather on the inside!'

The lady agreed with her and together they had an excited look at "Hello" magazine to see what the current celebrities were getting up to.

Afterwards Anna studied Miss Rae from every angle. 'Good, less Cinders and more Cinderella!' and added she looked younger, 'now everyone can see how pretty you are.'

Miss Rae didn't really know what to say as no one had ever said that to her, but it didn't matter because Anna had already moved on to the next thing and wanted to know where the van was.

Miss Rae drove and Anna directed and told her the plot of the latest Star Wars film; including her detailed recommendations of how it could be improved.

They stopped close to where the monster was and Anna said it was great Miss Rae could just stop where ever she wanted to.

'I've got a special badge,' Miss Rae pointed to the windscreen.

Anna got out to have a look. 'That is a very cool thing.'

'We can't park absolutely anywhere, I mean we couldn't just pull up in front of Buckingham Palace or at No 10 and I'm not meant to use it if I just want to buy a pie from Greggs. It has to be official business.'

'It's still great. He's in there,' Anna pointed to a fenced off area where a house had been knocked down, it had a big garden and the rubble had been dumped in a corner. The builders had put up a big picture of the block of flats they were going to put up.

Anna got out her machine and zoomed in so they could pinpoint where the little monster was hiding.

'He's under those trees,' Miss Rae pointed. 'What do you want me to do?'

'I need to have plenty of time to catch him before he gets out of the garden so you go to the smallest side and try and get him to come the other way.'

'Okay.'

'I'll make up the box,' Anna said, then she tapped Miss Rae's arm, 'put on your armour and gloves; that'll give you ultimate Team Anna protection.'

'What about you, I don't want you to get hurt.' Miss Rae asked.

'Hurt – smurt! Like I said that stuff would slow me down,' she said, dismissively.

When Miss Rae was ready she set off and realised Anna

was running so quickly she was already halfway round the plot. According to the machine the little monster hadn't moved. She got into position, slowly edged forward and when she was ten metres away she shouted and banged the box. Nothing happened and nothing moved. She stepped closer and shouted louder. The green dot didn't shift and now she was right on top of it, where was it? Where was the little bunny? BUNNY! ... oh god she'd started thinking like Anna now. She kicked at the undergrowth to see if she could shift it.

Suddenly there was a "HEERRHHH!" from above.

Startled she looked up and all she saw were gleaming white teeth as sharp as nails; it was like the edge of a saw was heading straight for her.

She ducked but as she twisted away it landed on her back with a fierce growl. She screamed in shock, lost her balance and landed heavily on the ground the monster clinging to her and biting furiously.

Chapter 27

Terrified, she wriggled frantically to try and shake the thing off, then the biting stopped.

'WHAT THE HELL DO YOU THINK YOU'RE DOING YOU GANTY LITTLE THING?' bellowed Anna. 'I'VE A GOOD MIND TO SPANK YOUR BOTTOM! I CAN'T BELIEVE YOU DID THAT …'

Miss Rae rolled over. Above her the little monster was hanging in a net and Anna was shaking her fist at it.

'YOU'RE IN SO MUCH TROUBLE, DO YOU KNOW THAT? IF YOU'VE HURT HER YOU'RE GOING TO BE IN MONSTER DETENTION FOR A HUNDRED YEARS …'

The little thing looked terrified as Anna shouted at it.

'Anna … ANNA!'

Anna stopped shouting at the thing.

'Anna I'm fine, I'm okay. I ducked to avoid it and it jumped on my back.'

'It was biting you!'

'The body armour, I'm fine …'

Anna turned to the little monster, 'you're bloody lucky!'

The thing quailed again and Anna slipped it into the box and slid on the lid.

'You're sure you're okay?'

She helped Miss Rae to her feet.

'Yes, not even a scratch. I ... I was expecting it to be hiding on the ground, like in the bushes, but it was up in a tree and it caught me by surprise.'

'Little bugger,' said Anna. 'Still we got him, eh?'

They crouched down together. The little monster had regained some of its belligerence and was gnashing its teeth then it saw Anna, stopped and retreated to the far side.

'You gave him such a telling off you frightened the ... er ... er ...'

'Shit out of him?'

'Well yes.'

'Good. He deserved it, jumping you like that. We need to write down what they're like. Maybe they could put that stuff on the machines then we can look it up and be ready.'

'You were worried about me ...' suggested Miss Rae.

'I was not! I was worried about my dosh. If anything happened to you I bet it'd be a real hassle getting my ninety quid.'

'Of course ... I forgot about the money.'

'Well don't,' said Anna. 'I need it for my lovely clothes.'

Miss Rae tried to stare her out but Anna stared back without blinking.

'We'd better get the bunny into the van before anyone sees it,' said Anna.

Miss Rae agreed. 'I'll give you a lift home.'

'Ta.'

Anna was quiet for ages, maybe five seconds, before she asked Miss Rae if she was going to wear her new kit the next day in the office. 'You've got to get out there in your fancy gubbins, you've got the haircut, you can do the makeup, now you have to see what happens.'

'I will,' she promised.

'Maybe I should spy on you …' said Anna.

'Maybe you shouldn't.'

'Maybe you'll tell me how you got on?'

'Maybe I will,' conceded Miss Rae.

Anna was satisfied with that.

'Anna, I forgot to give it to you earlier. In the side pocket there's a letter from Mrs Graham about the er … "voluntary service" you're doing …'

Anna picked the envelope up.

'And she got you an ID card. She was worried you might get into trouble if you were challenged so the card should help you explain.'

'An ID card, wowie! Hey it's got my name on it!' She touched it reverently. 'You know I hoped I'd get one, but I didn't really think I would. That's brilliant,' she hugged it to her chest. 'It's my first ID card ever, well my second because I've got a library card, I've got a passport too and I suppose that's like an ID card isn't it, my bank card has got my name on it, when we went to France mum got me a card for insurance and it says Anna Templeton …'

'So you've got lots of cards!'

'I don't have a bus pass,' complained Anna. 'I really want one but dad won't let me. He says buses are dangerous. Dangerous! Like the papers are full of people who die when they take the bus to go to Boots or Marks & Spencers. I don't think I've ever heard of people having bus related accidents. I've heard of plenty people being knocked down when they're walking along the pavement, or people sitting in their car listening to Radio Two being crashed into, so why can't I have one? WHY?'

'I don't know Anna.'

'I DO! If I have a bus pass I can get any bus and that equals freedom. I could go where I wanted when I wanted and he wouldn't know. That's why! But I can buy a bus ticket anyway, it's a bit more of a hassle but it's not like I have to learn Chinese or anything so "la" to him. Anyroads I can cross the city quicker on foot than most buses - free-running rules! I don't think you'd be any good at free-running Miss Rae, but I'd never be able to invent something as cool as the stuff you invented to put on the nets. That is amazing, that slimy one thought he could slip out of it didn't he, but he couldn't; that was real clever.'

Miss Rae blushed, 'I was just putting together stuff I've already learnt.'

'It was brilliant – I know because I'm brilliant and I know brilliant when I see it!'

Miss Rae grinned.

'Well I am,' claimed Anna.

They reached Anna's street and Miss Rae relunctantly pulled up.

'Good luck tomorrow …' Anna said as she got out.

'Thanks,' said Miss Rae.

Chapter 28

Miss Rae had to be in the office all morning so Anna couldn't go and speak to her. Caroline and Eliza had lessons but she wanted company so she decided to chum them.

'Why?' demanded Caroline, when she told them. 'Have you got some stupid plan to make us look stupid?'

'Yes,' she agreed.

'God Anna …'

'Course I haven't, why would I want to make you look stupid? You were really nice to Miss Rae yesterday and I just wanted to spend time with you. Can't you bunk off?'

Eliza sighed, 'no we can't, you know what dad is like!'

'Tell him to stuff it, come with me.'

They both looked at her sadly.

'So that means I have to come with you doesn't it? I promise I'll be quiet. I've stuff to think about.'

'I think that's highly unlikely,' suggested Caroline.

'The thinking or the being quiet?' asked Anna.

'Both.'

'I'll prove I can be quiet. I won't talk while you eat your breakfast.'

Caroline took a spoonful of muesli.

'You don't really like that mush do you?' Anna asked, 'I think they just collect the stuff from the bottom of rabbit cages, chop it up and stick it in a packet. It's probably full of rabbit poo … urgh. Look at it!' she shook the bag.

'A new record for you Anna,' said Caroline sarcastically. 'You managed to stay quiet for seven seconds.'

'We should give her a medal,' added Eliza.

'Yeah you should,' agreed Anna, not at all embarrassed. 'A big one, like the one I got when I won the cross country race.'

Eventually they said she could come along.

When they went to get ready Anna automatically checked her machine, she was surprised to see another monster in the city; they'd only caught the last one yesterday and it was usually three or four days between monster appearances.

She sent a text to Miss Rae. It was short by her standards, but an essay in comparison to most people.

It didn't feel right, the signal was so strong, much stronger than the last big one, that meant it must be bigger.

She checked where Miss Rae was. The little red light showed she was in the city. Good, she'd go with Caroline and Eliza, leave at coffee time, check the new monster and then go to Miss Rae's office. She could say thank you to Mrs Graham for giving her an ID card and find out if Miss Rae's boy had made a move.

On the way to their class she pointed out Caroline would be eighteen soon.

'I know Anna, I do remember how old I am.'

'Yes but the point is Caro when you're eighteen you're an adult, a grown up, you can scoot and do your own thing. Dad can't tell you what to do unless he says you're incompetent and can't look after yourself.'

'So?'

'Well I have a plan.'

Caroline sighed, 'I thought you might.'

'It's brilliant!'

'They all are, Anna.'

'Thank you,' she said. 'This one is especially brilliant. I've spoken to mum and she said you could stay with her. Then you could go to university and study what you wanted and you'd have somewhere to live and she would give you an allowance. While you're doing that and becoming super-clever, Eliza and I will be planning and scheming and speaking to lawyers so we can come and live with mum too.'

'Dad will never let me,' Caroline said.

'It'd be too late so tough titties! You like mum don't you and she loves you. You don't want to study engineering or stuff like that do you? Honestly Caro you've got to get away. Dad's been bullying you for too long. I'm right aren't I Eliza?'

Eliza nodded.

'But what about you two?' asked Caroline.

'Eliza will be sixteen soon after,' said Anna, 'I've read all about it, she can say who she wants to live with and the judge has to listen to her. We've talked.'

'You've got to go,' said Eliza. 'Anna's plan is a good one.'

'But you'd be stuck with him,' pointed out Caroline.

'Not for long, like Anna says I can ask to live with her mum. If they don't let me it'll only be a couple more years.'

'And let's face it Caro,' Anna pointed out, 'I don't do what dad says so it's not like it's any hassle for me. Anyway we're going to make another appeal, so maybe this time the judge will listen to me.'

Caroline admitted she hated the idea of studying engineering and really wanted to do something in design. 'But I just can't go … I'd need to speak to your mum first.'

'Because you don't believe me …'

'Because I can't turn up one day and say, "hi Natasha I've come to stay," it needs to be a bit more planned than that.'

'There's always jam in HER cupboard!'

'That's nice Anna, I still want to talk to her.'

'Okay, do you want to phone or do you want me to set up a meeting …'

'You set up a meeting I'm not going to do something this massive on the phone!'

'Good,' said Anna. 'So what are we studying today?'

'Chemistry.'

Anna groaned.

Eliza agreed, 'it's dull, but it could be useful.'

'I thought you wanted to be an archaeologist?'

'In a perfect world. Still I might need chemistry to analyse the things I find, that might help me tell how old they are,' said Eliza.

'There's no harm in learning things Anna,' pointed out Caroline.

Anna and did a handstand in front of them. 'I'll teach you how to do that then,' she said.

'We can learn the principles ...' said Caroline. 'We don't actually have to do stuff. Anyway this is where our class is, so you keep quiet, behave yourself and don't interrupt.'

Anna sat at the back put her headphones on and read a magazine. Every now and then her singing got too loud and one of her sisters would go back and hush her. After coffee she said she had things to do and was gone at a sprint.

The classroom felt a lot emptier without her.

Chapter 29

Anna raced through the streets, vaulting obstacles, leaping walls and singing along to the songs on her iPod as she went.

The monster was holed up in an old church, she opened the door a crack, slipped in and made her way to the gallery. The green dot showed the creature was somewhere near the altar and she settled down to wait.

It didn't take long, first a loud scratching noise echoed round the building, then a shadow moved and finally an sleek, gunge covered nose poked out from behind a pillar. It was a slimy monster like the one they'd caught before, but a lot bigger and a whole level slimier. It jumped onto the altar, picked up one of the shiny candleholders and sniffed the candle. It licked it, took a bite and instantly it spat it out. It then jumped down taking the candleholder and disappeared round the back.

As soon as it was out of sight Anna left and was on the street running at full speed.

She reached Miss Rae's office and went straight in the front door. She flashed her card at the receptionist, headed round the corner to the lift and pressed the button.

After a minute as nothing had happened she went back to the front desk.

'The lift's broken,' she complained. 'I've pressed the button a gazillion times and I've been waiting ages. You need to get it sorted. This is the government you know, you can't just have broken lifts in your building. Have you phoned the lift repair man, you should have done that, I can't be expected to hang around waiting I'm a busy busy bee!'

The receptionist looked down at her, slightly bemused. 'And you are?'

'I work with Mrs Graham, I've got a card and a machine and I'm an important team member. I'd go up the stairs but I can't find them. What would happen if there was a fire. You're not meant to use lifts when there's a fire. I've been told someone tried to use a lift and got roasted to death. Gruesome, think of the smell, they probably smelt like roast pork. I wonder if they tasted like roast pork. Do you think scientists have to eat roasted people so they know what they taste of? Yuck, that is not a job I'd like ...'

'Hold on, hold on pleease. You said you work with Mrs Graham?'

Anna flashed her card again.

Before she could start on another stream of consciousness the girl held up her hand. 'You seem awfully young to be a member of staff.'

'I'm a prodigy,' Anna retorted.

'Can I see your card properly?'

Anna held it up but wasn't going to let go of it.

The girl studied it. 'Okay Anna Templeton, so you're a member of staff, didn't they tell you how to use the lifts?'

'I'm new.'

'You put your card into the slot and press the button.'

'Okay, cool.'

'I'll say you're on your way up.'

'Pants' Anna said to herself, she had wanted it to be a surprise. 'Thank you,' she said out loud through gritted teeth and scooted round as quickly as she could. She put the card into the slot and pressed the button. The lift door opened and she pressed the button for the "**National Solutions Department**".

It was an irritatingly slow lift and when the door opened Miss Rae was barrelling out of one of the doors looking flustered.

'Anna ...'

'Hi Miss Rae.'

Anna ran around the reception area, checking it out. 'Cool you've got a water fountain and a drinks machine and look you've got a machine for crisps and chocolates, when I'm rich I'm going to have one of those.'

'Why would you need one if you were rich?' Miss Rae asked bemused. 'Couldn't you just buy all the crisps and chocolates you wanted?'

'But look at it, it's great!'

Miss Rae tried to shake off the distractions, 'Anna what are ...'

'You look cool. You're really pretty today ... Is Mrs Graham here. I'd like to say thank you. There she is. Hi Mrs Graham, how are you? That's a nice suit, that's even nicer than the one you were wearing the other day. Suits don't suit me, I love colour!'

Mrs Graham started to reply but Anna was already off again. 'Which one is your office, is it this one? Wowsers look at all the people, they look busy. Except him,' she pointed, 'is he asleep?'

Miss Rae hustled her into an office, Mrs Graham followed and shut the door.'

'What are you doing here Anna?' Miss Rae asked.

'Another big one has arrived,' she announced. 'It's really big! Big and slimy, big, slimy and bigger than any of the others and real slimy. Hey Mrs Graham, thanks for the ID card it's the best. Do you know it operates the lift? I guess you do or you'd have to work in the lobby wouldn't you?'

'Anna, please calm down,' said Miss Rae, 'I'm sorry Mrs Graham ...'

Mrs Graham was laughing, 'Anna you are a force of nature! So another one has appeared already? One word please.'

Anna's brow creased in concentration as she tried to think of the biggest word she knew, 'supercalifra ...'

'Yes,' translated Miss Rae.

'They're appearing more frequently,' Mrs Graham suggested.

Miss Rae pulled the imaginary zip over Anna's mouth. 'It seems. When Mr Goodman was here we maybe had one a week, now there have been three in four days ... we need to stop them at source.'

'You're right Miss Rae and we need to work out why they're coming in increased numbers ...'

'Mmmmffff …' came from a muffled Anna.

'I'm glad you agree Anna, you could learn a lot from Miss Rae,' said Mrs Graham, 'she is an excellent lateral thinker. I'm going to put pressure on the field teams to try and stop them coming in the first place. We're spending a lot of time repatriating them safely and I'm worried we're not going to be able to keep a lid on them. With so many about, the chance them being seen is getting too high.'

'Mmmmmffffmmff …' Anna was desperate to boast that was her idea too, but Miss Rae was holding the end of the imaginary zip.

'Are you going to try and pick up the new one this afternoon?'

Anna was wriggling about furiously now.

'Unzip!' Miss Rae zipped the other way.

The words tumbled out of Anna in a rush. 'I said there were more monsters coming I said you have to find out why so many of them were coming I said you have to stop them coming … I said all that! If we're going to catch this one we're gonna need some help 'cause it's a lot bigger.'

'An extra hand is fine,' said Mrs Graham, 'take whoever you like, be good for one of the techie boys to get out in the field,' then she was gone as she had a meeting to attend.

'HELP?' asked Miss Rae.

'Those were my ideas,' complained Anna.

'I know, I told Mrs Graham that's what you said, but it's easier for her to think it came from an adult.'

'You zipped me!'

'Anna I'm getting used to your stream of consciousness, but other people aren't and we need to be a bit more focused in the office.'

'It's a pretty okey dokey office,' then she remembered the other reason she's wanted to come. 'Where's your boy, can I see him, did your very cool look work?'

'Adam is a "smelly prat", Anna.'

'Oh dear,' she pursed her lips. 'What did he do wrong?'

'I'm not going to repeat it …'

'Was it rude, you don't have to worry about rude words, I'm a twelve-year old girl, there are no words me and my mates haven't looked up on the internet. Did he swear? Did he say "cor blimey you look fucking great?" Did he say "Phwoar!" Did he …'

'Okay Anna no more please, he made a number of remarks about my breasts and then said he wouldn't kick me out of bed.'

'In all the romatic films I've seen, which is a lot, that is not something the boy ever says,' conceded Anna.

'I thought he'd be clever and funny and sweet,' Miss Rae sighed, 'but he is just an unreconstructed lad. Said we should go down the pub after work! Do I look like the sort of person to "go down the pub".

'You do not,' said Anna firmly, 'although I haven't a clue what the sort of people who go down the pub look like. At least you talked to him.'

'Yes,' Miss Rae agreed, 'and I was a tiny bit flattered he thought I was attractive. Anyway why are you here?'

'I wanted to fetch you so we could catch the big, new, slimy monster, but I thought we might need someone to help so I thought we should ask Mrs Graham if she would let us have someone. I think a smelly prat should be first on the list. Yes?'

'Yes,' Miss Rae smiled back.

'And I'm very nosy so I wanted to see your boy.'

'Okay,' she said and led Anna into the office.

Anna had no interest in dad's office but she was excited to see this one. It looked like they'd set up desks in a stately home. The ceiling was high, the edges had fancy carvings along the length, a massive chandelier hung from the middle and old paintings were on every wall. The far end had been made into a small workshop area and people were building complicated machines there.

Miss Rae crossed the floor to one of the men, who was sitting in front of a three big computers.

'Adam …'

This was the boy. Anna stared at him curiously. He looked good, a little geeky, but he had a great haircut, cool jeans and his trainers were awesome.

'Yeah,' he said truculently.

The morning hadn't gone well for either of them Anna decided.

'We need help this afternoon. Mrs Graham thought it would good if one of you IT boys came. You'll be able to see what it's really like out in the field.'

'Mrs Graham?'

'Yes Adam. She thought it would help if you had first hand experience.'

'You mean catch a monster?'

'Personal development,' Miss Rae added firmly.

'Mrs Graham said, did she?'

Miss Rae nodded and as he wasn't prepared to challenge Mrs Graham he stood up sullenly.

'This is Anna Templeton,' Miss Rae introduced Anna, 'she's been helping me.'

'A girl!'

'You're pretty sharp!' said Anna, 'so anything wrong with that? Girls can do anything boys can do, except better. A hundred times better ... sometimes even more times better, yes usually more times! There's a girl Prime Minster, a girl is Queen, a girl is in charge of the Royal Mail and one runs an airline company, girls run TV stations ...'

'Thank you Anna ...' Miss Rae tried to interrupt the flow.

'... the stock exchange, hotels, universities, hospitals all run by girls,' she started to make it up but knew if she kept talking the boy wouldn't be able to challenge her.

'Anna, ANNA! We should get on!'

'What? Oh yes sure,' Anna agreed.

Miss Rae's boy stood up and put his jacket on.

'... and Greggs, and British Gas, and Kronenberg, and Zara, but she's not called Zara, and ...'

As they made they way down in the lift she began to list the many reasons why girls were better than boys. Miss Rae, tried to stop herself from grinning. The poor IT man had never experienced Anna in full flow and was quailing from the verbal barrage.

Miss Rae managed to stop Anna for a moment and told Adam he was to take one of the vans.

'We'll meet you there.' She showed him on the machine where the monster was.

'But, but ...' he stuttered.

'It's a chance,' said Anna, gleefully, 'to show you're better than a twelve year old girl.'

He muttered rebelliously as he got in the van.

They arrived at the church first, by the time the boy turned up Anna had given her opinion of him to Miss Rae and it was not totally unfavourable.

'It's in there,' Miss Rae pointed to the building. 'Here's a net, Anna has one too and I have the box, Anna says it's the biggest one yet, which is why we need you.'

'BIGGEST!'

'Look basically you and I will try to stop it getting away and Anna will try to catch it. Okay? That doesn't sound difficult does it?'

'This isn't really my sort of thing,' Adam complained

'It's not rocket science,' added Anna, 'I wonder what rocket scientists say? "Building a space rocket is easy peasy," they'll say, "at least it's not like learning to Foxtrot".'

Miss Rae used her lock-opening contraption and they slipped into the building. Adam had gone quiet and his face was pale.

'I heard you on the phone,' said Anna, 'it's good we've got you to help us, I bet you're great at catching monsters. You sounded like you knew all about it. We probably should let you get on with it, you'll have the thing boxed up in no time.'

'What?'

'You'll be able to tell the difference between a monster and a rock, not like us girls!'

'I ... I ...I was just joking, it was meant to be funny ...'

'Now ssshh ... remember to keep your eye on him!' Anna took a deep breath, held up the machine and played with the buttons. 'Look it was moving about before we got here, then it must have heard the door open because it stopped, now it's moving about again. I'll go round the side and you come through the middle.'

She was off and Miss Rae signalled to Adam to move forward.

They walked between the pews to the altar.

The monster was at the end tearing a prayer book apart and smelling the pages.

'Your net,' hissed Miss Rae, 'make sure you've got it ready.'

'What?' Adam whispered back.

Before she could repeat it, Anna leapt out with a loud shout, the monster jumped in surprise and raced away from her.

Adam was right in its path, he screamed, dropped the net and turned to run off.

He was too slow and because couldn't get out the way in time the thing jumped on his back, then onto his head and using the height leapt towards the pulpit.

A grinning Anna cartwheeled past, bounced in the air, swept the monster up in her net and somersaulted onto the top of the font.

'You slimy little buggle,' she said, holding it away from her. 'Phew you're well heavy!'

Miss Rae was ready with the box, Anna slipped the creature in and she snapped the lid shut.

'Urgh,' moaned Adam, tentatively touching his head and recoiling at the cold wet goo the creature had left there. 'That's bloody disgusting.'

'You should have caught it; you had a net! I think I know what the problem was, you was facing the wrong way,' said Anna smugly. 'If you want to catch something you have to look at where it's coming from.'

'I was a lot more worried about where it was heading, not where it was coming from,' he complained, 'that's because it was heading straight for ME!'

Anna had no sympathy, 'well you should have been ready, I did warn you!'

Miss Rae had a brief moment of schadenfruede, before she felt sorry for him and said there were paper towels in the van.

'Not as easy as when you're sitting in a nice comfy office playing with your computer,' said Anna. 'Luckily girl power saved the day, or "Judge Sludge" here, would have been off terrorising the neighbourhood. Now how do you feel about making fun of Miss Rae when she was trying to catch them all on her own?'

He muttered to himself and looked at the little monster in the box. 'He can't get out can he?'

'No,' Miss Rae confirmed.

'He's looked right fierce when he came at me,' Adam complained.

'I think he's sweet,' contradicted Anna.

Adam was a lot more humble when he spoke again, 'I didn't think it would be so scary. To be honest I actually thought it would be like collecting a hamster or a puppy and the most difficult thing would be bending down to pick it up. I was bloody terrified when he came at me, my heart's still going like a jackhammer. I suppose he was trying to get away.'

'And?' said Anna.

'I'm sorry. I admit it, it's not easy and it was unfair to make jokes, especially as I've never had to do anything like this.'

'What did you think?' asked Anna.

'I saw those teeth and I thought he was going to ... you know take a chunk out of me, I almost shitt ...!'

Anna started grinning.

'Adam!' warned Miss Rae.

'I was er ... sh ... sure I was in trouble.'

'You've seen them before,' Miss Rae pointed out.

'Not when they're coming for me, bloody great teeth and

claws at the ready!'

He carried the box back to the van and they got him some tissues.

'Going to the pub tonight?' Anna jumped onto the top of a pillar-box and stared down at him.

He was rubbing the top of his head trying to get the gunk off.

'What?'

'Please Anna …' asked Miss Rae.

'Okay, Miss Rae,' she said. 'What do you think of the little monster Adam,' she asked instead.

'He's like that one that came in last week, but a helluva lot bigger …'

'You've seen the others we've caught?'

'Yes, we usually go to have a look.'

'Have you been working there long?' Anna asked.

'About five years …'

'And the ones we've brought in, in the last few months are they the same as the ones over the last five years?'

'There have been some new ones recently and we've haven't seen some of the ones we used to see a lot of,' he decided. 'Why?'

'No reason,' admitted Anna. 'I talk a lot and I've been told to ask people things so they get a chance to talk too, otherwise they say it's just me speaking. Although to be honest that's a good thing because I have plenty of interesting things to say, whereas most people just talk about the weather or football or television.'

'You talk about the television a lot, Anna,' pointed our Miss Rae.

'But in an interesting way; I have an opinion about it, other people just say "did you see such and such" and I'll say "yes" and then … even though I've just said yes they'll tell me what happened. Well I saw what happened I don't need you to tell me! And worse they usually get it wrong, and I have to tell them what really happened and they say "are you sure?" Of course I'm sure, I watched the flippin' program!' she slapped her forehead to emphasise how stupid ALL the other people are.

Miss Rae said it was time to go and Anna slowly did a handstand on top of the post-box, then flipped backwards off it and landed softly in front of them.

'How did you do that?' Adam asked, plainly impressed.

'I'm a girl,' she replied, 'girls can naturally do clever things. Do you play football?'

'Yeah I play five-a-side once a week …'

'I bet I'm better than you,' she challenged.

He was about to contradict her but if she could somersault off a pillar box there was a good chance her boast about football was true. 'Okay I admit it, you're probably better than us, we just play as an excuse to go for a drink afterwards. It's a social thing.'

Anna looked satisfied and held out her hand. 'Thank you for helping us.'

'I'll see you tomorrow Adam, so we can put together the report,' said Miss Rae.

He gave a jokey salute, got in his van and drove off.

They watched him go in silence before walking to their own van.

'He's nicer than I expected,' said Anna, 'but he still deserved getting slimed.'

'You did that deliberately, didn't you?'

'I wasn't going to let him get away with ogling your boobs just because you had a nice, new top on. Actually he's probably as shy as you. I don't think he knows how to talk to girls; he only spoke to you that way because that's how his mates talk in the pub. He was smelly, but it was a nice smell of aftershave and he's a prat but only because he doesn't know any better.'

'What are saying Anna?'

'Who knows he might not be "The Boy" but … well he's a quick learner and … you know ...'

'I should talk to him?'

'Yeah, talk to him because he is kinda cool. Anyway this has been a great afternoon and since one of us has to go back to boiled carrots and nut burgers I need cake to help me survive!'

'Okay Anna, I'll buy you some cake …'

'… and a hot chocolate.'

'Yes and a hot chocolate.'

'With whipped cream on top!'

Chapter 30

Anna didn't see Miss Rae the next day, but she did get a lot of texts from her.

<I said good morning to him … nicely.>

<He's looking across.>

<Paul said the last one was the biggest they have on record.>

<This one is three times the size of the next biggest. Ever.>

<Adam is making me coffee.>

<Adam apologised for being an "arse".>

<Me and Adam did the report together.>

<Adam showed me the new program he is working on for the machine.>

<I made a joke and Adam laughed.>

<Adam said let's eat our sandwiches together.>

<Are you out? It's lovly out.>

<The ducks are in the park.>

<We're feeding the ducks crumps.>

<crumbs.>

<Adam gave me some of his crisps.>

<Mrs Graham said well done for picking up the "slimer" so quickly.>

<Adam was "totally" impressed you caught the monster.>

<Adam asked if you are a gymnast.>

<I said yes because you probably are.>

<Are you?>

<I'm making him a coffee.>

<He says the coffee is perfect.>

<Josie asked about the monsters.>

<She was pleased to hear they're not all slimy.>

<Adam said it was disgusting. The slime went right down his front.>

<He said he was glad we had tissues.>

<Ben asked if it was like Ghostbusters.>

<I said it was like when Slimer slimed Peter Venkman.>

<That's what you told me.>

<I hope that was right.>

<I haven't seen the film.>

<Mrs Graham is in a good mood.>

<She's bought us all cakes!>

<You'd like the cake. Creamy. Yum.>

<Did you have a good lunch?>

The texts continued all day and put Anna in a good mood so she sneaked some cakes into the house and had a midnight feast with Caroline and Eliza.

Chapter 31

Another monster found its way into town, it took them three hours of hard graft as it was tricksy, but by working together they eventually got it trapped. Afterwards Anna explained what sort of films she'd like to be a stunt person in; it was basically every sort of film. She thought it would awesome if she was doing the stunts in a film where her mum was the star. 'I'd have to grow a bit because mum is taller than me, but it would be cheaper for them because they wouldn't have splash out on make-up to make us look like each other as we already look like each other ... that's because she's my mum and genetics can do that to you, you know.'

'Yes,' Miss Rae agreed, 'I've heard that can happen with genetics.'

The interruption didn't break Anna's flow and she starting describing how you need to be able to act so you can pretend to be the actress who is meant to be doing the stunt, when she stopped in mid-flow. 'Hey, where did he come from?'

'Who?'

Anna held up the machine. 'Him, he suddenly appeared.'

She used the playback mode so Miss Rae could see.

'Look no monster, then boopty-doop he's there, like he fell out of an aeroplane.'

'You don't suppose this is the one that went missing,'

suggested Miss Rae.

'Oh …'

'Perhaps he's been stuck in a car since he disappeared.'

'Could be – got your smarts working today!' Anna twiddled with machine and the clock showed time flickering back. 'When was it?'

'About two weeks ago,' thought Miss Rae.

Suddenly the little green dot reappeared.

'That's where he was,' Anna said excitedly. 'It is the same one. You're right, either he hitched a lift or someone monster-knapped him.'

'Shall we take a look?' Miss Rae suggested.

Anna nodded. 'It's a bit of a drive.' She checked the time. 'Should be okay, don't want to miss the vegetable surprise an' all …'

They got in the van and before they'd even snapped on their seat belts Anna was quizzing her.

'Did you have a nice lunch with your boy today?'

'What makes you think we had lunch together?'

'You texted me,' Anna read the text aloud. "Going to Pret a Manger with Adam."

'Oh yes, I forgot … well I was going to buy my sandwiches and he said he was going too, so we …'

'What did he think of your tits today?'

'Funnily enough he didn't mention them, Anna.'

'They're just as sticky out, maybe he didn't have his contacts in …'

'He's learnt his lesson.'

'Has he Miss Rae? Or maybe you're proud of them now you don't mind his complimentary comments.'

'No he definitely didn't refer to them.'

'So?'

'You're as bad as my mother.'

'As thoughtful. Come on, yesterday the messages were whizzing over the internet. It was like a soap opera. I need to catch up with what's been going on.'

'Honestly nothing was going on. We went for sandwiches and then had a coffee on the way back …'

'And you talked in the office?'

'Yes … but about work.'

'Only work?' asked Anna.

'Well not just work,' Miss Rae admitted.

'Good. Just remember he might still be a "smelly prat" after all.'

'I know, but sometimes you have to kiss a lot of frogs to find your prince!'

Anna pulled a face, 'yeurgh! Kiss a frog, I'd rather eat fennel!'

'It's an expression, Anna, not to be taken literally.'

Anna grinned. 'I know.'

'I'm amazed you even made it to twelve without someone throttling you.'

'That's why I had to learn free-running then I could get away fast when I pushed things too far.'

'Are you like this at school?'

'Like what?

'Don't your teachers find you a handful?'

'I bet they love having me in their class,' said Anna, 'think what a boring job it would be if every student was as well behaved and hard-working as Caro. I'm the spicy chilli in the sauce! Here we go, it's on this road.'

Miss Rae pulled over to the side.

'The machine says he's somewhere at the back of that house,' Anna pointed to the third one along. 'Shall I nip over the fence and fetch it?'

Miss Rae thought for a moment. 'No, I'll knock on the door, I'll say the government is rounding up escaped zoo animals and one of them might have got lost in his garden. That'll give him a chance to hand it over without getting in trouble. If he asks any difficult questions I'll tell him it's top secret and warn him he could be arrested.'

'Could he?'

'Yes and held for an unlimited time without trial; according the regulations.'

'Scary!'

'It hasn't happened to anyone yet …'

'So far as you know,' pointed out Anna. 'Okay you do that. I'll have a "neb" anyway,' she said and scooted off down the road.

Miss Rae, headed for the house rather more sedately. She had just reached the drive when a man came out and got into a big, powerful car.

She went up and the driver wound down the window.

'YES!'

She held up her ID card so he could read it.

'I work for the government ...' she started.

'GET OFF MY LAND,' he bellowed. 'YOU GOT A BLEEDIN' WARRANT?'

'Warrant? I just wanted to ask a few questions.'

'I KNOW MY RIGHTS,' he shouted, 'SO JUST EFF OFF!'

'Er ...'

'I'll have my lawyer on you,' he said coldly.

It wasn't the way she'd planned it in her head and she wasn't sure what to do.

'GET THE HELL OUT OF HERE!' the man thundered.

She decided it would be better to leave and come back with some support, maybe even bring the police. He was a very intimidating man.

She started to walk back to van and then everything seemed to happen at once. A car engine roared loudly just behind her, she was pulled sharply to the side and there was an intense pain in her leg.

She hit the ground with a bump and the big car sped off down the road.

Anna was standing above her, she was taking pictures with her phone and repeating the car number plate loudly.

'Are you okay? He did that deliberately. He was trying to kill you,' she said angrily.

'My leg ... it's really sore ...'

Anna looked down. 'He's bashed it, it's bleeding. I'm

phoning the ambulance people.'

'It's okay, I'm sure it's okay …' Miss Rae said, she didn't want to cause any trouble.

It was too late. Anna was already speaking to the 999 number. She said it was an emergency, a hit and run. 'Can you send an ambulance as quick as poss?' She read the street and house number. 'Can I speak to the police?' There was a pause and then she repeated her friend had been knocked down in a hit and run. 'I've got a photo of the car and the number is …' she said the number. The person on the other line must have repeated it, because she said 'yes that's right.'

Miss Rae tried to move but her leg was really sore.

'Does it hurt?' Anna asked.

She nodded.

'You should stay where you are then,' said Anna, 'I'll put you in the recovery position …'

'I don't need to be in the recovery position, I'm conscious and breathing fine.'

'Okaaay … are you sure? If you do go all unconscious, don't you worry because I know what to do.'

'Thank you Anna.'

'Here,' Anna took her rucksack off and slipped it behind her. 'Lean on this.'

'Thanks, what … what happened?'

'I heard him shouting and I thought that's a bit odd, because you'd hardly had a chance to say anything. I decided to come back instead of checking the garden, I saw you walking away and he started his car. I didn't like the look on his face so I ran as fast as I could. He was definitely aiming for you and I managed to grab your arm and pull you to the side. What did you say to him?'

'All I said was I was from the government …'

'He must be a crim, he must be on the run from the law and if he wasn't before then he's definitely on the run now and from me. If I catch him he'll not be able to move for all the fennel I'll make him eat!'

There were sirens in the distance.

'That'll be the hambulance on its way to save your bacon. I'll phone Mrs Graham and say. She'll need to send someone to collect the van. You won't be driving and I can't.'

The ambulance arrived and they explained to the paramedic what had happened, two minutes later a police car pulled up so they explained again and ten minutes later one of the department vans turned up.

The paramedic examined her leg, he decided it needed x-raying to check if it was broken and as he started to explain what would happen next she realised Anna wasn't there and nor was the van driver. The paramedic went to fetch the stretcher and Anna reappeared. She squatted down beside her and squeezed her hand supportively while the driver put a box wrapped in a sheet in the back of his van.

'We're going to take your friend to the hospital now,' the paramedic said, 'do you need a lift?'

'No ta,' said Anna.

'What about the van?' Miss Rae asked.

'Someone's on their way in a taxi,' explained the driver.

'I'll take your key and wait for them, so don't worry.'

'I hope you catch the bastard!' Anna said to the policeman, who looked slightly shocked at her language.

'We'll do our best.'

'He's must be a proper crim,' she continued. 'Is he?'

The policeman didn't reply.

'Is he a murderer? He tried to murder Miss Rae. Maybe he's a drugs dealer, is he? Or a bank robber, has he been a-robbin' banks?'

'I really can't say.'

'You could give me a hint,' Anna persisted, 'you could do it in mime.'

The policeman opened his hands.

'Two words,' said Anna, 'first word?'

'No words,' laughed the policeman, 'no clues.'

The policeman's radio crackled and someone said something in code and he walked away to answer it.

The ambulance men put Miss Rae on a stretcher and put her in the back.

'What about you Anna?' she asked.

'I'll drop her at home on the way back to the office,' the driver promised.

'Text me,' said Anna as the doors shut and the ambulance set off.

Chapter 32

'Where have you been Anna Templeton?'

Dad opened the front door the moment she turned into the drive.

She simply handed him the note she'd got the policeman to write and stood opposite.

'Oh ...'

She continued to stare at him.

'A hit and run ... and you got the number-plate?'

'I've been thinking, you know maybe I'm more Anna Chambers than Anna Templeton.'

Chambers was mum's name.

'You were born Anna Templeton and that's your name,' dad said firmly.

'Yes but it's easy enough to change it, I just have to fill out a form.'

'I won't let you!'

'Why not? I'll still be me. Chambers is a cool name, Anna Chambers of Secrets. What's for dinner then? Something disgusting I expect.'

She bounced into the kitchen, her sisters brightened up when they saw her. 'I suppose it's too much to hope that Eliza was cook today?'

'Too much,' said Caroline.

'Oh well there's still plenty of wallpaper paste.'

'Anna T ...' dad caught himself. 'Anna just eat your dinner and stop making disparaging remarks about it. I think we'd all appreciate that.'

'Lasagne,' she sighed when the dish was put on the table, 'you know dad if you added mince it would actually taste nice and still be good for us.'

'It tastes delicious and it's much better for you without meat,' he retorted.

'I was a witness today,' she said to her sisters. 'I saw a hit and run. This man knocked someone down with his car and I was there. I took a photo of the car with my crappy phone and I remembered the number and then I phoned the police. They were well impressed. They said I had great presence of mind. I had to give a statement. They wrote down everything I said.'

'Did they have enough paper?' asked Eliza.

'They had three A4 pads,' said Anna, 'and they had to write on both sides!'

'I hope you behaved yourself, Anna,' said dad.

'I put my pants on my head and sang "The Wheels on the Bus", of course I behaved myself they were the bloody police.'

'Don't swear!'

'Is that the first thing you think of, I'm going to behave like a yoyo? Mum would have said I was a hero and well done for keeping my wits about me and you just ask if I behaved myself! I had to concentrate real hard because someone had been run over and it's difficult enough to remember car numbers even when there isn't someone lying on the ground, a moaning and a groaning and yucky blood spraying everwhere.'

'You're a hero, Anna,' said Caroline.

'Well done for keeping your wits about you,' agreed Eliza.

'You deserve a medal,' added Caroline.

Anna grinned at them, 'I do, don't I?'

'Just eat your dinner and stop being so self-congratulatory,' Dad said irritably.

'I understood that,' Anna stood up, 'high-five,' she raised her hand to her sisters, who slapped it back.

'If you paid attention at school you'd understand everything,' he retorted.

'Then I'll do it!' she said. 'There are lots of mysteries I want to understand like ...' She stopped. She wanted to visit Miss Rae the next day and if she pushed it too far he might make her stay at home or something. Instead she ate her lasagne as quickly as she could, so she didn't have to taste it.

'Chew don't just swallow,' ordered dad.

It was too late, her plate was empty and she was carrying it to the dishwasher.

She started singing as she put the dirty cutlery in.

"Working at the dish wash, Working at the dish wash, yeah, Come on and sing it with me, dish wash, Sing it with the feeling now, dish wash yeah"

'Are you putting the forks in the right way round,' dad asked.

"At the fork wash, woooh, Putting them the right way, yeah, Come on y'all and sing it for me, Fork wash, woh, fork wash yeah." She closed the door, did a little jig and danced out the room.

'What that all about,' dad asked perplexed, he turned and looked at Caroline and Eliza.

'It's a song by Rose Royce, "At the Carwash", explained Caroline. 'Anna sang it in the school show.' Then under her breath she muttered, 'one of the many you didn't go to.'

'Singing is a distraction, she needs to concentrate on her schoolwork.'

'She's not going to,' Caroline pointed out, 'that's not who she is.'

'THAT'S WHO SHE SHOULD BE!' he shouted.

The two girls recoiled and shrank back into their seats.

'She should work hard, she needs to be more like you two and less like some daft puppy that doesn't know its own mind.'

Caroline's hand tightened on her chair, she steeled herself to speak but in the end couldn't get the words out. Eliza put her hand on top of hers and when dinner was over they went up stairs to Anna's room.

'We've got to visit your mum sooner rather than later,' Caroline admitted. 'He's too much.'

'He wants us to do just what he says, he doesn't care what we might want or what we want to do or what our opinions are. If there were three machines sitting there and whenever he said something they said "yes dad", he'd be happy,' complained Eliza.

'Will do. Mum's learning lines at the moment so it can whenever you want, pretty much. Well not in the morning because she's got a personal trainer working with her. She needs to look super-fit, I could help her with that. I said I could be her trainer and she said no way. She mimicked her mum, "no way am I having my smart-arse daughter telling me what to do all day, it's bad enough as it is!" Not tomorrow either, because I'm busy. The next day, we could go for lunch the next day, she could take us for lunch.' Anna pouted, 'she can't take us to Burger King, it'll have to be some fancy restaurant,' she brightened up, 'I bet they can make us anything, burgers, pizzas, noodles, anything.'

There was a brief pause while she contemplated all the wonderful food she could order and Caroline managed to say that would be great. 'What are you doing tomorrow?'

'That person who was knocked down was Miss Rae. I wasn't going to tell dad because he'd be all, "what were you doing with Miss Rae?". By the way she was wearing the clothes you helped her buy and she'd done the make-up how you showed her and she looked super good and her boy is starting to be nice to her. I have hopes. Anyhoo, this car knocked her down. She texted me her leg wasn't broken but she's got a graze and a humungous bruise. I asked for a photo but she didn't send one. It's good it isn't broken but she can't walk, or drive or do anything except lie in bed eating chocolates.'

'Poor Miss Rae … but yummy chocolates.'

'But she doesn't have any, she just has raisins. Imagine that? I mean who'd take someone raisins when they're ill … apart from dad. He'd probably take Brussels Sprouts, bleah!'

Anna started a list of lots of other things that would be even worse to take someone who was ill but they managed to interrupt and got her to phone her mum and sort out lunch. Anna shooed her sisters out of the room afterwards so she could have a private chat with her mother.

Chapter 33

Anna went to bed and before she went to sleep she checked her machine; the little red dot showed Miss Rae was at home. It had disappeared when she was in the ambulance, then reappeared at the hospital, it stayed there for a while, she must have got a taxi or something because it disappeared again and re-emerged in the north of the city.

She decided she shouldn't visit first thing in the morning. Miss Rae would probably be feeling sore and that would be the mature thing to do.

Her resolve didn't last long and she was outside Miss Rae's house ringing the doorbell at 8.15.

A lady opened it and this time it was definitely Miss Rae's mum. She looked like an older Miss Rae, she was pretty, she had a nice flowery dress on and a bandana to keep her hair tidy.

Anna was about to introduce herself, but the lady interrupted. 'Anna Templeton herself,' she said with a smile.

'Can Miss Rae come out to play,' Anna asked.

'Come in. She's not up, she said you would probably give her plenty of time to get ready for your visit.'

'I was going to. Then I thought the earlier I came the quicker she'd start to get better. How did you know my name?'

'Erin has mentioned you once or twice.'

'Erin? What a nice name. You know I hadn't thought of Miss Rae having a first name but you should have called her Dawn or Faye or Sting ... I'm hoping she marries someone called De Ator.'

Miss Rae's mum looked blank.

'Then she would be Mrs Erin Rae–De Ator – Radiator,' she repeated with glee. 'Is she okay?'

'Why don't you go up and see, her bedroom is on the left at the top of the stairs.'

Anna sprang onto the banister and in an instant flipped herself onto the landing. She knocked on the door but didn't wait for answer before bursting in.

'It's ME!'

Miss Rae was sitting up in bed, a cup of coffee in her hand.

Anna jumped on top of the bed and looked around.

'It's just like my room,' she announced.

It was like a teenagers' room, there were posters on the walls, stuffed toy animals piled up on a chair and desk with a computer on it.

She sat cross-legged on the bed.

'How are you Miss Rae. Is it sore? It isn't broken? You poor thing I was worried about you.'

'Hello Anna. It's not broken, I'm just a bit bruised ...'

'Can I see it?'

'My bruise?'

'Yeah. You never sent a photograph like I asked,' she pointed out accusingly. 'Come on.'

'Anna you really are a pest.' Miss Rae moved the covers and pulled up her nightie.

'Oww, that is big, that's bigger than any I've ever had.'

'It could have been worse, Anna, but thanks to you …'

'We're a team. We look out for each other Miss Rae.'

Miss Rae's mother came in at that moment. 'Would you like a cup of coffee, Anna?'

'Yes please, I really need a coffee to wake me up properly in the morning.'

Mother and daughter looked at each other. The last thing Anna needed was to be any more awake in the morning.

'I think we owe you a ton of thanks Anna,' her mother said. 'If it hadn't been for you Erin might have been in intensive care, rather than being just a bit battered.'

'Like a fish finger?'

Miss Rae's mother smiled.

'I'm glad she's okay,' Anna added.

Mrs Rae went to make the coffee.

'I didn't think you'd live with your mum. I thought you'd have a big fancy flat. You've got an important job and whenever you see people with important jobs in the films they all have these big apartments with big tellies and cool kitchens.'

'I can't afford anything like that Anna. I had to borrow a lot of money to go to university and most of what I earn has to go to pay back the government.'

'That's not fair. They should have paid you to go to university because all that stuff you've learnt is good for them isn't it? If you hadn't known your chemistry you wouldn't have been able to make the boxes or the nets and then we'd be catching the monsters in laundry baskets and that would be useless! Has your boy been in touch?'

'Anna!'

'He has! I've brought you a present to help you get better. People always take grapes to patients in the hospital but that's not a treat, I've brought you Miniature Heros, you're a hero and they're tasty.'

'I did get a text.'

'What did he say?'

'He said he was very worried and would it be okay if he came round after work to say hi.'

Anna thought for a moment and then said that was good. 'I know this should all be about you. You're the one who got knocked down. Is it okay if I complain about dad?'

The door opened and Miss Rae's mum brought Anna a cup of coffee and some biscuits.

'Oooh Chocolate Hobnobs, I love them. Thanks ever. Has Miss Rae been a good patient or has she been fidgety and difficult. Can you guess what sort of a patient I am?'

'No Anna,' they said in unison.

'I'm a bloody awful patient, I'm a NIGHTMARE!'

'Erin has been a good patient …'

'A patient, patient,' suggested Anna.

'I'm not going to get better any quicker so I might as well stay quiet and calm.'

'I've got energy to burn so lying is bed is the worstest!'

admitted Anna.

The phone rang downstairs and Miss Rae's mother went to answer it.

'Dad was really bad yesterday. So bad Caroline wants to speak to mum and arrange to go and live with her when she's eighteen. If SHE can't put up with him any longer then it's really bad. I looked it up on the internet and it said you could leave home at sixteen. If that's real then Eliza can go next month but dad said something the other day about sixteen was too young.'

'I've never actually checked,' said Miss Rae, 'but I thought it was sixteen too. What about you? What if your sisters go and you're left on your own?'

'I'm going to run away!'

'But if your dad has custody it might get your mum into trouble, he might tell the papers she's encouraged you.'

Anna looked glum. 'I hadn't thought about that. She's just been cast in the most amazing film so bad stuff in the papers would be a nightmare.'

'You know I thought judges were meant to listen to what the children want and anyway it is usually the other way round. Children are sent to stay with their mother.'

'Yeah, that's what mum thought. Anyways it'd be good if my lovely stepsisters could get away. I can live with it.'

'He'd be on your case the whole time.'

'I don't know. Would he want that, the hassle I give him at the moment must be bad enough? He'd spend his time sending me to my room, stopping my television privileges and feeding me gruesome vegetarian food. He tried taking me to his office and I got banned for being a disruptive presence.'

'I can't believe it!'

'I know! I'm always such a sweet angel when we're together, aren't I?'

'A precious snowflake!'

'I wonder why he makes me stay, he doesn't like me, he doesn't like the things I'm interested in and he gets really annoyed when I don't do what he says. I make his life really difficult but he still won't let me go and live with mum.'

Miss Rae stared at her coffee cup.

'Are you okay?' asked Anna, 'do you need a Neurofen? I've got some Junior Neurofens you can have one of those.'

'I was just thinking it does seem odd.'

'He is odd!' Anna said forcefully. 'Can I have one of your Miniature Heros?'

'I thought you brought them to help me recover,' Miss Rae pointed out.

'My positive attitude has already put colour back in your cheeks, which means you're half ways to being better so I deserves a reward.'

'Okay so long as you leave me the Twirls!'

Anna stayed long enough to eat all the solid chocolate pieces, she even tipped the box out to make sure there weren't any left and then said she was meant to be at a free-running session. 'I'm glad that man didn't hurt you too badly, Miss Rae. I wonder if the policeman has caught him yet. Do you think the inspector assigns them a crim and says "don't you come back until you've got your handcuffs on him!" She pretended she was the constable next. "But Inspector can't you send someone else, the last time I tried to arrest Connor McConman he sold me a telly, a pair of Nike trainers and a "genuine" Rolex watch, the telly was just a big cardboard box with stones in it, when I looked closely at the trainers "Nike" was spelt "Mike" and the watch turned out to be made of Marzipan and I don't even like Marzipan!" She was back to being the inspector, "you're a very gullible man, Sergeant Copperbottom!" Hurry up and get better Miss Rae.' She did a twirl, 'I'll come back with Twirls.'

Miss Rae heard her talking to her mum for five minutes, then she shouted "bye", the front door slammed shut and the house was calm again.

Her mother came up to her room and sat opposite.

'Your Anna is an extraordinarily lively girl, Erin, where does she get the energy from?'

'I don't know mum.'

'She appears to have an opinion on everything too and … well she's forthright isn't she?'

'Yes, she has no filter. What did she ask you?'

'She wanted to know where my Mr Rae was. When I said I was afraid he'd passed on, she said that was a shame. There was the briefest of pauses and then she asked if I had a boy and if I didn't she would help me catch one!'

Chapter 34

It rained all the next day. Not that it bothered Anna, she spent the morning practising with Roy and the other free-runners and then met Caroline and Eliza so they could go for lunch with her mum.

At the restaurant the man on the door stood in Anna's way, gave her a very mean look and said something about dress codes in a supercilious voice. She ignored him and phoned her mum. Within seconds another man appeared, he gave the man on the door a row and ushered them in with an apology.

'What was that about?' asked Eliza.

'It's because … you know mum being … you know famous,' said Anna.

'Oh … right.'

'ANNA!' mum shouted when she saw them, Anna ran to her like a guided missile, leapt into her arms and hugged her tightly.

'Caro, Eliza come, come,' her mum beckoned.

They were more reserved as they hadn't been allowed to see her much since the divorce.

'You're both so grown up and as pretty as ever. Now let's sit … and before you ask Anna, yes you can sit beside me and yes you can have chips so long as you don't try to talk all the time and yes I do miss you and yes it is wonderful to see you.'

'Good,' Anna said with a big sigh of satisfaction, 'but what I was actual going to say was I watched you on the internet talking at the water aid conference and I thought you made some proper good points.'

'Which was the best one?' her mum asked, winking at her sisters.

'They were all so 'mazing I couldn't choose just ONE,' Anna claimed.

'That's kind of you to say Anna ...'

'I did watch the whole thing,' Anna said and then admitted she had been so excited at seeing mum at such an important event, what she was saying completely passed her by. 'Still people were clapping at the end so your speech-writer must have done a good job.'

'Speech-writer, little Tigercub?'

'If that had been me, I'd have given them what for, clean water should be a right not a luxury.'

'If you'd listened, you'd know that was my main point. Anyway let's not get too involved in what you'd have said if you'd been asked to talk. We should order some food and get on with the business of the day.'

'We have plenty water in Britain and some places don't have any so we should share it,' Anna continued despite her mum closing the conversation.

'Yes Anna ...'

'I'll have a beef burger and chips, with a side order of chips and plenty of tomato ketchup.'

'Anna we're in one of the best restaurants in London …'

'Yes you said, so the chips are bound to be extraordinarily good. Their tomato ketchup better be as good as …'

'Caro, Eliza?' mum talked over her, 'anything you want. It all looks great, I wonder if they'll do us a tasting menu then we can have a little of everything.'

'Could we,' asked Caroline. 'There are lots of things I'd like to try but I wouldn't want to choose something and then discover I don't like it.'

'Me too,' agreed Eliza.

Mum called the waiter over and asked for a selection of dishes … 'and a beef burger and chips as the food critic from "The Beano" has joined us.'

'And ketchup and more chips,' added Anna.

'So Caro, you'll be eighteen soon, legally an adult,' mum said.

'Yes, Natasha.'

'You can choose where you'd like to live, what you want to do with your life and to make your own decisions good or bad. Anna says you like fashion.'

Caroline looked down at her clothes. 'I love fashion. Dad won't let us buy much so I had to make these.'

'You made them!' interrupted Anna, 'I thought you'd been saving for ages and got them in the West End. You should have said; if I'd known I'd have got you to make all my clothes. To my specs of course, I hate boring clothes! I …'

'Wasn't the chips order was dependent on the rest of us having a chance to talk too Anna?' pointed out her mum.

'Oh yeah.'

'You made them Caro?'

'Yes, I go to the library, check out the magazines so I know what's going on and do drawings of them.'

'Just fashion?' mum asked.

'I'm most interested in fashion, but I like design generally.'

'So you're going to study that at college.'

Caroline's face fell. 'No, electrical engineering. Very specialised, good salaries and not everyone wants to do it so lots of jobs about.'

'Hmm …' mum put her finger to her lips to shush Anna. 'That's probably true. How long is the course?'

'Four years.'

'Four years of studying electrical engineering, then you'd get a job and probably do another … what … seven or eight years before you'd know the business and could go into management.'

'Yes,' agreed Caroline gloomily.

'And most working lives are forty years …'

Caroline groaned, 'forty years of electrical engineering!'

'I'm going to be a stuntwoman,' said Anna, 'and pop star, forty years isn't enough for all the songs I'm going to sing and all films I'm gonna be in.'

'Actresses can keep working until they drop dead,' mum said, 'and that's what I intend to do, because there are so many parts I want to play. I may not be a star all my career but I'll still be able to perform.'

'I could do archaeology forever,' said Eliza quietly.

'Well choices have to be made. You could go to university and change courses when you're there. You'd have to find a university that did the course you wanted to study in the long run or you could leap straight in and apply for a course in archaeology or design ...'

'Or stuntwomaning ...'

'Yes Anna, or stuntwomaning ...'

'But dad would never let us and we couldn't afford it,' Caroline said.

'It's your life, Caro. Did Anna say if you decide to move out you can stay with me while you sort things?'

'Yes but ... well Anna she says lots of things!'

'On this occasion she's right.'

'On every occasion I'm right!'

'But ... I couldn't afford ...'

'After my first big film, I put money in a trust to pay for you to go to Anna's school but your father wouldn't let you, that money is still there, you could use it to pay for your course, there's enough to cover rent for a flat too. You'd have to get a part time job if you wanted luxuries but you wouldn't starve.'

'Really?' asked Caroline.

'Both of you,' mum confirmed. 'Your father and I split because he wanted me to do what he said, no acting, no theatre and no socialising. It was tough to make the break but what sort of marriage is that? Anna talks to me all the time so I know he's doing the same to you. You're going to find it hard, he'll try to stop you and if he persuades you or forces you to stay now it'll be far more difficult to leave in the future. What I suggest is that you make plans, apply for college, move things to my house and then when you're legally an adult you leave. I'll give you any help I can'

'What about Eliza and Anna?' asked Caroline.

'My lawyer is putting another appeal together. I'll ask him to look at Eliza's situation. However Eliza will have to be sure what she wants, because it'll come down to that in the end.'

'I'd come today …' Eliza said.

'I'd love that, I miss you both, but until you're old enough your father has custody and he could cause all sorts of problems.'

They discussed it a bit more, Caroline and Eliza insisted they needed to leave. Maybe he was their dad but it was stifling at home and they couldn't keep doing what he wanted them to do forever.

Chapter 35

When she had a chance during lunch Anna surreptiously checked her machine but no monsters turned up.

After lunch Caroline and Eliza went to the library, looking a lot more cheerful and Anna met friends.

It was still raining and they got soaked but Kirstin's mum dried everything out for them and lent her an umbrella.

Afterwards she bought a multi-pack of Twirls and went to visit Miss Ray.

She rang the doorbell, Miss Rae's mum opened it, she looked pleased to see her and gave her a big smile.

'Come in Anna, Erin's been looking forward to your visit.'

Anna bounded in, crackling with energy.

'Where are you Miss Rae, hop to it,' she was half way up the stairs when she heard Miss Rae calling from the sitting room. She jumped back down and burst through the door.

'I had lunch with Mum, Caro and Eliza. It was a great lunch, chips, beef burger and chips but they did all the talking! Imagine a meal with out talking I was practically bursting. I had mum to myself at the end but she had loads to tell me so then I had to listen to her. How are you? You look better, you looked peaky yesterday but you don't today. Is that because you're feeling better or because you've got make-up on.' She looked closely, 'you've got make-up on …

ooh I know why …'

'Why Sherlock?'

'Because the boy is coming round! You texted me and said he visited last night, what did he bring? Did he bring those flowers? Those are from Marks and Spencers, classy.'

'Yes he brought them.'

'Good. So he should. Tough monster hunters like us can cope with anything, but people still need to treat us right. Was he nice, you know NICE?'

'He was sweet.'

'He's stepping up his game!'

'Anna!'

'Yes ma'am'

'My mum told me something after you left yesterday?' Miss Rae changed the subject, 'do you want to know what?'

'Yes! Because you're too nice to tell me if she said something horrid, so it's bound to be good. I bet she said, "Erin, that Anna is an amazing young lady, I will buy all her records when she becomes a pop star. You're a very lucky daughter to meet someone so amazing.'

'She said you offered to find her "a boy".'

'I did, but I was rather hoping your boy would help since I don't know any boys. Well obviously I know boys, but smelly Simon Robinson and his mates aren't really going to be all that interesting to a cool chick like your mum.'

'You think my mum is a cool chick?'

'Don't you?'

'She's my mother!'

'My mum is ultra-cool!'

'Your mum is a film star.'

'But she's cool even when she's not in films. We went for lunch with her …'

'You said.'

'You should have come. We were making secret plans, you'd have liked that.'

There was a moment's silence.

'Don't you want to know what we were planning?' asked Anna.

'You said it was secret …' said Miss Rae.

'Not from you silly, from the "prison warden"' Anna nodded knowingly, '… that's Dad by the way!'

Miss Rae raised her eyes to the sky, 'Anna you didn't have to spell it out, it was obvious you meant your dad.'

'I forgot you've got five degrees …'

'Two.'

'Only two,' said Anna, 'was it really worth going to university and only coming back with two?'

'Have you finished?'

Anna obviously hadn't and went on to say Miss Rae should have knuckled down and got far more degrees.

'Actually I was trying to be subtle, I was telling you you've finished and it's my turn to talk.'

'The adult world is so strange, I hardly understand it at all …'

'Shut up Anna.'

Anna held up her hand, 'High five, Miss Rae.'

She had to high five her.

'Anna you are a star. Now I have something to tell you.'

Anna looked up curiously.

'Actually I didn't think that would shut you up …'

'I thought it might be something important,' Anna replied.

'Okay … well because I'm stuck here getting bored I've been doing a little research …'

Anna gave her a sideways look. 'For me?'

'I was thinking about what you were saying, you know that your father got custody,' she paused, Anna looked expectant so she continued. 'I have wide ranging security access to government websites and I … er … checked the court sessions that applied to your custody.' She moved the screen so Anna could see it. 'The same judge presided over all of them.'

'Yes, isn't that what happens?' said Anna.

'Not really, judges are busy people, lots of cases to deal with, but each time your mother had more evidence or you attended to make a personal statement there he was, Lord Matthew Murray. It's unlikely he just happened to be free every time, surely he had other cases, or holidays, or was involved in some legal legislation or whatever. It's odd despite new evidence being presented and you expressing your wish with increasing vehemence his decision is exactly the same each time. I read up on how child custody cases are meant to be decided and the overriding focus is meant to be on what the child wants. And let's face it no one could be left in any doubt about what you want. There would have to be some pretty major reason why the child's view should be disregarded ... you know if one parent is Rasputin or Hitler and your mother appears to be neither.'

'She's not Ra Ra Rasputin, she ...' started Anna.

'I love listening to you Anna, but please let me finish.'

'Since you put it so nicely and since you are recovering and since your mother gave me an amazing chocolaty, orangey cakey thingy.'

'You know that's the longest speech I've been able to make since I've met you and the longest you've been quiet for.'

'Being with you is like having my very own soap opera with a crazy cast of characters,' said Anna. 'The boy and all the excitement of what he's going to do next, your mum who makes home-made Jaffa cakes and collects spoons and your mysterious dad who joined the army but you never hear from ...'

'Joined the army, Anna?'

'Yes, your mum said he'd passed on, so he's probably a soldier by now, perhaps an officer?'

'She was trying to tell you he's dead.'

'Dead? Why would the army want a dead soldier?'

'No, mum said he'd passed on, that's a gentle way of saying he's dead.'

'Are you sure?'

'Yes.'

'Oh poor you. Caro and Eliza's mum is dead, so I share mine with them. When did he die?'

'About ten years ago, but we're getting side-tracked. I'll tell you all about him some time but not now.'

'Okay.'

'The judge thing didn't seem right,' Miss Rae continued, 'so I looked at his background, he and your dad …'

'They're brothers!' interrupted Anna excitedly.

'No, but they might as well have been. They were at primary and secondary school together, studied at the same university, they're members of the same clubs and they're on the same online forums.'

'They're friends?'

'You'd think. There's no actual evidence they've been scheming, but Lord Murray has a connection to the case so even if he claimed they'd never talked in all that time surely he would've known your dad and they must have mutual friends?'

'That makes sense. I never felt he was listening to me, it was like everything was already sorted. Mum was always real nervous before court, but dad never was, so if he knew the judge was going to be on his side anyway, he wouldn't need to worry would he?'

'You need a different judge someone who will review the evidence and someone who'll listen to what you have to say.'

'I bet there's stuff at home that shows they know each other.'

'If you could prove it, it would be better because then you could show collusion …'

'Collusion?' asked Anna.

'That they planned it together!'

'If we proved it, then they'd have to say sorry Anna, sorry we cheated you out of living with your mum, sorry you had to eat crappy vegetarian food, sorry we tried to stop you playing football and hockey, sorry you were shouted at for having an opinion, sorry …'

'Is this a long list, Anna?'

'Pretty long Miss Rae.'

'Well I don't want to interrupt you …'

'Yes you do!'

'You're right I do, I wanted to check if any little monsters have turned up I was worried my machine wasn't working.'

'No, none.'

'It's funny there haven't been any since the rain came,' Miss Rae mused.

'They forgot their umbrellas?'

'I don't think they're bothered by water.'

'Well maybe they're at the shops buying jam?' suggested Anna.

'You have a serious suggestion?' Miss Rae asked.

'That's unlikely, but I do have a big pack of Twirls.'

'Twirls!' said Miss Rae licking her lips. 'So no monsters when it's raining, why?'

'The water washes stuff away, there's something they like and the rain washes it off so they're not bothered about coming here.'

'You're a genius …'

'I know,' agreed Anna, 'and I'm okay with that. And it's not just things like this, I'm a genius at singing, at maths, at wearing cool clothes, at free-running, at being a stuntwoman, at …'

'So perhaps they like something in the city and that's why they come …'

'… at catching monsters, at saving people from being run over, at …'

'So the rain comes, dampens it, washes it away or covers up the smell.' Miss Rae pulled out a notepad and made some notes.

'… at helping people, at eating Jaffa cakes … you're not listening to me. LISTEN TO ME!'

'Anna I'm always listening to you,' Miss Rae maintained, 'I'm just good at multi-tasking.'

'There's another thing I'm a genius at, multi-tasking!'

Miss Rae's mother came in at that moment.

'Hi Miss Rae's mum. I'm sorry Mr Rae is dead,' said Anna. 'I didn't know what "passing on" meant. Miss Rae has just told me. You know I thought you were saying he'd left you to join the army and that's why you were sad when you told me.'

'Thank you Anna. I am maintaining a positive attitude and Erin is a great comfort.'

'She grows on you,' said Anna. 'When I first met her I thought she was as sour as a lemon, now I know her a bit better I've discovered she's as sweet as strawberry jam, which I like … a lot!'

'You like me a lot,' said Miss Rae.

'No, you weren't listening properly I like strawberry jam a lot,' corrected Anna. 'I could eat spoonfuls of it and not just spread it on toast! Anyways time to go. See you tomorrow. Text me what the boy says this evening.'

'The boy?' Miss Rae's mother asked.

'IT Adam! Him that has the pash for Miss Rae and her lady bumps.'

Miss Rae went red.

'Say hello from me when he comes to cheer you up after a day playing games on those three computers of his.'

'If he does come I'll say hi.'

'And text me what you have for dinner, it'll give me something nice to think about when I'm chewing through my evening portion of oats and hay. Bye then, bye Mrs Rae.'

The room was suddenly very empty, the front door slammed and the house was silent again.

After a moment Miss Rae's mother suggested she put the radio on, 'it's … it's quiet.'

Miss Rae agreed, 'yes very quiet'.

Chapter 36

The rain had stopped by the time Anna got home and it was a lot warmer; in fact the streets were almost dry.

She wanted to search dad's office right then, but he would be home soon and she didn't want him to know she was onto him. She'd seen enough movies to know he'd come in, find her at just the wrong moment and then start "destroying the evidence".

She sat with Caroline and Eliza, who were both a lot more cheerful. Planning things with her mum had been a good idea.

She opened her window when she went to bed because it was so hot and in the morning the sun was bright and the clouds had gone.

A monster turned up mid-morning.

Eliza was in Caroline's room surreptitiously helping her pack. They were going to sneak her most important things to Anna's mum's house bit by bit and next week when she was eighteen she could just go. Anna wasn't needed so she decided to check the monster out. The dot was strong; it must be another big one.

She put her rucksack on, left the house through her bedroom window and sprinted down the road, a flash of clashing colours and revelling in the sunshine.

According to the machine the monster was close to the

ring road. What was it they had discussed last night? The monsters were attracted to something in the city, so far they had all been hiding in empty buildings or wasteland but always in places where the roads were packed with cars and lorries; they'd never found one in the suburbs where there wasn't much traffic. Miss Rae had said Anna was a genius for saying the rain had washed something away, so the monsters didn't come for the noise so perhaps they liked the smell of petrol. She texted Miss Rae. She had to text people immediately after she'd had an idea or she'd have moved onto something else and would never remember it.

A motorway cut through here. It went over the smaller roads on stilts and underneath there were footpaths, open areas and big concrete caves. Shoppers were milling about on their way to a giant shopping mall and it was a lot busier than any of the other places the monsters had hidden.

The monster was underneath one of the roads, Anna didn't want to draw attention to herself so she sat underneath a billboard advertising a new superhero film and pretended to text on her phone.

Some boys on skateboards whooshed in, laughing and shouting at each other. They dumped their rucksacks and began practising tricks close to where the monster was hiding.

One of the skaters messed up, fell off and his board shot away.

Bugger she thought, it's going under the road where the monster is.

The boy picked himself up, his mates laughed and he swore at them as he went to collect it.

Something moved in the shadows.

'Oi!' the boy shouted. 'Leave that it's mine.'

One of the others went over.

'What's the problem?'

'Some guy under there grabbed my deck!'

'Give it back,' the friend yelled, 'or we'll give you a kicking.'

The others gathered round.

'Gonna go beggin' on it, eh? Well get your own fuckin' board.'

There was a grunt.

Anna wasn't sure what to do. She didn't want anyone to know she was a monster hunter at the same time she didn't want them to hurt the little monster; it was probably just curious.

The boys went closer.

'You mate, you're in big trouble!'

The shadow moved again and teeth glinted in the dark.

The first boy stopped. 'What the hell?'

A loud growl echoed from the darkness.

'Who … who's there?'

On her machine the dot was pulsing. Anna had never seen it do that. Whatever was in the shadows wasn't like any of the ones they'd caught before. She decided to phone Mrs Graham. She rather thought she'd need help.

Before she could get her phone out, the creature grabbed

one of the other skateboards and wrenched it out of the boy's hand.

'AAArrrgh!' the boy shouted, jumping back in alarm.

There was a loud snapping sound, the two halves of the board were thrown out and landed in front of the lads. They stood for a moment and then all turned and moved well away.

'WHAT THE ...,' shouted the boy, whose board had been wrecked. 'Who the hell is under there?'

The boys stared into the shadows from a distance.

'He's gone, some weirdo.'

'Some weirdo nicking skateboards and trashing them!'

'I'm not hangin' round here,' one of the other boys said.

They all agreed and ran off.

People walking past heard the boys talking about a weirdo and didn't hang around either and soon the area was deserted.

Anna jumped up onto a portakabin and lay down to watch.

Nothing happened for a long time. Then something shifted in the shadows, it moved closer to the sunlight and as it did she was able to see it more clearly. It had a large body, short powerful legs and an ugly tail like a rat's. It was a pale yellow and hairless, wrinkly skin covered its body, its head was small and mainly seemed to be teeth and eyes.

One of the boys had dropped his water bottle. It stretched out an arm, grabbed it and chewed until it split. The water spurted out, it growled and tore the bottle apart.

246

'You're something fierce aren't you?' Anna said to herself. She looked at the machine again. 'And do you know what's weird is you're not moving but your dot is flickering around like it's packing to go on holiday.'

She had a sudden thought and enlarged the screen as much as it went.

Chapter 37

Anna rang the number Miss Rae had given her for Mrs Graham.

'Hi Mrs Graham, I've …'

'You've come through to Mrs Graham's secretary, can I help?'

'That is so cool, I didn't know she had a secretary, do you keep her right. If I was a secretary do you know what I'd tell my boss … hang on a sec I'm gonna have to tell you later, it's real important I speak to Mrs Graham.'

'She's in a meeting,' the man on the other end of the phone said.

'Is it a proper meeting,' asked Anna, 'or is that something you've been asked to say because she's busy, or eating a sloppy burrito, or doesn't want to talk to anyone because she's tired, or just doesn't want to talk to me …' then as after thought she added, 'or because she's drunk?'

There was a moment's silence.

'She's in a proper meeting, but who are you?'

'I'm one of her monster hunters,' Anna explained.

'You sound very young …'

'I am very young,' said Anna, 'I'm probably one of the youngest monster hunters ever and I'm probably one of the best too. I've already caught loads.'

'Is that Anna Templeton?'

'Yes and I …'

'Hang on Miss Templeton, Mrs Graham has just come out of her meeting and I'll pass you over.'

'Hello Ann …' started Mrs Graham as she took the phone.

'Were you really in a meeting Mrs Graham, have you really just come out of it?'

'Yes Anna, what …'

'Dad pretends he's in a meeting when he wants to avoid people …'

'Does he, well I WAS in a meeting, is this important?'

'YES, mega important. I've just seen another monster and it's real big, like the size of a big dog, not one of those black ones, the Labradors, bigger than that and it's a lot more bolshie too. It nicked a boy's skateboard right out of his hands! And do you know what's worse?'

'What Anna?'

'There are four of them! I didn't see the other three but the machine showed four dots if you got it focussed right. I was very sensible, I "monitored the situation from a distance", now I'm "reporting in". If someone hadn't attempted to murder poor Miss Rae I'd have phoned her first, but what could she do, she can hardly walk let alone catch giant monsters. You were the next on my list because you're the boss, I don't mean for you to go down and catch them, I wanted you to know so you could "draw up plans". I could probably catch one on my own but I've only got one net and I've have to be real lucky to catch all four in it.'

'What did it look like Anna?'

She gave a long description of the one she'd seen.

'Can you come to the office?'

'Sure Mrs Graham, I'll be there soon as ...'

Mrs Graham put the phone down. 'Oh dear,' she sighed. Her secretary looked quizzical.

'More monsters and they're bigger than ever, we're lucky with Anna Templeton she's turning out to be one amazing young lady.'

A slight figure bounced through the door. 'yeah I am, totally 'mazing!'

Mrs Graham and her secretary looked up very surprised.

'I was here all along!' she announced joyfully. 'Look there's IT Adam, he helped us catch a monster. Hi Adam!'

He waved back.

'So, even if an experienced monster hunter like Miss Rae was fit it would be tricksy. Do you have any other monster hunters, you know like a secret SAS monster hunter unit all ready to spring into action?'

'A standbye unit?'

'Yes, since Miss Rae is out of action I need help.'

'Yes poor Miss Rae ...'

'Usually I'm useless at picking up hints,' said Anna, 'but even I can tell there isn't anyone here who can help!'

'No,' admitted Mrs Graham despondently. 'Everyone is good at what they do, but what they do isn't catching the little monsters.'

'No one waiting in a special helicopter?'

'Not even in a special helicopter.' Mrs Graham's phone rang. She was irritated at the interruption but answered it anyway. They could hear a man talking. He told her he'd just had a reporter asking about an incident in one of the underpasses in central London.

'He was implying it was some sort of creature and wanted to know what the council is doing about it. Is there anything there?' the man asked.

Mrs Graham gave a very vague reply, full of long complicated words concluding, 'so you understand?'

The person obviously didn't but wasn't going to admit he didn't know the meaning of most of what she was saying and rang off.

'That was a pretty big fib,' said Anna admiringly.

'Not a fib,' claimed Mrs Graham, 'merely obfuscating reality.'

Anna looked completely blank.

'I was avoiding the truth,' Mrs Graham explained. 'We need time to sort this out and keep the monsters secret.'

'I'm good at keeping secrets! If I wasn't going to be a stunt girl when I grow up I'd be a spy. What's that guy doing?' she asked pointing into the room.

They both turned and when they turned back to their surprise Anna had disappeared. There was a noise behind them and they looked to see if it was her, no one was there! They turned back and she was right in front of them pretending to speak on her phone.

'Of course Prime Minster, if James Bond is on a mini-break to Alton Towers I'll fill in until he gets back. I'd make such a great spy.' She laughed with glee. 'You look like you think I'm magic, like Hermione, it wasn't magic I just ducked behind your desk when you were distracted!'

Mrs Graham's secretary laughed out loud and even Mrs Graham managed a smile. 'Right Anna, I'll try and sort out some help for you,' she said. 'It might take some time so would you like to see what the techie boys are working on?'

'Yes I would. Why are they all boys?'

'They're not,' admitted Mrs Graham.

'We have three techie girls,' confirmed her secretary.

'I don't know why we call them boys ...'

'I suppose it runs off the tongue better,' suggested the secretary.

Chapter 38

Anna was introduced to the technical team and was soon enthusiastically demanding more features for her machine and discovering some of the extra things it could already do.

'This is so cool,' Anna said whenever she learnt a new trick.

'You're the first person to ask us about the other features,' said Josie, who was one of the techie girls, 'all the other field operatives simply use the monster scanning screen.'

'But it's brilliant,' Anna averred.

Josie showed her a screen she hadn't seen, 'if a type of monster has been captured before, you can see what it looks like and if it's got any special characteristics.'

'This is a very good thing, I was going to give you a hard time because I had that idea and I didn't think you'd thought of it,' she said, 'do the other monster hunters know about this?'

'We've offered them training days but they're always too busy.'

'Hmm … well I'm glad I know.'

At lunch time she went out with Josie and it gave Anna the opportunity to tell her about one of the musicals she'd been in at school, sing her the songs and act out the most exciting bits.

Half way through the third song Josie asked if she had played all the characters.

'No but I learnt all the lines and all the songs because they were so good. My school is an all girls school and I got to play Bugsy, it was brilliant fun. Do you sing, singing is the best … after doing stunts. Stunts are the best, I'm going to be a stuntwoman when I grow up, I'll be jumping off bridges, driving cars into buildings and crashing through windows. It's not really glass you jump through in a film, it used to be made of sugar, yum yum, but now it's a sort of plastic. If you tried to jump through that window,' she pointed to the window of the restaurant, 'you'd most likely knock yourself out but if you went so hard you did break it you'd probably kill yourself because the broken bits would cut and stab you because they'd be sharp as kitchen knives. People think being a stuntwomen is just a question of being tough and not minding bruises but it's not.'

'No?'

'Definitely no Josie, a stuntwoman has to be smart and totally plan everything because the director wants to do it in one take, he doesn't want to waste time and of course it's well expensive. If my mum's acting and says the wrong thing when they're filming, that's okay because she can say it right the next time and it just costs a bit of time. If you drive a car through a building, smash into a bus and blow up the petrol lorry it costs mega-millions and if you blow up the wrong petrol lorry it'd be a nightmare and you'd probably run out of them petrol lorries bloody quickly.'

'Oh.'

'Luckily I'm sharp as a bag of squirrels and if I'm good at one thing at school it's maths so I'll be able to plan things properly.'

'How old are you Anna?'

'Twelve.'

'Twelve and you already know you want to be a stuntwoman?'

'And pop star. I'm going to have two jobs it'll be brilliant.'

It took Anna the rest of lunch and most of the walk back to sing excerpts of the songs she was going to have on her first album.

She stopped in mid song, 'did you want to be a techie boy when you were growing up Josie?'

'What?'

'Are you living the dream?'

'I ...'

'You're not are you? What do you really want to do?'

'I ...'

'Well? I've told you what I really want to do. Dad wants me to study hard and be an engineer or a chemist or a something boring, but screw him! So what about you?'

Anna stared until she gave in.

'I'd like to be a furniture maker.'

'At Ikea?'

'No, I mean a proper maker of furniture. Starting with a piece of wood, carving it, bending it, sanding and ending up with a chair, or a table or a cabinet.'

'Is that because you're no good at being a techie boy?'

'I'm brilliant at being a techie boy, Anna,' the girl replied, 'but you asked me what I'd really like to do.'

'Good for you. How much does a chair cost?'

'I don't know.'

'Could you make me one for mum's birthday!'

'I ...'

'I have money from catching loads of monsters and there are only so many jars of jam and Kentucky fried chickens I can eat. I'd like to buy my mum something that says I love her. You could make her a chair and carve hearts on it. No that would be just too cute, a chair with my name on one arm and hers on the other. Wait, wait ... her name carved on the back or maybe my name carved on the back so she knows who it's from. Actually don't make it yet I'll have to think about it. Perhaps a desk, a beautiful desk, a beautiful desk she can sit at and write beautiful thoughts. Yes that would best. How long will it take?'

Josie went red. 'Er ... I'd have to learn first and that could take a couple of years ...'

'That's okay. She's thirty now, so a desk for when she's thirty-two would be cool. Do you think a desk would be five hundred pounds? I could give you two hundred and fifty quid now and pay the rest when it's ready. Would that be a good deal?'

'Hang on a bit I've not even got a course to go to ...'

'Oh yeah,' said Anna, 'you can't be a techie boy one day

and go off and learn how to make furniture the next. But I want to be first in line when you're making desks.'

When they got back to the office Mrs Graham was talking to a man; she beckoned Anna over.

'You're new,' Anna said, staring at him closely. 'Who are you?'

'This is Commander Johnston …' Mrs Graham said.

'Are you a history teacher?'

'No, I'm not … wait a minute why would I be a history teacher?'

'You have a history teacher's beard,' Anna explained.

'Commander Johnston was in the navy, Anna,' Mrs Graham said.

'It's a sailor's beard but now I work for the government Miss Templeton and I've been looking forward to meeting you.'

'Me?'

'Yes I'm often on the phone to Peter Goodman and he's told me a lot about you.' He held out his hand, 'I'm pleased to meet you at last.'

'What did he say about me?'

'Who?'

'Mr Goodman. Was it good? It'd better have been good because I helped him so much. I caught the monsters much quicker than he could because I'm so quick. Did he say I was amazing? Did he like my singing?'

'I … I' stuttered the Commander.

'I'm going to be a singer, you know. I have big plans …'

'Anna perhaps we could concentrate on monsters for a little bit, that's why Commander Johnston is here,' Mrs Graham interrupted.

'Are you a monster hunter then?' Anna asked.

'Yes, Mrs Graham asked me to come down and ... you know be ready if you needed an extra pair of hands.'

Anna looked pleased he was offering to give her a hand rather than coming to take charge.

'It's an unbelievable situation, four monsters at the same time.'

'... and they're way, way bigger ...' Anna said.

'Let's go into my office,' said Mrs Graham, 'and Anna can tell us what she saw.' She called Adam over.

'Yes Mrs Graham?'

'More monsters and I think we need as much experience as we can get,' she explained.

'Of course,' he said, 'I'd like to make up for last time.'

'May I come,' asked Josie. 'Adam told me about it and well ... I'd like to help.'

'Yes Josie, thank you,' said Mrs Graham.

Chapter 39

The technicians had worked a miracle in the time and made bigger boxes to cope with the new monsters. These were loaded onto the London van. Josie and Adam went with Mr Janda, one of the London drivers, and Mrs Graham and Anna went with the Commander in his van.

When they arrived the police were standing across the path.

'I asked them to seal off the area, just to be on the safe side,' explained Mrs Graham, 'it'll give us a bit more space.'

'A police cordon great,' said Anna. She got out her I.D card, flashed it at the surprised policemen and walked past. 'You're doing a great job,' she said 'keep up the good work.'

Behind her Mrs Graham raised her eyes to the sky and the Commander tried not to laugh.

'Did you see that?' Anna said to them as they headed to the underpass. 'This is the best; they saw my card and just let me through! Do you think I could use this at any police cordon?'

Mrs Graham shook her head.

When they arrived Anna pointed out where the monsters were. 'We should do what they do on that sheepdog programme on the telly,' she suggested.

'What do you mean?' asked Mrs Graham.

'What sheepdog programme?' asked Josie

'One Man and his Dog?' suggested Commander Johnston.

'I've seen that,' said Mr Janda. 'Are you going to whistle to the monsters?'

Anna thought that was a great idea, 'although it'd be better if I sing to them, my singing is so soothing they'd be ever so relaxed and they'd actually want to be to caught.' She started to suggest songs she could sing until Mrs Graham interrupted and asked what her plan was.

'My actual plan?'

'Yes Anna, your actual plan' Mrs Graham said patiently, 'is it something to do with sheepdogs?'

'Not actual sheepdogs. Unless we have some. You don't have actual sheepdogs in your van do you Commander Johnston?'

'No, but I have apples. I mean I have other things but the monsters like fruit; there can't be much to eat in the middle of an underpass so an apple might cheer them up once we've caught them.'

'That's brilliant. Wait 'til Miss Rae hears it, she'll be well impressed.' Anna got out a notebook. 'I shall add it to the Annalog. This is where I write important things down,' she held it up to Mrs Graham. 'See, these are my notes, look at this one I had a great idea for a telly show, it's about these kids who …'

'So no sheepdogs,' said Mrs Graham, learning the hard way how easily Anna could be distracted.

'Sheepdogs? … oh yeah so you're going to have to be

pretend sheepdogs.' Anna started to explain her plan. 'We can't catch all four at once so we have to split them up and catch them one at a time. I'll be the shepherd, the box will be my sheep pen and you'll be the sheep dogs. Do you see?'

Mr Janda and the Commander thought it was a clever plan.

'Very sensible,' agreed Mrs Graham.

'What, what ...' asked Josie.

'I don't know what you're talking about either,' admitted Adam

'It's the most boring telly show in the world ... EVER!' said Anna. 'Dad makes us watch it in case we get over excited by programmes about curtain making or how to paint ceilings.'

'I like it,' said Mr Janda, 'it's very soothing and the countryside is beautiful.'

Mrs Graham explained shepherds train dogs to respond to whistles and then use them to herd their sheep ...

'Yes, yes,' Anna agreed excitedly, 'and on the telly the shepherd, that's me, has to shut the little woolly bullys in a pen. If he does it super quick he gets more points and points mean prizes; perhaps we should all have a go and see who does it fastest ...'

'Let's just try to catch them, Anna,' said Mrs Graham.

'Well okay, if you think. Of course this'll only work if they're scared of us,' Anna mused. 'They might all be Bobby Rutherfords, then we'll be in trouble.'

'Bobby Rutherfords?' asked Adam.

'Bobby Rutherford, he's the brother of my mate India and he is not frightened of anything. Well he is ... but there aren't any giant vampire bats in London so nothing in London scares him,' Anna explained. 'Except he runs away from Ruth Keyes, but that's because she has a pash for him and he's still only interested in sport and Lego and doesn't know how to stop her pash. So what are you lot waiting for, we've got monsters to catch! We'll make up the boxes now. Commander Johnston, if you've got body armour you should put it on. I saw in our van there are some smaller boxes ... you could use them as shields.' She looked round at the blank expressions. 'Tch! In case the monsters jump you!'

'Jump us?' asked Mrs Graham.

'Well I don't know if they will, I'm just trying to plan ahead in case. The one I saw had a lot of teeth, you know more than we've got and more than dogs and cats have ... lots basically and you wouldn't want it to bite you with all of them.'

Anna was suddenly focused. She sorted out the bigger perspex boxes, distributed the smaller ones as protection and at the same time told them what she expected them to do. 'You've got to work as a team, split the monsters up so one is on his own and if you do that I can try to catch him. If he gives me trouble, Commander Johnston should come and help because he's caught monsters before, but the rest of you gotta make sure the other three wrinkly, yellow bellies stay put. Okay!'

The switch to serious Anna was so unexpected they all

said yes. Even Mr Janda who thought he was only there to drive the van.

'You've got some of the new nets?'

Commander Johnston nodded.

'Good,' said Anna, 'we're ready to rock. Mrs Graham and Commander Johnston, that way.' She pointed. 'Adam, Josie and Mr Janda on the other side. I don't know if they're fast or strong or clever, basically I'm going to find out when the first one makes a break for it. It's gonna be fun.'

Anna stretched, flexed her muscles and bounced excitedly. 'Right let's go!'

They did as they were told and headed towards the space under the main road. The Commander checked his machine and went first. The others followed nervously, perspex boxes held out in front for protection. It was dark but as their eyes became adjusted to the gloom they saw four shadows along the back wall.

The creatures edged away in a line, the Commander directed them to make a circle then suddenly leapt between the first and second one.

Startled the first creature ran off into the sunlight and Adam, Mrs Graham, Josie and Mr Janda hurried into position to stop the others following.

For the first time Anna got a good look. It was bigger than she'd expected and was muttering to itself. When it saw her, it stopped, shook itself and the wrinkles rippled down its body.

Some of its eyes focused on Anna while others checked

around to see if any one else was there. Its teeth were sharp, there really were plenty of them and it gnashed them at her as it stalked closer.

'I'm not happy about those teeth,' Anna said. She did a little jig, '"See this girl, watch this scene, digging the Dancing Queen,"' she sang. She moved closer to the monster, 'hey mellow yellow, you a dancer too?'

It backed off and she thought it was going to make a break for it so she went onto the balls of her feet ready to chase.

Instead without warning it sprang at her head.

She threw herself to the ground, rolled under it and bounced back to her feet.

'Oh pee-ew! You don't 'alf need a bath!'

The monster skidded to a stop, wheeled round and launched itself at her again.

This time it kept low and she sprang over it.

'You are one tricksy buggle Wrinklystiltskin,' she told it. 'You're not going to the same thing every time are you? You've got some smarts. "Hey, It's murder on the dancefloor, but you better not kill the groove, murder on the dancefloor, but you better not steal my moves."'

It paused as if entranced by her dancing and then leapt again, this time aiming at her hips.

Anna had a big smile on her face, she sashayed to one side and held the net where she had been. The creature's momentum took it slap bang into the middle and it landed on the ground with a rather sad "Oooftt".

She kept a tight hold of the edge of the net, wrapped it round until it couldn't move and then tried to drag it to the box. It was way too heavy, the Commander saw she was struggling and as the other monsters were surrounded asked Mr Janda to go help.

Mr Janda took hold of the net so the creature couldn't get away, Anna fetched the box and between them they rolled it in and slid the lid on.

Anna sat on the top.

'I'm glad you didn't bite me because you've a ton of pointy teeth, you must have kept the tooth fairy busy when youse were growing up. Does your breath smell as bad as the rest of you? That would be most dis-gust-ting! Right …' she leapt up, fetched the second made-up perspex box and shouted to Commander Johnston to let the next one out.

Commander Johnston cautiously stepped away from the second creature in line, keeping a wary eye on the others.

The monster saw the gap and made a break for freedom. It must have seen Anna catch its friend because it headed in the opposite direction.

She followed, trying to herd it towards the wall. It back-pedalled a few steps, then charged towards the pedestrian tunnel. On the way it barrelled into a heavy rubbish bin, tipped it over and carried on as if it hadn't noticed.

'"Or should I give up? Or should I just keep chasin' Monsters,"' Anna sang as she raced after the monster. She overtook it, ran up the rounded side wall of the tunnel and dropped her second net over it then somersaulted and landing in front.

The net twisted around its legs, it stumbled and fell over. It began to wriggle furiously but that got it even more snarled up and within seconds was in too much of a tangle to move.

It was bigger than the first so she didn't bother trying to shift it and waited until Mr Janda arrived and helped him box it up.

'Goodness Miss Anna,' he said appreciatively, 'what a manouvre, that was amazing, it was like watching something out of the movies!'

Anna was about to reply when there was a loud growl followed by an anxious shout from Commander Johnson.

'Watch out Mrs Graham,' he called.

There wasn't time for Mrs Graham to react and before she knew it the monster jumped up at her. She let out an involuntary scream, it crashed into the box she was holding, barged her over and she landed on the ground with a thump.

'Mrs Graham, are you ...' Josie started.

'Don't worry about me,' Mrs Graham shouted, as the creature ran off, 'catch him!'

Adam yelled to Anna and followed.

In the confusion the remaining monster saw its chance and it was off too, darting between Josie and the Commander

'Damn!' shouted Commander Johnston and set off too.

'ONE AT A TIME ... PLEASE,' called Anna; a grin on her face.

The first one paused, glanced at Adam, decided it would be easier to barge past Anna and accelerated towards her.

Anna had her net ready. She waited until the very last moment, leapt over the on-rushing creature and dropped the net on it. The monster was going too fast to stop, ran into the net, stumbled and fell.

As Anna landed the second monster arrived.

'ANNA!' Adam bellowed a warning.

There was a collective intake of breath and all they could do was watch in horror. It crashed into her, bounced her high into the air and raced off.

'WHAT THE HELL, YOU BLOODY THING …' Adam roared.

'YAAAAR …' screamed Anna.

'CHRIST!' yelped Mrs Graham.

With everyone's attention on Anna, the monster made its escape unnoticed.

Chapter 40

Adam desperately ran forward as fast as he could but he was never going to get there in time to catch her.

Anna started to fall, then just before she hit the concrete she twisted, flipped over and landed on her feet, hands in the air.

"'Yaar've got to roll with the punches to get to what's real … JUMP!'"

Adam skidded to a stop. 'Anna! You okay? I thought …'

'You were worried about me IT Adam!' she replied.

Commander Johnston grabbed hold of the net before the monster she'd caught could wriggle free.

'Of course,' Adam said, out of breath '… Erin warned me I'd be in big trouble if anything happened to you.'

'Really?' asked Anna.

Behind them the last monster scrabbled up the concrete wall and disappeared over the top.

'It's getting away,' Josie interrupted.

Anna pulled out her machine. 'I think we're okay, it's not gone far.'

'I'll give you a hand,' Mr Janda said to the commander. 'You have to be careful, some of these fellows can give you a nasty scratch.'

Despite its vigorous attempts to escape, the two men managed to roll the creature into the third box and put the lid on.

Mrs Graham picked herself up, came over and apologised. 'Sorry, sorry, it was my fault they got away ...'

'They're a tricksy bunch Mrs Graham, but we've got three,' Anna pointed out.

'They look hungry,' said Josie bending down to look at them.

Commander Johnston slipped an apple into each box. The monsters sniffed them and started eating.

'Our wrinkly Houdini must be checking something because he's stopped moving,' said Anna, monitoring the screen.

'Could we get these ones into the van and out of sight, before you go after him,' asked Mrs Graham.

Mr Janda and the commander lifted up the first box and carried it to the van. '

You were amazing Anna,' said Josie.

'I'm always amazing,' agreed Anna, 'although I'm not as amazing in French class as I am on the hockey pitch.'

'Weren't you scared?'

'No. It was fun,' Anna explained. 'I didn't know what they were going to do or what was going to happen so it was like a surprise birthday party.'

'I was really scared,' admitted Josie.

'Me too,' agreed Adam.

'I didn't think they were going to be so big, I was terrified when that last one ran into you,' Josie continued. 'I thought it was going to really hurt you.'

'They're big. They're chunky too. The first one was heavy enough, but you,' Anna squatted down to look at the second monster, 'you ate all the pies didn't you? Isn't that a great way to say someone is fat? He ate all the pies. You haven't eaten any pies Josie, you're a twig girl like me. Mr Janda you've eaten plenty of pies.'

Mr Janda laughed, 'it is all muscle, Miss Anna.'

He lifted up the side of the second box, the Commander took a corner.

'Phew,' gasped Commander Johnson, 'I think we need a hand.'

Adam took a corner and the three of them lugged it over and slotted it in the back, they collected the third monster and placed it carefully in the van.

'Bloody hell they're some weight,' said Adam rubbing his arms.

'Thanks,' said the Commander, 'so one to go. I'll help Anna corner it and when we do, it'd be best to bring the van round. He looked the biggest of the four and I don't fancy dragging him all the way back here.'

Anna agreed, 'yeah great idea.'

'I'll come,' offered Josie, 'you know to be a sheepdog.'

'Me too,' said Adam, firmly.

'Umm … if you followed the way he went Anna,' suggested Commander Johnston, 'we could go along on either side and maybe a pincer movement will catch him quicker.'

'Sure.' She ran up the wall, caught the top, vaulted over and disappeared from view, singing as she went.

Josie and Adam headed through the tunnel on the left and Commander Johnston went to the right.

On the other side of the wall was an empty street. It would have been a bustling shopping area once, now there was just a row of boarded up shops and a vandalised phone box.

There was no need for Anna to check her machine, the monster was on other side of the road scratching the door of an old decorating supplies store and she edged behind a post box to wait for the others.

Commander Johnston arrived first. When his head appeared she slowly raised her arm and pointed.

He waited until Adam and Josie arrived and then signalled they should all go closer. Before they could move, the shop door crashed over and the monster disappeared inside.

They gathered at the entrance

'We should try and trap him in here, we don't want him getting away again,' the commander suggested.

'No we do not!' agreed Anna, 'his numerous teeth, his many eyes and his wrinkly skin would give your average publican a hell of a shock!'

'Publican?' asked Commander Johnston.

'Yeah ... you know a member of the public,' Anna explained with a sigh.

'Of course,' the commander replied sarcastically.

'What ... WHAT?' Anna demanded. 'You've spent too long at sea!'

'A publican is someone who runs a pub, Anna,' Josie gently explained, 'you know a landlord.'

Commander Johnston nodded in agreement.

'This is the biggest,' said Anna, without pausing to admit she might be wrong, 'we're going to have to be the most careful ever. I ... I ... we need to play to our strengths like I keep saying to Miss Rae. There won't be room in there for me to dodge about and this is the biggest and I'm the smallest so I should be a sheepdog along with techie boy. We'll try to steer it to you Commander Johnston 'cause you're bigger and stronger than us and you'll have a better chance of catching him. Techie girl, you should stay here and if it tries to get out the door you can warn us. Is that a good plan? I think that's a good plan, do you think that's a good ...'

'An excellent plan Miss Templeton,' said the commander and opened the door.

The shop was filled with shelf after shelf of dusty rolls of wallpaper stretching up to the ceiling. Somewhere at the back the monster was pulling them out with grunts of curiosity and then dropping them. At the far end was a hatch in the wall and beyond it the room where the staff used to stand and serve.

Anna crept down the middle row, Adam the left and Commander Johnston stayed out of sight at the end of the right aisle.

At the end Anna turned, looking very pleased with herself and caught the Commander's eye. He nodded to say he was ready.

'WWRRRAAaaar!' she whooped loudly.

What happened next was quite unexpected. Instead of

272

running away from the noise, the monster barged one of the towers of shelves over towards Anna.

'LOOK OU ...' bellowed the Commander.

Anna was already moving.

The shelf crashed against the wall, the heavy rolls of wallpaper cascaded out and a cloud of dust erupted, thick as smoke obscuring the whole of the back of the shop. The last they saw of Anna was a flash of colour leaping towards the back wall.

Chapter 41

Commander Johnston raced down through the haze. 'Oh god, OH GOD!'

A frantic Adam was already half way there, 'ANNA!'

The door at the side opened and Anna re-appeared. She put her hand out as if she just done a magic trick.

'Ta-daa,' she exclaimed, 'I jumped through the ha...'

There was a shriek from the door.

While they had been distracted the monster had made a bolt for the exit.

Josie was standing her ground, the box held out in front, but her hands were shaking.

Mouth open, teeth white in the gloom the monster hurtled into the makeshift shield and knocked Josie off her feet. She hit the ground winded, looked up, saw the monster was about to pounce and screamed again.

Commander Johnson frantically threw himself at it, grabbed the thing round the middle and brought it crashing to the ground inches from her head.

It snarled, twisted to face him, its lips dripping with green slobber and the smell of its rancid breath hit him.

It stretched open its jaws, the sharp rows of teeths glinted and it lunged for him. Before it knew what had happened it had a mouth full of wallpaper.

Anna was holding the other end of the roll. 'You're not

playing nicely are you,' she said, wagging her finger at it. 'I'm very disappointed.'

It spat the paper out, wrenched itself free from the commander's grip and made a dash for the door.

Josie, white as a sheet, grabbed its leg, it kicked her hand off but she'd slowed it down and Adam, panting heavily, reached the entrance first.

The monster reared up, roared angrily and launched itself at him.

Adam thrust his box forward, braced himself but was knocked out the way as if he was made of cardboard.

The commander scrambled to his feet and grabbed a back leg, but the creature was so powerful it pulled him over and dragged him along the floor.

'OH NO YOU DON'T!' shouted Anna, she stuck her foot out, caught the monster's front leg and tripped it. She hooked her net around its head and before it could wriggle away Commander Johnson twisted his net over its upper body. Together they wrapped the nets tight and soon all it could do was squirm ineffectually.

Adam picked himself up, fetched the box and between the three of them they rolled it in and shut the lid.

'Helloooo ...' Anna was on the phone. 'Mr Zanda, we've got it; you can bring the van round. You can tell Mrs Graham it's been totally exciting but it's totally sorted.'

Commander Johnston stood up straight and wiped the sweat from his forehead.

'Miss Templeton, thank you, I thought I was in big

trouble, I thought he was going to take a chunk out of me.'

'And me,' stuttered Josie. 'God I was so scared.'

'Hhew, hhew,' Adam panted. 'Anna …'

'Proper monster hunter now Adam, but you need to do more exercise, perhaps you should take up running around football 'coz I think you musta been training for walking about football!'

He raised his eyes to the sky, 'what are you like Anna?'

'I'm cool,' she replied and then saluted. 'You're tough as old boots aren't you Commander, you took on old Henry Wrinkler and saved Josie.'

The Commander helped Josie up.

'I was useless,' Josie said, 'if it had got away it would have been my fault.'

'You did an amazing job, Josie,' he said. 'You were very brave, if you hadn't got in his way and then grabbed his leg he'd have been away and god knows what trouble he might have caused.'

'Yeah you were brilliant,' agreed Anna.

The van pulled up outside and Mrs Graham and Mr Zanda got out.

'Well done, well done,' she said.

'We're amazing,' agreed Anna.

'That was some jump when the shelves came down. I thought, I thought … you know …' said Commander Johnston.

'Shit I was freaking … !' admitted Adam.

'The very best free runner in the world, who by the way is

a girl, she came to our gym and helped me learn that move,' explained Anna. 'Meraud did it in a film, my teacher Roy showed me the beginning of the film, he wouldn't let me see all of it, I think there must of been people without any clothes on kissing and stuff, I bet he thought I was too young, it was really annoying because the start was so exciting, it was about these crims who have stolen money from another crim ...'

'Crims?' asked Mrs Graham, bemused.

'Criminals,' explained Adam.

'Don't interrupt,' continued Anna, 'it was so cool ...'

'You know,' said the Commander, 'we should probably get this lot away, then the police can re-open the path.'

'Yes sir!' Anna saluted. 'Quick march, bunnies home, on the double. One two, one two, about turn, time to visit Miss Rae, one two, tell her what she's been missing.'

They loaded the last monster into the London van and helped Commander Johnston put the spare boxes back into his.

'Thanks for helping Sir,' said Anna. 'I know a lot about catching monsters but I could always learn more; I don't suppose you could perhaps teach me some of the clever tricks you use?'

'Of course Miss Templeton just phone or text me, it was a pleasure to meet you but I'd better go. I've got to be back in Birmingham this evening.' He got into his van. 'I'll complete the form and email it to you Mrs Graham, ma'am.'

'Thanks for coming at such notice.'

'I'm pleased I could help.'

'I'm off too,' said Anna and she was up the wall, over the fence and away in an instant.

Chapter 42

Miss Rae's leg was a lot better and she was able to walk, if a little gingerly, so when Anna burst through the door she suggested they get some fresh air as she was tired of being cooped up inside.

There was a park near by and they went there. Anna couldn't wait and told her of the thrilling day she'd had and how Commander Johnston was amazing. 'He let me be the boss; he didn't mind I was a girl or I was twelve. He's like Roy he can see being a girl or being twelve doesn't stop you being good at something.'

She started to act out how they caught the four monsters. 'The last one tried to jump poor Josie and Commander Johnston had to nab it super quick because she was mega scared. It was a bloody scary one, it was bigger than any of the others, it had a gazillion teeth and sharp claws and it was NOT shy. Commander Johnston was so cool about everything. He just boxed it up, neat as you like … are you okay, is your leg sore?'

'It's fine …'

'You look sad,' Anna said.

'No, no …' Miss Rae said.

Anna hugged her.

When she let go Miss Rae looked dazed.

'What's wrong now?' asked Anna.

Miss Rae looked as if she was about to start crying.

'You're leaking,' Anna said and touched her cheek, 'you should get a plumber to see to that.'

Miss Rae wiped away the tear.

'Okay, spill the beans, Miss Rae. I'm twelve I haven't a clue what's going on. I thought you needed a hug, but it's okay if you don't, you just have to say "don't hug me Anna" and I won't. I mean I'm not really a huggy person ... except for my mum and I could hug her for days with out stopping. I'm told a hug cheers people up but obviously it doesn't!'

'It does Anna, it really does, it cheered me up.'

'You don't look any more cheerful,' Anna said, viewing her critically from different angles.

'I was being stupid and over sensitive ...'

'Miss Rae you have to spell it out, I really do not have a Scooby doo!'

Miss Rae sat on a bench.

'Okay Anna. Your hug did cheer me up. I just wasn't expecting it, I've never had any close friends so no one has ever really hugged me, well mum did when I was a little girl. I was sad because Commander Johnston is a proper monster hunter, he's smart, he's tough and he's the sort of person you should be hunting monsters with, not a miserable, geeky loner like me.'

'WHAT! You're exactly the person I should be hunting monsters with,' Anna said vehemently. 'You're not miserable, you're not a loner and when does being geeky stop you being cool.'

'Cool?'

'Sure Miss Rae, cool clothes, cool hair and super cool brain! We're a team, we look out for each other, we're practically family.'

'Family?'

'When your boy decides to marry you I'll be your bridesmaid. It'll be awesome, I'll have a princess dress and scatter flowers in front of you and eat too much at the party and fall asleep in the middle of the dance floor.'

She lay on the ground and pretended to snore, then she leapt up.

'So let me get this right, you were sad because when I telling you about the Commander, you thought I wanted to go off and hunt monsters with him and you were also sad because you thought I thought you were miserable and then you were more sad because I hugged you and no one else hugs you. Phew that is complicated, are all grown-ups so complicated?'

'I don't think so, just me,' admitted Miss Rae.

'So that we both know what's going on … I don't want to go monster hunting with anyone else, I don't think you're a miserable cow …'

'You did!'

'When?' challenged Anna.

'When we hunted those first monsters.'

'I most certainly did not,' Anna retorted hotly, 'and I have a most amazing memory. However I can't work if you're also saying I shouldn't hug you ever again or what.'

'I don't mind a hug every now and then if I'm really down, but I'm like you, I'm not really a huggy person.'

'Okay. So we're good?'

'We're good Anna.'

'I told mum about what you found out about the judge and she said "coo-er!"'

'Your mum said "coo-er!" Anna?'

'No. What she actually said was, "that judge is a fucking bastard and I'm going to rip off his balls and make your father eat them!" Now I can't understand most of what Mrs Graham says, but I understood all of that.'

'Umm ... perhaps you're concentrating your learning in the wrong areas?'

'She did calm down in the end and agreed you were right; we need actual evidence. I'm a-going to sneak round his study and mum is going to get someone to look at school rolls, talk to the teachers and see if they can prove dad and Michael Matthews knew each other. She said you were also right that whatever we've got to speak to a different judge. She said you must be real smart and I said you were mega smart, I told her how you'd been to university and you'd got ten degrees.'

'Ten Anna! It's going up each time.'

'When you meet mum you'll have to complete the list I told her you had degrees in chemistry, in inventing, in law, in tromboning and in jam-making. She was well impressed.'

'I keep telling you I have two. I hope you're teasing?'

'You look better now,' decided Anna. 'Maybe the hug did

work. You're walking a bit better too, let's have a look at your bruise.'

'Not out here.'

'The sooner it's better, the sooner we can get back to catching monsters together. So what's the latest news about your boy?'

'He's been texting to check how I'm doing and asked if he could come round.'

'Again? Good, so what time?'

'He said he'd … hang on a sec why do you want to know what time?'

'So I can spy on you, obviously!'

'Well maybe I'll keep that to myself.'

'You should be safe, it's bound to be in the evening and I'll be stuck at home pretending to eat quorn but actually spooning it into a cleverly hidden plastic bag. Do you like living with your mum?'

'Anna you are the queen of the non-sequiturs!'

'I'm the queen of everything … even them.'

'It means you change what you're talking about to something completely different without even a pause,' Miss Rae explained.

'Is that good or bad?' asked Anna.

'It's disconcerting.'

'Keeps you on your toes. So do you?'

'I love my mum.'

'Don't you think you should be moving on?' asked Anna. 'Shouldn't she be moving on too? I mean getting a boy of her own, doing stuff. I mean it's lovely she looks after you and she makes the best cakes ever but shouldn't she be bringing back hot sexy boys and having wild fun. I bet she daren't do that if you're going to come home and interrupt her pashing. She pretended to be Miss Rae, 'mum, mum, I'm home where's my spag bol and jam pudd ... Mum are you KISSING THAT BOY!'

'My mum and hot, sexy boys Anna?'

'Yeah she's a hot chick. You know I had a brilliant idea on my way here.'

'All your ideas are brilliant ...'

'I know,' Anna agreed, 'and this one is right up to scratch. You like Caro don't you?'

'Yes ...'

'And you like Eliza too?'

'Where's this going?'

'The three of you should get a flat together!' she said triumphantly. 'That would be the greatest. It would be like "Friends". Mum and I could visit and you could cook us meals and tell us exciting stuff about work and university and it would be all messy, because you're messy girls and you could play practical jokes on each other ...'

'Your sisters struck me as quite tidy people and neither of them looked remotely like practical jokers.'

'So you think it's a good idea?'

'I didn't say that ...'

'But you didn't say no. Caro will be eighteen any day now, in fact next Tuesday, and she's going to need somewhere to live. Mum's offered her a room but there might be less hassle with dad if she moved into a flat with you. She'll be able to afford it because Mum has put money in her Piggle Bank. The money was meant for her to go to my school but Dad wouldn't let her. She's put money away for Eliza too, so you could get a real cool place.'

There was a pause.

'You're thinking about it!' Anna gushed excitedly

'Actually I was trying to work out how you ever get a chance to breathe,' said Miss Rae.

'As we both know I'm the queen of multitasking!'

'I hate to admit it but you're probably right …'

'I always am …'

'About me still living with mum; I do need to move on. I've never lived away from home. I went to university in London so I just stayed with mum and now of course it's handy for my job.'

'Great, I'll tell Caro this evening …'

'Hang on Anna, it needs a bit more thought and what about Caroline? You've only just come up with this; I bet she doesn't know you're planning to send her off to live with someone she hardly knows.'

'Pfft, the three of you need start fending for yourselves,' said Anna. 'You think about it Miss Rae, but I still want to tell Caro and Eliza my brilliant idea.'

'You can mention it … but only as an idea.'

Anna was happy with that and moved back to monster hunting and told Miss Rae about all the tricks the machine could do that they never knew. She brought it out and showed her some of them. Then she said they should trick the Commander and steal his monster catching ideas. Finally she wondered if Miss Rae had decided why the monsters were coming.

'I have been thinking about it,' Miss Rae said. 'There are a few waiting to be taken back home so we could test my theories on them. Petrol, exhaust fumes, perhaps they're using something to clean the roads or the pavements. I suspect it must be something new because they've been coming more frequently. Mr Goodman used to catch no more than four or five a month and he said he thought they had wandered into the city by mistake, but now they seem to be deliberately coming and they're getting bigger.'

Anna nodded. 'You know Miss Rae, when it was just the bunnies we could catch them without any special things, just your amazing nets and girl power. Now unless we stop them coming we're going to have to come up with some mega clever plans.'

'Yes, you're right. We have to try to stop them coming!'

Chapter 43

Anna went round to Miss Rae's the next morning and bounced in eating a doughnut.

'Anna ...?'

'Just wanted to be sure you got into work safely,' she said, by way of explanation.

'And?' asked Miss Rae.

'Check you have a proper breakfast, you know proper homemade muesli with dried fennel,' said Anna.

'And ...'

'Well if things went well with your boy, I want to hear about it and if they didn't I'm going to hold my nose and call him a smelly prat and he'll be in a whole load of trouble when I see him.'

Miss Rae smiled, 'we had a nice evening. We went for a curry and chatted and ... yes we had a lovely evening.'

'Good,' decided Anna. 'I had a lovely evening too. I'm still not allowed to watch television but Caro and Eliza sat with me and told me jokes. Some of them were grown-up jokes and they explained them,' she fanned herself with her hand, 'phew, they were rude.' She hugged herself with glee. 'I did say they should share a flat with you and they loved the idea. Caro said it would be great to live with my mum but if she is going to university she probably should leave home. She said that's what people do, so she should too.'

'It's a scary thought, Anna, leaving home.'

'Not as scary as some of the monsters we've caught so after them everything is easy peasy. Do you want a doughnut?' Miss Rae took one and Anna went into the kitchen and offered Miss Rae's mum the last one.

When they arrived at the office Adam fussed over Miss Rae.

'You should have said you were coming in Erin, I'd have given you a lift. Your house is hardly out of my way.'

Miss Rae had to avoid looking at Anna, who she knew would be smirking.

'I had some ideas about why the monsters might be coming,' she said instead. 'More and more have been turning up so the sooner we find out what's attracting them the better.'

Josie appeared and the four of them went to the holding area. They'd caught so many recently the hall was full of Perspex boxes. The monsters looked quite content. Mr Julian, who looked after them, said they didn't seem to mind being in the boxes so long as they were fed regularly.

'What do you think of them?' demanded Anna.

'I like 'em,' he said, 'now I admit some of them aren't the bonniest but they've got character. Him for instance,' he pointed to one of the monsters, 'I wouldn't like 'im loose in my sitting room roaming all over the place and knocking over me model boats, but he looks like he's got spunk, you know a bit of fun in 'im.'

'What about them?' Anna pointed to the four big

monsters.

'They're a bit different, look tougher than the others.'

'Does anything make them more lively,' Miss Rae asked.

Mr Julian tapped the ends of his fingers together. 'It's odd, but when the doors are open, you know for a van, now it's not every time, but sometimes they all go to that side of their boxes.'

'I don't suppose it's any particular time of day?' Miss Rae wondered.

'I can't say I've noticed.'

'I like him best,' Anna pointed to the little one with three eyes on stalks. 'The first one I caught was like him … or her. That's the one that slimed you Adam,' she bent down to say hello. 'And you're the little bugger who jumped Miss Rae and tried to bite her.' She shook her finger at it and to everyone's surprise it looked guilty and shoved a bit of fruit towards her, as if it was saying sorry.

She sat cross-legged in front of it. 'You shouldn't have done it but I don't suppose you really wanted to hurt her, you were just standing up for yourself. You look quite cute and it's cool you can fly.'

It seemed to like the sound of Anna's voice, settled down, ate a carrot and listened to her random musings.

'Do they get fiercer the bigger they are?' Adam asked.

'None of them have been fierce in 'ere,' Mr Julian affirmed.

'Perhaps it's you Mr Julian,' said Anna, 'you sound nice, perhaps they think you're their granddad.'

'It's calm and peaceful in here too,' added Josie.

'I don't suppose any of them have been fierce out in the city either,' suggested Miss Rae. 'I mean they've been active and defensive, but we haven't heard of them attacking people.'

'That one tried to bite me,' Josie pointed to the biggest one, shivering at the memory.

'Yeah but only coz you were in its way,' Anna reminded her. 'It'd seen it's mates being boxed up and it was probably getting a bit paranoid. You know, "they're out to get me and I ain't done nuffin!"'

'Could be,' she agreed.

'Right,' decided Miss Rae. 'I can't go hunting at the moment but I can monitor the ones here and see if I can work out what's bringing them into the city. Anna you can check on any that appear. If they're manageable catch them and call up the van. If they're not you have to promise to come back and we'll think of some way to get you help.'

'I promise, Miss Rae.'

'I've also thought of some improvements to our equipment so this'll give me a chance to get those sorted. Adam could you ask Jake and Sandra to come and give me a hand.'

'Who are Jake and Sandra?' demanded Anna.

'They're part of the technical team and can conjure up pretty much anything I ask.'

'Like Twirls and Jaffa cakes?'

'More like they helped me build the boxes.'

'I suppose that's cool too.' Anna agreed. Out of habit she pulled her machine out to check.

'We've got you an updated one, Anna,' said Josie. 'Improved screen, some of the features we talked about are easier to access and its got a camera.'

Anna left the office with even more of a spring in her step than usual. The new machine was awesome and as they were showing her the new features another monster appeared. They checked what it was and since it was one of the chameleon types that looked a bit like a tortoise they decided she should pick it up. She turned down the offer of a lift, said she'd see the driver there and was soon crossing the city at full speed, practising tricks.

Before she captured the little monster she turned on the video camera and sent back pictures of it moving across the floor. As it plodded along whatever was beneath it appeared on its back. She put a magazine in its path and the grinning face of famous model appeared incongruously there. She unfolded the box, put it in front of the monster and it just walked into it. She rolled in an apple for its dinner, slid the lid shut and let the van driver know it was ready for pick-up.

Chapter 44

When Anna appeared in the office the next day she was bouncing off the ceiling. She headed straight to the holding bay, ignored all the high-tech equipment surrounding Miss Rae and jumped on her desk.

'I would make such a great secret agent. I've been so sneaky and I've discovered so much.' She looked around. 'Hey what's going on down here, you building a space station?'

'Like I said yesterday I had some ideas about why the monsters might be coming ...'

'Well you'll have to wait your turn. I've been investigatin' and you were right Miss Superbrain. I had a search round dad's study, it's okay I was ultra-careful, I didn't want to be caught. Secret agents gotta be smart, I mean what if the door opened just as I discovered a vital bit of evidence, I'd be caught red handed and there'd be a mighty punch up ...'

'A punch-up?'

'Yeah, do you never go to the movies? There'd be a massive WAM! BAM! KABLAM! punch up. I'd put up proper fight, but there'd be so many of them I'd have to jump out the window ... which wouldn't bother me of course. So what I did is I went to dad's work and told them to tell him Anna was there. When I went up I said "last time my work experience was interrupted because you all had to have a meeting so I thought I'd come again to find out what it's like in the real world," then I stared at them like I did before. All the people in the office got real edgy, real quickly. Eventually the boss came out and said how nice it was to see me again but they were just about to go into a big conference. He said it was a shame but they had a lot of meetings to go to. I said "oh" like I was proper disappointed and then I stared a bit more and dad had to give me more money for a taxi, ha ha. That way I knew for sure he was there and couldn't sneak up on me.'

Miss Rae said that was a good plan.

'I didn't have to look far. Dad has everything in boxes and there're labels on them. There was a box called CUSTODY and a box called COURT and a lot of school boxes, ANNA SCHOOL, MY SCHOOL, CAROLINE SCHOOL, ELIZA SCHOOL, and even a box called WEDDING. I looked at his school box first. It was full and Dad and Matthew Murray were deffo friends, there were letters to each other, photographs of them doing stuff and they even went on school trips together. I scanned some of those. When I looked in the wedding box Matthew Murray had been invited the first time dad got married, but he wrote to say he couldn't come because his little boy had swallowed a piece of Lego and had to go to hospital to have it taken out. I scanned that too.'

'Even invited to the wedding,' said Miss Rae, 'he really should have declared that.'

'When I looked in the box called "CUSTODY" there were hardly any bits of paper, well compared to the other boxes and compared to all the stuff mum took along. I scanned all that. It was basically dad saying I needed proper supervision and I needed discipline and that mum was an "actress"; there were cuttings from newspapers and magazines about actresses who had got drunk or took drugs. In the box marked "COURT" there were plenty official documents but they were mainly about what dates the hearings should be. It looked like the dates were changed a lot but only when dad asked for a change. When mum asked for a change she never, ever got a different date. I scanned most of that too. I've emailed it all to mum and she's going to give it to her lawyers. I'm only twelve but …'

'Yes Anna, I know you're twelve …'

'You don't know when my birthday is, I might have had one so I might be thirteen now!'

'It's in December,' said Miss Rae, 'anyway Anna I'm sure you'd have mentioned it because you'd have wanted a present.'

'That would be nice, what will you get me?'

'Let's not get sidetracked, finish your story.'

'Oh yeah, I'm only twelve but even I can tell it's a set-up. Dad and the judge are deffo friends, their evidence is "feeble" and like you said the dates of the hearing must have been sorted so Matthew Murray could be the judge. Wouldn't a judge get a telling off for doing stuff like this? Why do you think they went to so much trouble?'

'I don't know …' said Miss Rae, 'well I suppose I do, your father likes people to do what he says. Your mum was very young when they married?'

'She was eighteen.'

'How old is your dad?'

'I think he's fifty five now.'

'That's a big age gap, twenty years at least.'

'Twenty-five. She's thirty, I was born that first year.'

'I was still a child when I was eighteen, I hardly knew myself let alone the world,' said Miss Rae.

'Caro is eighteen and she's far too young to marry anyone,' agreed Anna. 'Mum says dad wouldn't let her do anything, eventually it got too much and that's why she left.'

'Perhaps he thought she would come back if you had to stay ... or ... well maybe he wanted to punish her for leaving.'

'That's really not nice,' complained Anna.

'No,' agreed Miss Rae. 'He probably wasn't trying to be nasty but maybe his brain works in a different way.'

'Yeah it deffo works in a different way.'

'Anyway,' Miss Rae continued, 'the courts really should consider all this.'

'Yes, I just want to live with mum,' said Anna, 'and eat proper food because I'm not a sheep. Okay it's your turn. What you doing, you inventing?'

Miss Rae turned on her laptop and opened a file with a number of maps. The first one showed all the places in London where monsters had been found in the last three months and the second where they had been found in the two years before. 'Odd don't you think?' she asked.

Anna agreed. 'The new ones, they're all together.'

'Yes, now let me put the local boundaries on the map.'

She pressed a button and the outlines appeared. All the monsters she and Anna had caught were in just three districts. 'In previous years, they're all over the place. I wondered if it was the same in the other big cities so I checked the data. In Birmingham, Leeds, Manchester and all the others the pattern hasn't changed. The monsters are randomly dispersed …'

'Dispersed?'

'Spread out and there's been no increase in numbers. But what do you think happened in Glasgow?

'More monsters?'

'Yes. There's been a similar increase as here but …'

'Like in just one district.'

'Yes.'

'Coo. You know why don't you Miss Rae, but you're making it like a television show for me,' said Anna.

'Yes, I thought you'd like that.'

Anna sat down in the middle of the desk and smiled, 'thanks.'

'Mr Julian said sometimes when the big door was open the monsters would move towards it. So I kept it open and he was right, in fact it was quite frequent. Why do you think'

'It was when they washed the pavements?'

'No, but it is to do with washing.'

'When the lady across the road does her dishes?'

'It happened whenever a bus went past.'

'They wanted to read the adverts on the side?'

'Could have been, so I decided to check with the bus companies …'

'I'd have done that,' interrupted Anna.

'… and found some of the depots had recently changed the stuff they use to wash their buses – and it turns out the Glasgow company changed to the same thing.'

'So what're these machines for?' Anna gestured at the shiny machines all around.

'I'm using them to find out what the chemical is.'

'Have you?'

'Not yet Anna. At the moment I'm collecting data. I'll break it into its constituent parts and I can test each one on the little monsters. I don't think the bus companies would like being told to stop washing their buses but the people who supply the detergent might be able to remove the one chemical.'

'And you can do that?'

'Yes.'

'Wow!' said Anna.

'We've been working on other things too.'

'More stuff, you are the superwoman of monster hunting, tell me, tell me!'

'Could you bring that box over?' Miss Rae asked.

Anna picked it up and studied it carefully before bringing it. 'This panel is bigger.' She pointed to a small grey section.

'Have you got your new machine handy?'

Anna nodded.

'Then make up the box and put the lid on.'

Anna did as she was told without any more questions, she was so curious she didn't want to slow things down.

'There's a square button on your machine, press it once.'

She pressed it and the see-through box went completely opaque. 'Woah!' she exclaimed.

'There's another trick, press the button and hold it for two seconds.

Two seconds later the top of the box pinged off.

'That's fantastic …'

'I don't know when we'd need that but we'd developed it for something else and it was easy to add it to the boxes so we did.'

Adam came through and Anna waved and shouted to him.

'Have you seen this Adam,' she put the lid back on and pinged it off.

'We've improved the nets too,' said Miss Rae,

'How?'

'Catch me in one Anna,' said Adam.

She picked one off the desk and threw it over him. As the sides flicked round his body they locked together behind his back so he was completely trapped.

'If I tried to move I'd just fall over,' he explained, staying very still, 'it's not sore, it just holds me.'

'The green button on the machine releases it,' said Miss Rae.

Anna pressed it, the net was loose again and she pulled it off.

'Do me, do me,' she demanded.

Adam caught her in the net and she felt it wrap around her. He was right she was completely trapped, her legs were held so tight together if she tried to walk she'd keel over. 'I suppose if I was really desperate I could make a very slow getaway by jumping,' she suggested.

Adam smiled.

She tried to flex her legs to jump but the net kept her in the one position and it was impossible to get any spring in them.

'You could roll,' suggested Miss Rae.

'Is this the cleverest thing you've done?' asked Anna, 'because it is really clever isn't it Adam? Miss Rae must be one of the cleverest people on the planet; I am speechless! How does it work? Is it glue, no it can't be glue because how would the machine be able to unstick it.'

Adam released the net.

'I think it must be some sort of magnet. A magnet that works on electricity so you can turn it off.'

'Very good Anna,' said Miss Rae.

Anna climbed up on the desk again and sat opposite.

'Looking pretty "fly", Miss Rae, you're getting good at doing makeup and your hair is just lovely,' she fluffed it. 'What do you think Adam? Does she look "fly"?'

'Anna you can't ask people questions like that,' said Adam.

'Because?'

'Because it's embarrassing.'

'I'm not embarrassed, and Miss Rae's not embarrassed because she hasn't gone red and anyway she's gotten used to me. So it must be you. I'll say it for you.' She put on a deep voice, 'Miss Rae you are looking well "fly" today and I'd like to take you to a movie so everyone can see how "fly" you look. What sort of movie would you like to see? Even though I am a boy I will go to a girl movie with you.'

She pretended to be Miss Rae next. 'I would like to see a cool action film with super cool stuntwomen doing cool stunts,' she flicked her hair, 'I would like popcorn, chocolate Twirls, a hot dog, a blue slushy drink and an ice cream.' Then she was back to own voice. 'Right gotta go, they'll be checking the cells at HM Prison Templeton soon, enjoy your evening out.'

Chapter 45

Anna bought a pack of sausage rolls on her way home, ate one and saved the other two in her rucksack for Caroline and Eliza. It was just as well because the bean and parsnip stew was truly horrid.

The three of them were going upstairs when dad called Caroline back. He often did that but this time Eliza looked anxious.

'What's wrong Eliza?' Anna whispered.

'I don't know for sure, Anna. He's been talking about university a lot recently. Maybe he's going to make her sign up for that degree in electrical engineering.'

'I'm going back,' Anna said.

'Are you sure?'

'Yes, he shouldn't be forcing her to do stuff.'

When Anna walked into the kitchen Caroline was curled up in her chair shaking and dad was standing over her.

'Why are you disobeying me? I told you never to disobey me,' he shouted at her.

'Stop bullying her!' yelled Anna getting between him and her sister. 'Leave Caro alone. You can't keep telling her what to do.'

Caroline lifted her head, her eyes were red and tears were streaming down her cheeks.

'YOU'VE MADE HER CRY!' Anna bellowed.

'Get out Anna!'

'Your own daughter and you've made her cry. Caro is coming with me. Come on Caro.'

Caroline stood up and Anna took a firm hold of her hand.

'You are a horrible bully,' Anna yelled at her father, 'you don't deserve children!'

'I told you to get out Anna, stop your infernal meddling. Caroline will do what's she told, as will you!'

'Shouting at us doesn't make you any more right,' Anna said defiantly.

'Yes stop shouting at us,' Caroline said. She wiped at her tears.

'How dare you speak back to your father!'

'We going upstairs,' said Anna, 'Caro is a grown-up and you can't tell her what to do.'

Dad was white with anger. 'I am your father. You do what I say or face the consequences,' he banged on the table with his clenched fist.

You're meant to look after us, not make us cry!' Anna snapped back.

'Stop it dad, you're wrong, you're wrong to make me do things I don't want to do,' Caroline managed to stammer.

'I say what's right or wrong,' dad replied.

The doorbell rang.

'Tell them to go away!' he yelled.

'We're going upstairs dad,' said Anna.

'You're still disobeying me you little monster.' He swept

the dinner plates of the table and they fell on the floor with a crash.

Anna and Caroline stared at the mess of crockery in shock.

'I'm going to teach you a lesson you're not going to forget.' He charged round the table and swung his open palm towards her head.

Anna automatically swayed back out of reach.

He stepped closer but with Caroline behind her Anna couldn't move any further away and he slapped her on the cheek.

'You hit me you fucking bastard!' she yelled outraged.

'I've warned you enough times about swearing,' he shouted back, clenched his hand into a fist and raised it above his head.

'Stop it dad, STOP IT,' Caroline pleaded desperately.

Chapter 46

Before Dad could hit Anna again, someone caught a hold of his wrist.

'LET GO ELIZA OR YOU'LL BE IN FOR A HIDING TOO!' he bellowed furiously and turned.

It wasn't Eliza, it was a big man in a blue uniform.

'I think you should calm down, Mr Templeton,' the policeman said.

'Let go, let go of me or I'll report you for misconduct,' Dad demanded and tried to wrench his hand free.

'If I have to cuff you I will sir. You've already assaulted a minor, you don't want to get in any more trouble.'

'These children are the ones in trouble, disobeying my direct orders, talking back and an almost daily pattern of misbehaviour.'

A policewoman squeezed past to Anna and Caroline.

'Are you girls alright?' she asked.

The red slap mark on Anna's face was throbbing, his ring must have caught her because a little trickle of blood ran down her cheek but her eyes were shining.

'He hit me!' Anna was rigid with anger, clenching and unclenching her fist.

'Yes we saw.'

The policeman turned dad around and marched him out of the room.

'You alright Caro?' Anna looked up at her eldest sister.

'Yes,' she managed in a weak voice. 'I was so frightened when he slapped you.'

'Anna, you're bleeding,' said Eliza, red-eyed.

'I've had worse playing football,' Anna beckoned and took her hand.

The policewoman wanted to be sure and examined her cheek.

'What ... what's going to happen?' asked Caroline.

'It's just a scratch but you'll probably have a bruise,' the policewoman said and then explained their father would have to go to the police station. She said they would need to question him. He might just get a caution, but he would probably be there until tomorrow or until he calmed down.

'Oh,' acknowledged Caroline.

'Well done you, Eliza, calling the police,' said Anna.

'It wasn't me, I thought it was you ...'

The doorbell rang and the policewoman went answer it.

'Can I help?' she asked.

'I'm a ... I'm a friend of the family ...' a familiar voice said.

'MISS RAE,' yelled Anna excitedly.

The policewoman brought her in. 'You know this lady?'

'You've come at just the right time, we've been in uproar!' said Anna.

'I was ... Anna you're bleeding ... your father ...'

'He HIT me!'

The policewoman interrupted and asked who she was and

why was she here.

'I ... I ... Anna does some voluntary work with me,' Miss Rae explained, 'I was worried about her so I phoned 999,' she said.

'You phoned, why?' said the policewoman.

Miss Rae explained she'd been texting Anna, but hadn't been getting a reply. 'As that has never happened before I ... I had a bad feeling and Adam, my ... er ... boyfriend, said if I had a bad feeling then it would be better to phone and he'd bring me over so if I was wrong I could explain. He's parking the car.'

'Just as well you called,' the policewoman said. 'Okay girls you can't stay here over night on your own. Are there any relatives you can go to?'

'My mum's away, there's nowhere else safe to go,' said Anna.

'They can stay with me,' offered Miss Rae.

'Really!' Anna looked overwhelmed for a moment. 'Yeah, Miss Rae is well responsible, she works for the government.' She added Mrs Graham would be able to say how responsible Miss Rae is, 'Mrs Graham is her boss and is even more responsible than Miss Rae.'

The policewoman gave her a look. 'I'm afraid I'll need more than that!'

Miss Rae said of course and suggested they went into the other room, 'I'll get in touch with my director, you can talk to her and she can provide references.'

After they left the room, Anna asked, 'you okay Caro?'

and nudged her.

Caroline was still shivering and dabbing her eyes, 'thank you Anna, thanks for standing up for me.'

'I'll always stand up for you, you're my sister, we're ...' what ever they were would have to wait because the doorbell rang again. Eliza came back with Adam.

'Blood! Anna there's blood all over your face are you alright ...' he looked horrified.

'I'm a girl, IT Adam, I'm tough!'

The policewoman came back and said it was fine for them to go with Miss Rae. First she needed to talk to them separately and take statements. When that was finished they collected some overnight stuff and settled in the back of Adam's car.

'Are you sure you three are okay?' Miss Rae asked, once they were moving.

'I ... am ... so ... in ... shock,' said Anna, 'you know I can hardly speak. He went completely video rental, shouting and screaming at Caro. It's just as well you phoned the police because he really was well off the shelf. Were you at the movies? Is that where you were? Did you buy her popcorn Adam? He hit me, it was just a slap but if the police hadn't stopped him he was going to punch me. What sort of person does that, you knows punches a girl?'

'I don't know Anna, someone who has lost control? What, why Caro ... ?'

'Yes, what, why?' repeated Anna.

'He ... he wanted to check my application for the course

in Electrical Engineering and … and I realised I had to stand up to him,' Caro explained. 'If I didn't, I never would. I told him I didn't want to study electrical engineering and he went ballistic. He started shouting and screaming and I curled up into a ball I was so scared, then Anna came in and tried to get me away. He went even madder, I think I'd have ended up doing what he said if she hadn't been there but I decided if she could stand up to him and she's only the size of pixie then I could.'

'The size of a pixie!' Anna exclaimed, affronted.

'I heard him shouting and screaming and I thought he was going to kill them,' Eliza said. 'I was so scared I didn't know what to do; I was so glad when the policeman came to the door.'

'Thanks Miss Rae,' Anna started singing, "did he think we'd crumble? Did he think we'd lay down and die? Oh, no, not us! We will survive."

By the time they reached the house, Anna was as high as a kite, she danced into the sitting room, Miss Rae's mum was sitting watching television and she vaulted over the sofa and landed beside her.

'Hi Mrs Rae, what-cha watching?'

'It's the finals of … oh hello Anna … er … what are you doing here?'

'This is a surprise isn't it Mrs Rae, there's nothing on your television that's even like half as exciting as what's happened to us this evening! Look I've brought my sisters, aren't they lovely!'

Mrs Rae greeted them, 'how nice to meet you, and are you as er … lively as Anna?'

"Er …' started Caroline.

'They're well not!,' interrupted Anna. 'Sometimes they move so slowly you can't tell if they're asleep or awake.'

'Anna can I leave you, Caro and Eliza here for a mo, I'd like a quick word with mum,' Miss Rae asked.

'She going to tell you what's been happening,' Anna confided loudly. 'My version would be so exciting you wouldn't be able to sleep for days for thinking on it.'

'Once I've heard Erin's report I can devote tomorrow to listening to yours Anna, then I'll compare them and rate them, for accuracy, thrills and length.'

'I'll win,' Anna claimed.

Miss Rae and her mum went into the kitchen to talk privately.

Anna called her sisters over and made them sit on either side. 'Right, you've got to remember I'm your little sister, you have to look after me, you know give me treats, buy me presents, praise me … a lot. In return I'll continue to be messy, difficult, annoying, a pain in the butt, that bloody girl, I won't shut up and I'll keep interfering!'

'Sounds a bargain to me,' said Caroline.

'We could help you with your homework and carry your books home from school too,' offered Eliza.

'Sweet,' said Anna.

Chapter 47

Since it was late, Miss Rae's mother decided it was time they got some sleep.

Miss Rae found a couple of sleeping bags and there was a bed in the spare room so she left them to it. Anna didn't consult her sisters, 'Caroline you take the bed,' she said, 'Me and Eliza will have the sleeping bags I mean ...' she made a snoring sound, 'Eliza actually sleeps anywhere!'

Miss Rae had just slipped under the covers when Anna appeared and plonked herself on the end of her bed.

'Thanks Miss Rae,' she said, 'for rescuing us.'

'Like you said we're a team Anna ...'

'Yeah we're the best team ever,' she said. 'Miss Rae?'

'Yes Anna?'

'What do you think will happen? The policewoman spoke to you, what did she say?'

'She just wanted to check it was safe to let you come with me, nothing more.'

'Of course it's safe to come with you, you work for the government, you're serious, sensible, hard-working and a super clever person ...'

'I could still be a danger to children so she had to be sure,' Miss Rae explained. 'I got in touch with Mrs Graham and she forwarded my Disclosure and Barring document ...'

'What's that?'

'It means the police have checked my background to see if I've done anything bad. Of course I could be a sneaky witch with a ton of secret evil schemes they don't know about, like selling your sisters into slavery or tipping you in the pot for dinner.'

'Well I'd make a delicious meal, because I'm so sweet.'

'But I'm not a sneaky witch, so you're okay.'

'They took dad away. Will they keep him?'

'I don't know.'

'I don't want him to go to prison but I don't want to live there any more. I don't trust him, what if he goes mental again? I just want to be with mum.'

'The policewoman said she saw your father hit you, her colleague had to stop him from hitting you again. There's a law against corporal punishment but it was more than that. Have you told your mum?'

'Not yet. She's got a super important meeting tomorrow and she doesn't need any distractions, if she knew she'd fly back and that might spoil things and she's worked so hard for this. You'll look out for me Miss Rae, and Caro and Eliza, they're here, I'll tell her when she gets back to the airport. She always phones from the airport.'

'Anna ...'

'I'm fine. Okay it was a shock he actual hit me, but I've been hurt a lot more by the footie boys, they deliberately kick and barge me and knock me over. I pretend I'm okay, 'cause if they think knocking me over will stop me going for the ball they'll do the same thing again and then they've won. So I get up and you know, kick them back. This evening I couldn't let him win I had to get Caro out of the kitchen somehow, but I'm ever so glad you called the police.'

'Your mum needs to know this, it'll be part of your case …' Miss Rae decided.

Anna nodded, 'but that wasn't only why I came in. I wanted to check you'd brushed your teeth and your mum … is she okay with us staying and you never said what you and your boy were doing, was it adult stuff, kissing and things?'

'Of course I've brushed my teeth,' said Miss Rae, 'I always do. I told mum and she said she would have been more angry with me if I hadn't I brought you over. She likes you and she said your sisters seem very well-behaved …'

'She likes me even though I'm not well-behaved?'

'Yes.'

'See! And what about your boy?'

'Adam and I did as you suggested. We went to see a film. It was an adventure film and it had a happy ending. Then we went to a café and yes we were doing adult stuff … talking to each other. I sent you a few texts to say we were having fun …'

'And …'

'Well … you didn't reply to any of them and I got a chill.'

'A chill?'

'Yes like something bad was happening.'

'Maybe you're psychic, Miss Rae!'

'No, I think as your sisters were planning to move out I was simply anxious about your father's reaction.'

'Thanks Miss Rae. Your boy, is he getting better or worse the more you know him.'

'Better …'

'He must be because you said boyfriend to the police lady.'

'It was easier to explain it that way …'

'And you? Does he think you're better or worse?' Anna asked a twinkle in her eyes.

'I didn't ask so I don't know,' Miss Rae replied.

'I'll ask him tomorrow and then you will know.'

'You will not!'

'I think I will!' contradicted Anna.

'That was an order not a prediction.'

'Was it, I can't tell. Anyway it's good you're talking and having fun. What do you think about sharing a flat with Caro now? She's got nowhere to go, I don't want her to be a down and out.'

'I thought she was going to stay with your mum?' Miss Rae asked.

'Yeah but only temporary like. I can't be having her hanging about eating all the jam and hogging the bathroom. I'd want Eliza out sharpish too when she's eighteen, her and her German accordian music and collection of foghorns!'

'Anna I can't begin to think how you come up with such mad rubbish.'

'I told you before, I'm a genius!'

Chapter 48

Three weeks later Anna was in the office chatting to Josie and amusing herself by slowly doing handstands. She was wearing her favourite clothes, the ones with the most clashing colours and the hippy beads Miss Rae had given her, which she hadn't taken off in two weeks.

The door to the office opened and the familiar shape of Mr Goodman hoved into view.

She flipped the right way up, dashed across and held her hand up. 'Yo!'

'Yo! Miss Templeton ... yo? What on earth does that mean?'

'It means hi, it means long time no see, it means welcome back to England, it means why were you away sooo long, it means you abandoned poor Miss Rae and put her in a bad place, it means I had a rotten time after you left, it means we sorted things out even if you weren't there because of girl power, it means things have changed big time, it means I'm an official monster hunter with a card and everything, it ...'

'For such a short word it has an extensive range of connotations.'

'Do you and Mrs Graham have the same dictionary, because I can't understand her either. Can I tell you stuff?'

'Miss Templeton I'd be delighted to hear your er ... stuff. Perhaps at lunchtime, Erin might like to come too, but first

I have to speak to Mrs Graham, is that okay?'

Anna said it was and cartwheeled back to Josie.

When he came out of Mrs Graham's office he only had to look in Anna's direction and she was at his side.

'I've said to Miss Rae,' said Anna, 'and she said she'd love a free meal even if she has to listen to my endless prattling. We could go for fish an' chips, "gor blimey!"'

Miss Rae joined them. 'Welcome back Mr Goodman.'

'Thank you Erin. It seems you two have been busy while I've been away.'

'Well busy!' said Anna. 'We've been battling monsters, saving the world and coming up with the best ideas history has ever seen,' said Anna. They were out of the building, down the road and waiting for the lights to change before she stopped describing all the monsters they'd caught.

'And …' said Mr Goodman when she paused for breath.

He was too slow and she told him how clever Miss Rae was, how she'd worked out what was attracting so many more monsters and how she had been able to change the detergent so it worked just as well without the chemical the monsters loved. He also found out about the man who had driven his car at Miss Rae, because Anna remembered about that in the middle of telling him about the machines that analysed the smells.

Mr Goodman sensed another gap, but Anna talked over him until Miss Rae put her hand up.

'Anna remember how you talked about giving people a chance to contribute to the conversation?'

'Oh yeah,' agreed Anna. 'How are you Mr Goodman?'

'I'm well, I've had a very interesting time, very informative and the food was excellent so I probably ate too well.'

'Yes,' agreed Anna, 'you're a lot fatter than when you went away.'

'Anna,' scolded Miss Rae.

'What? WHAT? I'm only saying because he might not have noticed. It's best to address these things the sooner rather than the later when we're squeezing him through doors and buying him two seats for the train!'

Mr Goodman sucked his stomach in, 'I don't think I've got a two seat body!'

Anna circled him, 'not yet,' she said darkly. 'Okay, did you teach them a lot?'

'Yes …'

'Were they plagued with monsters like we were?'

'No, they …'

'Did they need you more than we did?'

'Anna, let Mr Goodman say more than a couple of words,' said Miss Rae.

'And then it'll be my turn to speak again?'

'Yes,' agreed Mr Goodman.

'Okay.'

Miss Rae pretended to zip Anna's mouth shut.

He told them he had helped his German colleagues get the most out of the machines, they had shared experiences and he had taught them about the variety of monsters they'd had to deal with in Britain. 'In return they explained some of the tactics they used. It was an excellent opportunity to swop ideas.' He stopped and there was a long silence.

They both looked at Anna and she stared back.

'You can unzip now Anna,' said Miss Rae

'I'm a real pain in the neck aren't I?' she suggested happily. 'Were the bunnies the same?' she asked.

'Most were familiar, there were differences but that's to be expected. However they were all small, much like we'd been dealing with until recently. I was very surprised to hear how big some of the ones you've had to sort out were ... and how frequently they'd been turning up.

Miss Rae said it had been scary and Anna said no it hadn't, it had been exciting.

At the restaurant they sat down and once they'd ordered. Miss Rae said to Anna it was her turn to talk. 'I know you've plenty to say.'

'I have, because everything, like EVERYTHING is better thanks to Miss Rae.'

'Everything?' asked Mr Goodman.

'Everything, everything EVERYTHING! I'm living with mum now and so are Caro and Eliza, they're my step-sisters. I'm getting to train longer at free running and I'm allowed to go to stage school at the weekends to learn singing, acting and stunting. It's weird how quickly it changed too.' She told him about the night dad got really angry and how Miss Rae had rescued them and let them stay with her and how when mum had come back she'd spoken to her lawyer. 'But we never had to go to court. There was just a bit of paper that said I could stay with mum. I did have to talk to a judge. This was a different judge, not the one from before; the one from before was dad's mate! I also had to speak to a social worker and to a policeman …'

'They must have enjoyed that,' said Miss Rae.

'I'm sure they did, I'm an interesting talker,' Anna said.

Anna admitted she had been worried about what would happen, like dad going to prison, or his friend the judge telling her off and mum being in the papers, but there was nothing. She and her sisters had visited dad, with mum, her lawyer, a policeman and the nice social worker lady.

'He hadn't calmed down at all. He shouted "what's all this about," to the lawyer and "what are YOU doing here?" to mum. Then he shouted at Caro she was not to disobey him. He told her she had to go to study electrical engineering at university. He shouted at the policeman that he was going to take him to court and he shouted at the social worker that mum had stolen his children and he expected her to make us come back. Caro started crying and had to leave the room. He shouted at me. "You Anna Templeton, you are becoming a tearaway, you've got to learn to do as you're told. You are grounded for the next month, no television, no radio and you are not allowed to visit any of your friends. Perhaps then you will learn some respect." Mum didn't say anything and she'd zipped me so I didn't either. She looked kinda sad the whole time. The policeman, his name was Inspector Hussain, Labeeb Hussain. He plays hockey, not for Britain, he's too busy being a policeman for that, but he plays for a club. He

318

said if I liked hockey I should join a club like his. They're always looking for people. I'm a forward like him. They train on a Tuesday evening and that would work because …'

'Anna,' interrupted Miss Rae, 'weren't you telling Mr Goodman about your dad?'

'Oh yes … Inspector Hussain looked pretty shocked at what dad was saying. He was there when we went to talk to the judge so I think he must have talked to the judge too. The judge said I could go home with mum right then. I couldn't believe it. That was the best moment of my life! He said Caro and Eliza could stay with mum too and they looked like different people, they had big smiles and they bounced about just like I do.'

'You do look happy, Miss Templeton,' Mr Goodman admitted.

'It's like I've been given a free season pass to Disneyland, that's how happy I am.'

'And your father?'

'I don't know, I've not been to see him since we went on that visit two weeks ago. I hope he's calmed down. The social worker lady said he has to go to "Angry School", that's so he can learn NOT to be angry rather than the other way round. I don't really want to see him. Do you know what?'

'What, Miss Templeton?'

'He wasn't angry if people did exactly what he said, but he got real angry if you wanted to do your own thing. I think Miss Rae is right when she said after he and mum split up he got so angry he wanted to do something that would really hurt her.'

'And that was?' Mr Goodman asked.

'Stopping me living with her!'

Miss Rae said she really didn't know the "ins and outs" but it had seemed an odd situation. 'For someone who wants revenge on a mother, stopping her seeing her child is about the worst thing you can do. It is cruel, but he didn't seem like a cruel person, leastways not when I met him.'

'Anyways,' decided Anna, 'maybe if he goes to Angry School they'll teach him to be nicer. For the moment Caro and Eliza aren't going to see him either, they want to get settled first.'

'What happened to the judge?' asked Mr Goodman.

'Dunno,' said Anna, 'maybe he'll have to go back to "Judge School" and they'll remind him he has to listen to what the children want and not just what his mate asks him to do.'

Chapter 49

They were walking back to the office when there was a bleep from Anna's machine.

'That's the first monster since you sorted things out, Miss Rae,' she said.

Mr Goodman said things seemed to have gone back to normal in London. He had heard the crowds of monsters had stopped turning up in Glasgow too.

'Let's all go catch it,' Anna suggested.

Mr Goodman said Anna and Miss Rae should go since they were a team. He'd return to the office but would be ready if they needed backup.

They checked what type it was.

'Yucko, it's the same as the one that sprayed gunge over you, Mr Goodman, that was so funny.'

'Well it'll be spraying gunge over you Miss Templeton and I'm sure it'll be just as hilarious,' retorted Mr Goodman.

'We've got Pac-a-macs,' Anna replied smugly.

'And they'll keep you perfectly dry?'

'Maybe,' said Anna.

'You know despite your assumption I was on an eating holiday I did pick up some interesting tips from our German colleagues,' Mr Goodman said '... and one of the things I learnt was how they dealt with these little chaps. Much as I'd like you to experience the full gunge experience they can

321

be placated …'

'Eh?'

'If they're fed dried fruit they calm down: apparently apricots work best.'

'Apricots stop me from being bunged up, if they're any less bunged up they'll be going like fountains,' suggested Anna.

'It seems to work the other way with them, stops them spouting gunge and you should be able to catch them without getting a soaking.'

'Okay, we'll try it but I'll be wearing my Pac-a-mac just the same.'

They said goodbye to Mr Goodman and set off.

The little monster had holed up in the courtyard of an old petrol station. The yard was cool and quiet but it was shuffling about in the middle looking fidgety and anxious. They tossed it an apricot from a distance. It stared at the dried fruit for a moment, sniffed it, licked it and gobbled it down. It sat back looking a lot calmer. Anna laid a trail to the box and it followed eagerly scooping up the pieces of apricot. It walked straight in to collect the last piece and she shut the lid. It didn't seem bothered and sat contentedly as it chewed on the fruit.

Anna pressed the button, the perspex went opaque. 'Cool, just like we've picked up a box from the shops,' she said.

As they weren't far from the office they decided it would be as easy to carry it back and started walking.

'Have you found a flat yet?' asked Anna.

Miss Rae had talked to her mum and they had agreed they both needed a bit more independence. She and Caroline were going to find somewhere together, with space for Eliza when she was ready. Anna had wanted to come on the flat-hunting adventures but Miss Rae could only look in the evening and Anna was spending the evenings with her mum.

'They're all dull,' Miss Rae complained. 'Beige walls, beige fittings, the pictures on the walls are boring, they're all just ... you know nice!'

'Duh! Once you move in you put up your Metallica and Slipknot posters and "la" instant home from home!' Anna pointed out.

'Why would you think I'm a fan of heavy metal?'

'When you showed me your bruise I saw a tattoo of Iron Maiden on your butt!'

Miss Rae snorted.

'Well if not heavy metal, get posters of your boy.'

'I don't think so.'

'Is he pleased you're going to be in your own flat? When you get settled he can come round and do manly jobs about the house, unblocking the loo, catching mice ...'

'He's not so much of a handy man ...'

'He's quite handy, his desk is close to yours, I think it's nice you spend all day smiling at him.'

'I don't smile at him all day!' Miss Rae claimed.

Anna pulled out her notebook and pretended to read from it. 'Annalog: Monday. Eight-thirty subject arrived at work. Subject turned on computer. While waiting for computer to boot up, subject smiled at boy sitting three desks away, boy smiled back. Subject watched boy when he went to help Mrs Graham …'

'You have a vivid imagination, Anna Templeton, what you need to do …'

Miss Rae stopped in mid-sentence.

'What, what do I need to do?' Anna asked.

'That man!' Miss Rae kept walking. 'The man in the car, he's the one who tried to run me down.'

'No way!'

'It's a different car but it's the same man.'

'I'll phone a policeman,' Anna said.

Before she could get her phone out, the car pulled up in front of them with a squeal of brakes and the man wound down the window. He was well dressed, smart suit, sharp tie and carefully blow-dried hair, he was smiling but it was not a friendly smile.

'You two are going to get a lesson in keeping your mouths shut,' he snarled and reached over to the passenger seat.

'Who the hell do you think you are?' shouted Anna. 'You ran over Miss Rae!'

He grinned nastily and held up a big knife.

'GET IN!'

Without a seconds pause Anna shoved the box up against the window, pressed the release button on her machine, the lid popped off and the little monster realising it was free jumped out onto the man.

It immediately started spurting cold gunge from its

feelers. The man got such a shock he dropped his knife out the window and tried to grab the creature. That made things worse and very quickly the windows were covered in the stuff. The little monster was so slimy the man couldn't keep a hold of it and it kept squirming out of his grip.

Miss Rae kicked the knife under the car, they retreated to a safe distance and phoned 999.

By the time the police arrived, the man was covered in slime, his beautiful suit was soggy from the goo and the monster was sitting on the back seat occasionally spraying a fresh jet.

The man heard a car approaching, saw it was the police and reached down to start the motor.

Anna jingled the keys in front of him.

'Give 'em to me you little brat!' he yelled.

She shrugged, 'ain't going to do that,' she said and handed them to the policeman.

The man realised he wasn't going to get away and instead demanded they catch the "bloody" creature!'

Anna cautiously opened the back door, tossed in some dried apricots and once it had settled down, scooped it back into the box.

'What on earth is that?' asked one of the policemen.

Miss Rae held up her ID card. 'It's an escapee from the zoo, a very rare Balinese mammal,' she explained. 'Poor little thing was frightened.'

'Bloody disgusting thing ...' the driver snarled.

'It was probably allergic to the smell of your perfume,'

said Anna wrinkling her nose.

'Aftershave,' the man corrected.

'Whatever.' She turned to the policeman, 'go on then arrest him, read him his rights!' demanded Anna, 'bloody crim had a knife. He was going to stab us.'

'Course I wasn't going to stab you, pet, you've got me wrong.'

'So the knife was just for scratching your bollocks,' retorted Anna. 'What's he done? He's a proper villain. He must be a bank robber! Do we get a get a reward for catching him, how much do we get? You should pay us the same each since we both helped arrest him. I get ninety quid for catching these little zoo animals, but he's much bigger than them. They're only a kilo while he must at least a hundred kilos. You should pay us nine grand for catching him! By the way his knife is under the car. Miss Rae kicked it there so he couldn't use it.'

The policeman didn't answer any of her questions but took out a notepad. His colleague handcuffed the man, locked him in the police van and carefully picked up the knife with a plastic bag.

The first policeman asked what had happened, wrote everything down and when that was done, explained they'd have to go to court as witnesses.

'No probs, I'm free all week,' said Anna.

The policeman cleared his throat and said, 'that's good to know Miss, but it's more likely to be in a few months.'

Miss Rae managed to pull the pretend zip across Anna's

mouth before she could complain.

'Wow!' said Anna, as they watched the policemen drive off with the man handcuffed in the back. 'We're living such exciting lives, aren't we? Who'd have thought a year ago we'd be hunting monsters AND arresting crims?'

'A year ago I'd just finished my degree and was struggling to find a job,' said Miss Rae.

'Now you're an important big cheese, your inside loveliness is on the outside too, you're moving into your own flat and planning adventures with your boy!' added Anna. 'A year ago I was stuck in Annacatraz, with my bonkers dad and today I'm living with my mum, who as everyone knows is almost perfect, I've been taught the most incredible moves by the best free runner in the world, my plans to be a stuntwoman and pop star are well on track, I met you and you turned out to be the most amazing person and you rescued me and took me and my sisters in, even though I can be one of the most annoying people in the world!'

She took hold of Miss Rae's hands and spun round her, a huge grin on her face.

'Isn't life absolutely brilliant?' she asked.

Miss Rae agreed wholeheartedly, 'yes Anna, it is absolutely brilliant!'

THE END